The Silver Serpent

Andy Bazan

Iron Tarantula Books—McAllen, TX
ISBN: 978-0-578-66254-1
Library of Congress Control Number: 2020905297
Title: The Silver Serpent
Author: Andy Bazan
Digital distribution | 2019 Paperback | 2019

Dedication

I would like to dedicate my first book, *The Silver Serpent*, to the two most gorgeous and golden hearted ladies that I know. The adorable and charming loves of my life. My divine daughter and princess, Cassie, and my blessed lovebird, Valerie. They are the wind in my sails, and they inspire me every day. I love them with all of my heart and soul.

Chapter One
Slick

A Silver Serpent named Slick lived in the Atlantic Ocean in the early 1900's. Slick's elusive reputation made some people doubt that he even existed. Very few people had seen him and those that had were slaughtered and devoured by him. Slick's monstrous size made him dangerous, and his thirst for blood made him ferocious.

Slick also had a voracious appetite. He could slay anything and anyone that crossed his path. His favorite meals were sharks and humans, but he devoured anything with flesh and blood. His diet consisted of every sea creature in the ocean along with birds and humans.

Slick was 150 feet long and weighed thirty metric tons. His body was armored with leathery scales and razor-sharp claws and teeth. His entire body was shiny silver with traces of emerald green and sapphire blue on the tips of his scales. His eyes were an ardent ruby-red. Slick was without a doubt, the king of the sea, and sat on top of the food chain. His long, sleek, and powerful body enabled him to slash and dash through the water with streamline precision and he often reached tremendous speeds of up to seventy-five mph.

He was the only sea monster of his kind to survive the brutal years of evolution. His lover, Sandy, had been slayed two years ago, in 1902, by some whale hunters while she was out hunting by herself. Slick had never forgiven himself for letting her hunt on her own, and he never forgave the humans for taking his true love away from him. When her body was brought to shore, the entire world learned of the dead Silver Serpent, but they had no idea that one was still alive. They sent the world's best scientists and hunters to try and find another Silver Serpent, but they gave up after a year of no signs or sightings. They figured they had slayed the last one of its kind. Slick knew that they were looking for him, and that he was outnumbered. He stayed deep under the Atlantic waters and out of sight and far away. He was merely biding his time and waiting for the right opportunity for vengeance. The Silver Serpent was not only devastatingly dangerous, he was also incredibly intelligent. That being the case, he felt lonely sometimes. His best friend was a whale shark named Bo. Bo was 40 feet long and weighed twenty metric tons. He was one of the few creatures in the ocean that was safe from the jaws of Slick, because he was a friend. It was midnight, and the ocean's surface resembled obsidian in the moonlight. There was an ominous and ghostly silence across the Atlantic waters. Slick stuck his spiky head up above the surface for some fresh air.

Bo swam up to Slick to say hello.

"What's going on, Slick?" Bo asked.

"Say there, Bo. How's it going? I'm just getting some fresh night air before I go slay a midnight snack for myself," Slick replied.

"Sounds good buddy. What's on the menu for tonight?" Bo said.

"I'm thinking of some yellowfin tuna or some mako shark," Slick replied.

"You're a cold-blooded killer man. Don't you get tired of all that blood, guts, and bones?" Bo said.

"No way man. I love that stuff! Don't you get tired of all that krill all the time?" Slick replied.

"Yeah sometimes. That's why I like to eat fish also," Bo said.

"We all have our own needs. That's just the way the great Sea God made us," Slick replied.

"Do you feel like devouring any humans tonight?" Bo asked.

"I would if there were any around. Do you see any boats around this late at night?" Slick replied.

"No. There usually aren't any boats around this late at night and this deep in the ocean. The only ones that you see sometimes, are the shrimp or crab boats this late and this deep," Bo said.

"Yeah, I'm sure there are some party boats closer to the shore, but I don't feel like swimming that far right now. I'll just wait for some tuna or sharks," Slick replied.

"OK man. I'm gonna call it a night and go get some rest. I'll see you tomorrow," Bo said.

"OK Bo. Have a good night. I'll see you later," Slick replied.

Bo swam off and Slick swam deeper into the ocean to a place where sharks and tuna liked to swim and hunt. Slick spotted four mako sharks feasting on and tearing up some type of carcass. The carcass looked to be human. Slick seized the opportunity to feed and attacked them from behind. He grabbed one shark in his jaws and another in his claws. He immediately bit the head off one of the sharks, and the other he grabbed with his two upper limbs and sunk his claws into their hearts and brains and slayed them instantly. The other two sharks swam away. Once the two mako sharks that Slick grabbed were dead, he devoured them piece by piece until there was nothing left but a blood trail.

"AHH, that was delicious," Slick said to himself.

It's time for some rest he thought. He swam to his ocean cave located deep in the depths of the mystical Atlantic.

Slick arrived at his cave and swam inside. Inside it was decorated with different color seaweed all over the place. There were also bones and skulls of fish, sharks, and humans on his cave's ocean floor. He also had a couple of treasure chests that he looted from sunken pirate ships years ago. Pirate ships that he had sunken, and pirates that he devoured. The chests had gold, silver, rubies, emeralds, and sapphires. Slick swam to his favorite corner of the cave where he had his extra spongy bed made of kelp. He flopped onto his comfortable bed and fell asleep. In his dreams he dreamed of his lover, Sandy, who had been slayed by some whale hunters a couple of years ago. He truly missed her a great deal. They were happily swimming together in the Atlantic and hunting sharks. That's how he liked to remember her.

He also dreamed of his mother and father who had died of old age about 5 years ago. His mother and father were so in love, that when his father died, his mother died a week later of a broken heart. Those were his only loved ones, and they had all passed on to the eternal sea kingdom in the sky. He missed them all very dearly and wished that he could see them again someday. Then Slick's dreams turned more violent as he found himself battling some whale hunters and their harpoons and guns. He destroyed the hunter's boats and devoured all of them. That's the way he liked to end his dreams.

He woke up and found himself hungry again. Slick decided to swim out to Boat-Wreck Lane to hunt for something to devour. It was called Boat-Wreck Lane because there were sunken boats there. When he arrived at the surface, he saw that it was day time and there was a party boat there. Slick decided to attack the party boat for a quick meal.

The Silver Serpent swam as fast as he could towards one of the party boats and slammed into its hull. The jolt from the hit put a big hole in the hull and knocked four passengers overboard.

Slick swam to the overboard victims and lunged at one of them and grabbed her in his lethal jaws. He chomped down on the young female in the bikini and split her in two. Slick devoured her torso while her legs fell into the ocean.

"Holy shit man! It's the Silver Serpent! He just ate Nancy!" Craig exclaimed. Craig was the owner of the party boat.

"Get the guns!" Billy yelled.

Billy and Craig rushed to the cabin and grabbed the guns.

Slick went after another one of the overboard party goers.

"No! Please don't kill me!" Nate yelled.

After devouring Nancy's torso, Slick raised his upper body and head above Nate, and darted down and snatched Nate in his jaws. Nate screamed out in agonizing pain. Slick violently grasped Nate with his two upper limbs and ripped him into three bloody pieces. Nate's head stayed stuck in Slick's jaws, while his legs and torso were pierced with the claws of Slick's upper limbs.

"He got Nate too! Shoot that son of a bitch!" Craig exclaimed.

Craig and Billy fired off rifle and handgun rounds into Slick's body. As Slick was chewing on Nate's head, he felt the lead slugs penetrate his scaly skin. He dove deeper into the ocean with Nate's mangled body parts skewered his jaws and claws. The rifle and handgun slugs didn't go too deep, but they broke the first layers of his armored scales and caused some bleeding. He swam back to his cave with the bloody stumps of what was left of Nate to finish them there.

"Did we hit him?" Billy asked.

"Yeah, I'm sure we did, but I don't think it did much damage. Did you see the size of that monster?" Craig replied.

"Yeah, that's the biggest creature in the ocean I've ever seen. I didn't think that mythological creature really existed. I guess I was wrong," Billy said.

"Throw some lifesavers to Molly and Marco quickly before that monster comes back," Craig ordered.

Molly and Marco were the other two overboard party goers.

Billy threw out some lifesavers so that Molly and Marco could grab a hold of them and pull themselves back onboard the boat.

"Damnit! I think our boat is sinking!" Craig exclaimed.

"That creature must have made a whole in the hull when it rammed us," Billy said.

"Help us! Somebody, help us!" Craig yelled.

A nearby shrimp boat heard all the commotion and guns and headed over that way to see what was going on.

"I think that boat is coming towards us," Billy said.

"Yeah, me too. Thank God," Craig replied.

Marco and Molly climbed back on board the sinking boat.

"Oh my God! That monster ate Nancy and Nate right in front of us!" Molly exclaimed.

"What the hell was that thing?" Marco asked.

"That was the Silver Serpent. You've never heard the legend?" Craig replied.

"No. I've never heard about that," Marco said.

"Yes. I've heard about that God-awful creature. My grandpa used to tell me stories about the Silver Serpent," Molly said.

"Well, now you've seen it first hand for yourself. I'm sorry you had to witness that," Craig replied.

"I can't believe that Nate and Nancy are gone. We have to kill that thing," Billy said.

"That's much easier said than done. People have been trying to slay that beast for years, and none have been successful," Craig said.

"That's not true. There was another Silver Serpent about two years ago that was slayed by a group of hardcore whale hunters. That Silver Serpent's head was supposedly mounted in the Captain's den. Few people have ever seen it though. That's why not everybody believes in it," Billy replied.

"OK. Are you saying that these Silver Serpents can be slayed?" Craig asked.

"Yes, that's what I'm saying. I don't know how they did it, but I bet if we ask around, we can find out," Billy replied.

"The shrimp boat was getting closer. Maybe they know something about it," Craig said.

Molly was crying hysterically, and Marco was panting like a tired dog. The shrimp boat finally arrived at the sinking party boat.

"Please help us sir! Our boat is sinking!" Billy said.

"Lord have mercy. You guys better climb aboard my boat," the Shrimp Captain said.

He pulled his shrimp boat right next to the sinking party boat.

"What happened to your boat here?" The Captain asked.

"Did you not see that creature? It was the Silver Serpent! It slammed into my boat and made a hole in it!" Craig exclaimed.

"Then it slayed and devoured two of our friends," Billy replied.

"Are you kidding me? I didn't see that monster. I just heard the guns and the commotion. That's why we came over here," the Captain replied.

"We fired our guns at that Silver Serpent. I know we hit him, but I don't think it did much damage," Craig replied.

"So it does exist. I knew there was some truth and sense to those stories. Yes, I imagine that is like trying to slay a Tyrannosaurus rex with a pea shooter. Go ahead and climb aboard," the Captain said.

The traumatized party goers jumped over to the shrimp boat. The party boat was sinking fast.

"It looks like that boat is history," the Captain said.

"Yeah, not much we can do to save it now. Damn. I loved that boat," Craig replied.

"It's just a boat. Boats are replaceable, lives are not," the Captain said.

All the passengers were safely onboard the shrimp boat, so it headed back to land. The boat arrived back at the docks.

"I'm sorry about your friends. You have my condolences. It's a real tragedy when they go so young like that," the Captain said.

"Yes it is. I sure am gonna miss them. Thanks for your condolences," Craig replied.

"Rest in peace Nancy and Nate. May God protect your souls on their journey into the afterlife," Billy replied.

"I pray that they go to heaven," Molly said.

"I need a drink," Marco said.

"I'm sure they will go to heaven if they were decent, God fearing human beings," the Captain replied.

"How can we slay that Silver Serpent, Captain?" Craig asked.

"If I had the answer to that I'd be rich. A wealthy sea captain by the name of Captain Golden has been offering a $10,000 reward the last couple of years to the slayers of the Silver Serpent. I had heard that some whale hunters slayed one a couple of years ago, but they feared that one was still out there due to all the recent humans disappearing," the Captain replied.

"Damn. There has to be some way to destroy that beast," Craig said.

"I've heard that a silver harpoon through its heart can kill it, but that theory has yet to be proven," the Captain replied.

"How did they kill that other one a couple of years ago?" Billy asked.

"Nobody knows. The whale hunters don't always let the community in on their little secrets. They are very secretive and discrete," the Captain said.

"There must be a way to slay that abomination. We need to do some research on this Silver Serpent," Craig said.

Chapter Two
Boat-Wreck Lane

The Silver Serpent named Slick, by his legendary parents, woke up at noon the next day to find a bloom of colorful jellyfish slowly propelling themselves around, just outside the walls of his cave.

"What a lucky day to see these jelly filled donuts right outside my cave," Slick said to himself.

Slick rose from his cushy, kelp bed and lethargically swam to the jellyfish. He arrived at the jellyfish bloom, and quickly devoured a mouthful with one quick snap of his mighty, steel trap jaws.

He gulped.

Then Slick saw his other friend Oliver the octopus swimming towards him. Oliver was a giant, purplish-blue, octopus with a head the size of a small house, and tentacles that stretched over one hundred feet long.

"What's up, Slick? How does it feel to be the king of the ocean?" Oliver asked.

"What's up, Oliver? How you doing man? It feels great. Nobody can mess with me or my buddies. I am the fiercest sea monster in all the seven seas," Slick replied with a chuckle.

"That's great man. I wouldn't mess with you either," Oliver said.

"That's good buddy. We have each other's back," Slick said.

Just then a ruckus from the surface erupted.

"What the blazes is that?" Oliver asked.

"It looks like another fishing boat roaming around Boat-Wreck Lane," Slick replied.

"Let's go check it out," Oliver said.

"OK," Slick replied.

The colossal Silver Serpent and the gigantic octopus swam towards Boat-Wreck Lane, where the commotion was. They arrived there.

"Yup, it's another fishing boat," Slick said.

"Why is it snooping around Boat-Wreck Lane?" Oliver asked.

"I don't know. Maybe there was an accident here or something," Slick replied.

"What kind of accident?" Oliver asked.

"I don't know. Maybe some humans got attacked or something like that," Slick said.

"Slick, did you devour some humans here last night?" Oliver replied.

"Yeah, just a couple," Slick said.

"You devil you. Don't you think that's gonna draw more attention to you, and there will be more humans out here hunting you?" Oliver asked.

"Not really. It's been that way for years and will never change. I'm not scared of them, but they sure as hell should fear me. They killed my one true love, and I will have my vengeance. Besides, I love the taste of humans," Slick replied.

"I know you see it that way, but does it always have to be like that?" Oliver said.

"The humans don't respect us, and they hunt and slay us. Why should we respect them and not slay them? We live on a creature planet where only the strongest creatures survive," Slick replied.

"I guess you have a point there. I'm getting sick and tired of their boats hanging around our territories," Oliver said.

"So am I. Do you honestly believe that if I didn't devour humans, that they would stop coming around? You are smarter than that. The humans go wherever they want, whenever they want," Slick responded.

"So what do you want to do?" Oliver asked.

"Let's hit that fishing boat from underneath it and flip it over," Slick replied.

"OK, let's do it," Oliver said. The two sea creatures positioned themselves directly under the boat. Then they torpedoed themselves towards the hull and savagely slammed into it with brute force. That caused the boat to flip over.

"Damn! What the hell was that?" A passenger exclaimed.

The two fishermen fell overboard.

"They fell overboard. Let's go get them," Slick said.

"I don't like to devour humans Slick. You know that," Oliver replied.

"So what? Just help me scare them and slay them. You never know, you might enjoy it," Slick said.

"OK, let's go," Oliver responded.

The two sea beasts swam over to the overboard fishermen and got right in front of their faces.

"Holy shit! Do you see those things?" The fishermen yelped.

"How can I not see them? They are right in front of us! That's the Silver Serpent and that other creature looks like a giant octopus!" The other fisherman exclaimed.

The Silver Serpent stuck his long upper body out towards the fishermen and grabbed one of them in his jaws. Slick's sword-like teeth skewered the fisherman's body parts like a shish kebab.

"AHHH, it's got me!" The fisherman exclaimed.

Slick chomped down on the fisherman and crunched multiple bones in his body. Blood squirted out of the wounds like red liquid gushing out of a busted pipe, while Slick continued to demolish and devour the shredded body.

"Get the other one," Slick said to Oliver with a mouthful of flesh and organs in his jaws.

Oliver wrapped his long tentacles around the other fisherman's head and squeezed it until it popped like a ripe melon.

"Good job Oliver! That's the spirit!" Slick exclaimed.

"What do you want to do with him?" Oliver asked.

"I'm going to devour him. What do you think?" Slick replied.

"Well then go ahead. He's all yours. Enjoy," Oliver said.

Slick grabbed the headless fisherman with his two upper limbs and tore the still-beating heart out of his chest.

"This is my favorite part," Slick replied.

Slick popped the heart into his mouth like a delectable morsel and chewed it with savory satisfaction. Next, he savagely devoured the rest of the body parts, bones and all.

"Are you all done there buddy?" Oliver asked.

"That hit the spot. Yes, I'm all done. Thanks for your help Oliver. You are a real pal," Slick replied.

"No problem man. That was rather fun after all. I'm kind of drained though. I'm gonna head back to my place to get some rest," Oliver said.

"OK buddy. I'm gonna return to my cave to let my food go down and get some rest. I'll see you later," Slick replied.

“OK Slick. See you later,” Oliver said.

The two sea monsters swam back to their places of residence for some rest.

Chapter Three
The Hawkeye

The next day it was Wednesday, August 2, 1904. The Silver Serpent laid sound asleep in his cushy bed of colorful kelp. He awoke and swam outside of his cave. Slick spotted some hammerhead sharks swimming around some coral reef just above his cave. That was a perfect breakfast opportunity for the Silver Serpent.

He stealthily slipped out of his cave and dashed at them before they could even see what was coming. He slayed and devoured them on the spot.

"That hit the spot," Slick said to himself.

While Slick chewed on the remaining pieces of the sharks, he saw Bo swim by above him just below the surface. Slick swam up to Bo.

"How's it going, Bo?" Slick asked.

"Say, Slick. I came to the surface to see what's going on above us. It's good to know that, you know," Bo replied.

"You are an excellent look out, but you sound a little paranoid," Slick said.

"That's easy for you to say. They could be hunting either one of us at any time and you know that. Why do you have to be such a smart-ass Slick?" Bo responded.

"I'm just kidding man. I'm just saying I don't worry as much as you do. It's not healthy, you know," Slick said.

"Well you should worry. The more humans you slay, the more they are gonna be out here hunting our skins," Bo replied.

"Whatever man. I'm not scared of any humans," Slick said.

"I'm not either. But we always have to be prepared," Bo replied.

"I agree pal. So what is going on up there on the shimmering surface?" Slick said.

"I don't know. The same old stuff. You are here too. Why don't you stick your eyes above the surface and see for yourself?" Bo replied.

"OK wise guy, I will. Do you really think I'm scared to be seen by any humans? I'll devour them alive before they even know what hit them," Slick said.

"I'll do it too. I'm not scared of them either," Bo replied.

The two gargantuan sea monsters stuck their eyes just above the glossy, royal-blue, ocean's surface. They saw a boat named *The Hawkeye* that patrolled the waters around Boat-Wreck Lane, since that was where their friends were slayed by the Silver Serpent.

"Do you see that? Who do you think it is?" Slick asked.

"I don't know. It could be anybody. Maybe it's somebody snooping around because of the humans you devoured recently," Bo replied.

"Maybe you're right. Who knows?" Slick said.

Bo was right. It was Billy and Craig. The two friends of Nancy and Nate whom the Silver Serpent had just devoured a couple of nights ago.

"Craig, do you have the silver harpoons ready to go?" Billy asked.

"Yeah. They are all ready to go," Craig replied.

"OK man. Get that stuff ready, because we are entering Boat-Wreck Lane. The last area that the Silver Serpent has been seen," Billy replied.

"Great. We are right on top of that," Craig said.

The two fishermen lurked about the waters of Boat-Wreck Lane in *The Hawkeye*. Bo and Slick swam below the surface to remain low-key and unseen.

"We better hit something with these silver harpoons. They cost thirty dollars each," Billy replied.

"Don't worry. We will hit something with these babies!" Craig exclaimed.

The two serpent hunters snooped around Boat-Wreck Lane hoping to spot the Silver Serpent. Slick said goodbye to Bo and decided to swim back to his cave for a while.

It was about 2:00 in the morning the next day. The Silver Serpent swam outside his cave looking for a late-night snack. Boat-Wreck Lane was located a couple of miles away from Slick's cave. Slick's sensory skills were so sharp and keen that he detected *The Hawkeye*. That meant that he heard them underwater through his hydro-sonic sonar hearing abilities.

Slick decided to swim to Boat-Wreck Lane to see what was going on. When Slick arrived there, he saw that *The Hawkeye* boat was still there hanging around. Slick's arrival caused some eruptive waves around the boat.

"Holy Smokes! Did you see that Billy?" Craig exclaimed.

Just as Craig was saying this, *The Hawkeye* flipped over.

"AHHH!" Craig said.

"Yeah, I saw that! AHHH!" Billy shouted as the boat flipped over. Slick quickly found the overboard victims.

The colossal sea creature saw Billy and Craig helplessly flapping around like some crippled dogs in a pool of jelly. The large rogue swells caused them to bob up and down like popping corks. The king of the ocean swam over to the struggling victims and bit both of their heads off in a matter of seconds. Their lifeless bodies floated there in the red and black waters of Boat-Wreck Lane.

Slick wasted no time as he clamped his jaws down on Billy's torso and ripped him in half. He crunched down devastatingly hard on Billy's upper body and chewed on it for a while. He crunched on flesh, bone, and organs alike, and then swallowed it. Then he tore the torso off Craig, chewed on it, and swallowed that also. Slick grabbed the lower halves of his victim's corpses in his claws and swam back to his cave. On his way back he spotted Bo devouring a massive amount of krill.

"Say, buddy. How you doing?" Slick said.

"Gulp. Say, buddy. I'm getting my share of krill for the morning," Bo replied.

"I see that. I'm heading home. I'll see you later," Slick said.

"OK man. Take care," Bo responded.

Slick swam back to his cave while Bo continued to swallow massive amounts of nutritious krill. Slick arrived at his cave and found his other good friend, Oliver, waiting outside his cave's entrance.

"What's going on, Oliver?" Slick asked.

"Not much. What's new with you Slick?" Oliver responded.

"I just finished devouring a late-night snack. It was glorious," Slick replied.

"Let me guess. Did you devour some more humans?" Oliver said.

"You know me too well Oliver" Slick said.

"Man, you are just a human devouring machine. You are a true original," Oliver replied with a chuckle.

"That is how the great Sea God made me. I am what I am," Slick responded.

"So what do you have going on for today?" Oliver asked.

"Not much brother. I'm just gonna lay low and get some rest. This killing business can be exhausting sometimes," Slick replied.

"Get outta here. You are the king of the ocean," Oliver said.

"Thanks man. But being on the top of the food chain isn't easy all the time. Sometimes I need to battle other creatures trying to take over my spot. I must protect this ocean and my throne," Slick said stoically.

"I understand. I imagine it can get lonely at the top sometimes," Oliver replied.

"Exactly man," Slick said.

"OK. I'm gonna go look for some squid to devour. I'm in the mood for calamari," Oliver replied.

"Isn't that like cannibalism buddy?" Slick said.

"Just because we are in the same family, doesn't mean we can't devour each other," Oliver replied.

"We must slay or be slayed out here. The law of the ocean. Am I right? Take care and I'll see you later my brother," Slick said.

"OK Slick, you go get some rest so you'll have more energy for slaying and devouring, and you can protect this vast ocean and your royal throne," Oliver replied.

Oliver swam away to the east to Squid Alley to hunt some squid. Slick swam inside his cave for a good night's rest on his bed of cozy, colorful kelp.

Chapter Four
Marco and Molly

The next day it was Friday August 4, 1904. Marco Gumwood woke up next to his girlfriend Molly Thompson in his bed, with the radiant, yellow sun beaming its golden rays through his bedroom window. Molly was gorgeous with long, silky, onyx hair and sparkling, peridot-green eyes. Marco was barrel chested with dark brown hair and eyes.

"Good morning, sunshine. How did you sleep?" Marco asked.

"Good morning, baby. I slept okay. I'm still so sad about Nate and Nancy's death. I can't believe they were eaten by that monstrous Silver Serpent," Nancy said.

"I know babe. I can't believe it either. I think we should go down to the Sandbar to see if anybody knows anything about the Silver Serpent," Marco replied.

The Sandbar was a local bar in the harbor town of Cape Crusade. Cape Crusade was located in the borough of Staten Island, New York, where Marco and Molly resided. It was also a hangout for the local fishermen and whale hunters. The whale hunters and fishermen were the ones who had the most knowledge pertaining to the Silver Serpent. Molly and Marco took a shower together, got dressed, and headed out the door. They jumped into Marco's horse drawn buggy and rode to the Sandbar. It was about 4:00 on that sunny and pleasant Friday afternoon. The couple arrived at the Sandbar and saw that there were quite a few horse drawn buggies in the parking lot. Most citizens of Cape Crusade owned horse drawn buggies because they were more affordable. There were some wealthier citizens who owned automobiles.

They parked the horse drawn buggy and walked inside the Sandbar. Inside there were lots of fishermen and whale hunters with their friends and girlfriends. Marco and Molly walked up to the bar and ordered some beers. They spotted an old fisherman sitting by himself drinking an Irish whiskey on the rocks.

"How you doing?" Marco asked.

"Good afternoon, young man. I've seen better days. How about yourself?" The old fisherman replied.

"I'm okay. I'm Marco, and this is my girlfriend Molly," Marco said.

"How you doing, Molly? It's a pleasure to meet you. My name is Walter," the old fisherman replied.

"I've been better. It's nice to meet you Walter," Molly said.

"It's nice to meet you Walter," Marco replied.

"It's a pleasure to meet both of you. What can I do for you youngsters today?" Walter asked.

"We were wondering if you know anything about the Silver Serpent," Marco replied.

"The Silver Serpent you say. Why do you ask about that God-awful monster?" Walter said.

"A couple of our friends were slayed and devoured by it near Boat-Wreck Lane. We witnessed the horrific events for ourselves," Marco replied.

"I'm sorry to hear that. Yes, I know a thing or two about the Silver Serpent. How do you think those wrecked boats sunk there? The Silver Serpent sunk those boats and devoured their crews," Walter said.

"What else can you tell us about it? Can it be slayed?" Marco replied.

"I can tell you that it is nothing to take lightly or tangle with. It's a highly-advanced, bloodthirsty, lethal, killing machine. If you try to slay it, you better be ready to be slayed yourself because many people have tried to slay it and ended up losing their own lives," Walter said.

"Oh my God! How many people have tried?" Molly asked.

"I don't know the exact number, but it has been quite a few over the years. The Silver Serpent has a taste for human blood, and he despises humans because they are responsible for the death of his lover," Walter said.

"How do you know all of this?" Marco asked.

"I've been around these waters for many years, and that is how I know. I was on the crew that slayed the Silver Serpent's lover while she was pregnant with his offspring. My crew hauled her body onto the shore and dissected her. We found the growing offspring inside her belly. That is why the Silver Serpent hates humans from the depths of his soul and why he slays and devours so many of them. We robbed him of his true loves, his lover, and his unborn offspring. And more importantly of his bloodline," Walter said.

"Holy Shit man! There is no wonder why he attacks so many humans. They took his true love and his unborn whelp. Shit, I'd be pissed off too," Marco replied.

"Oh, that poor creature, I feel bad for him now. But he did kill some of our good friends. I'll never forget that," Molly said.

"Yes, that he did. He's slaughtered and devoured many people's friends, sons, daughters, brothers, sisters, fathers, mothers, and grandparents. That is why so many people want to destroy it. But not all of them try, because they don't want to be the next meal on his menu," Walter replied.

"Is there a way to slay it?" Marco asked

"Yes, there is a way to its demise. Only a silver harpoon through its heart can slay it. It has to be made of pure silver," Walter said.

"I don't know if I want to do this yet, but if I do, where can I purchase some silver harpoons?" Marco asked.

"You can buy some at the Purple Octopus. The deep-sea fishing supplies store located on Blackberry Street," Walter replied.

"OK man. I have some thinking to do. C'mon Molly. Let's go home," Marco said.

"OK babe," Molly replied.

"Walter, it was a pleasure to meet you and thank you for this valuable information," Marco said.

"Yes, thanks mister," Molly said.

"It is no problem youngsters. It was nice to meet you two as well. You all take care now and beware of the mighty Silver Serpent. It is still out there, and it has a taste for human blood on its slithery, forked tongue," Walter replied.

"Oh, just one more question. What did your crew do with the bodies of the Silver Serpents you slayed?" Marco asked.

"That's a good question. Once we brought her to shore, the entire northeast coast, nation, and world, learned about it through reports from the Coast Guard, Navy, Law Enforcement, and media. Our Captain ordered us to cut off her massive and menacing head, so that he could mount it in his den above the fireplace. It is still there to this day, but the Captain is growing more senile every day. He only allowed close friends and family to see it, if anybody at all. We donated her body and the offspring's body to the world's most sophisticated forensic labs. Extensive studies that focused on blood, bone, and tissue were conducted by those labs. The Silver Serpent's existence was shrouded in mystery. The scientists couldn't figure out how long they had existed or how they came into existence. They could only determine that the Silver Serpents were some kind of prehistoric carnivores that reproduced, and they could live up to 100 years. When the offspring was discovered in the belly of the dead female Silver Serpent, most people were convinced that another Silver Serpent still existed. The world sent its best scientists and hunters to search for another Silver Serpent, but they never saw one and gave up their search after about a year. I was out fishing by myself about six months ago near Hammerhead Hedge, and I saw the Silver Serpent about fifty yards away stick its long, silver, upper body and head above the surface. I know it must have seen me too, but for reasons only God knows, it chose to let me live. I still thank God everyday for allowing me to live this long. I told the people of Cape Crusade that I saw another Silver Serpent and that one was still out there. They didn't believe the word of an old drunk anymore. I can still remember those glorious days and nights out at sea. They were the best days of my life. Our crew was called the Manta Rays and our Captain, was Captain Gusto. We were the best whale hunters in all the seven seas, and the only ones with a Silver Serpent kill, under our belts," Walter replied. Suddenly, Walter didn't seem drunk at all. All of his memories became fresh and clear in his mind at that moment. It was nothing short of divine intervention.

"Wow, that definitely answered my question and then some. I'm amazed. That was an incredible and mind-bending story. The world needs to know that another Silver Serpent still exists and is still out there hunting the Atlantic waters. And somebody needs to slay it before it causes more death and destruction," Marco said.

Marco and Molly finished their beers and said their goodbyes again. They were still in awe from Walter's story about the Silver Serpents. Then they walked out of the Sandbar and into their horse drawn buggy. They rode home and made passionate love to each other before and after dinner. Then they ate some cookies and cream ice cream for dessert and fell asleep together in each other's loving embrace on Marco's comfortable, king-sized bed.

Chapter Five
Hammerhead Hedge

Slick woke up the next day on Saturday, August 5, 1904. He swam up to the surface to scope out the scene. The Silver Serpent saw his great friend Oliver the octopus lurking about the glistening, cobalt surface.

"What's going on buddy?" Slick asked. Oliver saw Slick and almost squirted his ink on himself just because of the sheer size and menacing look Slick possessed.

"Hi there, buddy. Damn, you nearly scared the ink out of me!" Oliver replied.

"HAHA, you are a regular joker my friend," Slick chuckled.

The two friends swam over to Hammerhead Hedge, which was about three miles to the west of Slick's cave. It earned the name Hammerhead Hedge because of all the hammerhead sharks that congregated there to feast on the sea life that lived around a huge hedge of seaweed and kelp.

They arrived there and spotted a gam of five hammerhead sharks.

"Look, it's Hank the hammerhead and his shark goons. What's up Hank? How you doing, old friend?" Oliver asked.

"What's up Oliver? Not much man. I'm just looking for some fish to sink my teeth into. How you doing Slick?" Hank replied.

"I'm great, Hank. How about yourself?" Slick said.

"There goes some bluefish right there. Let's get them!" Oliver exclaimed.

A school of blue fish swam just under the large hedge of sea vegetation. Slick and Oliver darted after the bright blue fish. Oliver grabbed some of them with his tenacious tentacles as Slick snatched some in his jaws of death. Hank and his shark buddies accelerated after the school of blue fish as well. They too got their share of fresh, fish fillets.

"Just like the old days, huh Slick?" Oliver said.

"Yeah man. You said it. This stuff never gets old," Slick replied.

"AHH, those sure were some delectable blue fish," Oliver said.

"Yeah man, those were some fat, juicy ones," Hank said.

"Has there been any word on the fishermen and whale hunters?" Slick asked Hank.

"Yeah, my gang and I saw some whale hunters here earlier this morning lurking about. I think they were looking for humpback whales," Hank replied.

"Is that a fact? Exactly how many boats were there?" Slick said.

"Two," Hank replied.

"OK, thanks for the update," Slick said.

"No problem Slick. Ocean creatures like us have to stick together, right?" Hank said.

"You know it," Slick replied.

"Alright then gents, it's time to go take my mid-afternoon nap. I'll see you sea animals later," Oliver said.

"OK Oliver. Take care bud," Slick replied.

"Yeah buddy, see you later Oliver," Hank said.

"That sounded like a great idea, Oliver. I think I'll go back to my cave and do the same," Slick replied.

Slick and Oliver swam back to their caves for a midday siesta. Hank and his goons spotted a school of Atlantic bluefin tuna, so they swam after them for some dessert. Sharks loved to devour bluefin tuna just like Slick did.

As Slick was swimming home, he heard a boat's engine rumbling on the surface. He stuck his eyes just above the surface to spot the boat. It was a fisherman's boat with three fishermen onboard. Slick tried to keep his distance from the boat, so they would not see him. The fishermen were fishing for sharks, but they were also looking for Slick, because they had heard of the recent attacks and killings of some of the locals.

"Keep your eye out for that monster?" Rusty said.

Rusty was the Captain of the fishing boat.

"Aye-aye Captain," Travis replied.

Travis was another fisherman on the boat. The boat was named *The Barracuda*.

"I'll drop the anchor here at Hammerhead Hedge," Milo said.

Milo was the third fisherman on *The Barracuda*.

"Let's throw the lines out," Rusty ordered.

Milo and Travis dropped four fishing lines into the sparkling, greenish-blue, ocean abyss.

"I heard there have been some giant sharks caught here lately. Hammerhead and mako sharks mostly, but even some great whites have been spotted," Milo said enthusiastically.

The four lines were rigged with solid weights and large chunks of bloody bonita at the end of the hooks. The lines drifted further and deeper away from the boat.

"Do you see any activity around us?" Travis asked.

"Yeah, some schools of fish are at ten o'clock, so there should be some sharks around as well. Let's chum the water for good measure," Rusty replied.

Milo and Travis grabbed a couple of chum buckets and tossed them into the majestic Atlantic.

Slick was observing the boat's activity from about 100 yards away with his eyes barely sticking out above the surface. He was too far away for the fishermen to see him and his green and blue tipped scales helped him camouflage with the water nicely. He decided he was going to have a little fun with them. Slick ducked his head back under water and swam stealthily to a chunk of bait on one of the lines. It was about 100 yards under the surface. The Silver Serpent snatched the chunk of bonita in his jaws and tugged ferociously on it. The rod bent violently and Rusty was the first one to grab it.

"Fish on!" Rusty exclaimed.

Rusty grabbed the rod and pulled back as hard as he could to set the hook. The hook set hard in Slick's upper jaw, and it stung him quite a bit. That really pissed him off. Slick pulled back on the line with tremendous force, and that sent Rusty flying overboard into the ocean like a flying fish. Rusty hit the water hard with the pole still in his hands.

Slick sped away in the opposite direction of the boat and dragged Rusty down under the water with him.

"Holy smokes! Let go of the rod Rusty!" Milo exclaimed.

Finally, Rusty was smart enough to let go of the fishing rod. Slick felt that Rusty was no longer at the end of the line, so he stopped swimming away for the moment. Rusty began to swim back up to the surface.

"Help! Help me!" Rusty yelled as he surfaced.

"Hold on Rusty! We're coming for you!" Travis exclaimed.

Rusty was about thirty yards away from the boat and about fifty yards away from the Silver Serpent. The boat headed towards Rusty to pick him up.

Slick swam rapidly towards Rusty to slaughter him before he could get away. *The Barracuda* got right up next to Rusty, and Travis threw him a long rope so he could pull himself up. Just as he and Milo were pulling Rusty up the side of the boat, Slick popped up out from the ocean's crystal surface and grabbed Rusty by the legs with his jaws and then snapped them off violently from Rusty's waist. Rusty's top and lower halves of his body laid floating in an expanding cloud of syrupy, red blood that stained the ocean's pristine shade of royal blue.

Then Slick grasped Rusty's top half in his jaws and the lower half with his upper limbs and dragged the two bloody pieces of human carnage down into the depths of the murky Atlantic Ocean.

"NOOO!" Travis exclaimed.

"Holy shit man! Rusty!" Milo yelled.

"Did you see that thing? That was the Silver Serpent!" Travis exclaimed.

"Yeah, I saw it! It was enormous! That damned beast just killed our friend!" Milo replied.

Travis and Milo were shocked and started to suffer from post-traumatic stress disorder. They were shaking uncontrollably.

"Should we go after it?" Travis asked.

"I don't know man. What kind of weapons do we have onboard?" Milo replied.

"We have some rifles and harpoons," Travis said.

"Do you think that's enough to kill it? How do you know it's not long gone by now?" Milo replied.

"I don't know. What do you want to do?" Travis said.

"How can we go after it if we don't know where it is?" Milo replied.

"You're right. It's probably long gone by now. Let's head back to shore, so we can report this and get some more man power and fire power to kill that thing," Travis said.

"OK man. Let's do that. That thing is probably 200 yards under the water by now. Let's come back when we have a better arsenal and more man power to attack it with," Milo replied.

The two fishermen headed back to shore on *The Barracuda* still traumatized from the absolute terror and gore that they just witnessed. They arrived at the docks and headed straight to the Sandbar to report the horrific events that just took place. Slick swam back to his home with the mangled stumps that used to be Rusty in his jaws and claws, so that he could devour them in the cozy confines of his own cave.

Chapter Six
The Silver Serpent Bounty

Travis and Milo rushed over to the Sandbar to report the horrific events that they just witnessed that Saturday. They stormed in and rushed over to a table of notoriously fierce whale hunters.

"You guys gotta help us! The Silver Serpent just killed our friend Rusty!" Travis exclaimed.

"Calm down buddy. Did you see that yourself?" Rocky replied.

Rocky was the Captain of a whale hunting crew called the Bloodhounds. They earned their name, the Bloodhounds, because they were also avid game hunters on land during hunting season. They hunted wild game such as white-tailed deer, black bears, red foxes, cottontail rabbits, woodchucks, and red, gray, fox, and flying squirrels. Each Bloodhound crew member owned a bloodhound dog to aid them in tracking their game.

"Yeah we saw it for ourselves! That monster devoured him right in front of us!" Milo said.

"That beast is getting outta control! It sounds like the Silver Serpent has struck again! That beast must be slayed!" Christo exclaimed. Christo was another member of the Bloodhounds.

"How can we do that?" Travis asked.

"Captain Golden said he would pay a $10,000 reward to the slayers of the Silver Serpent," Rocky replied.

Captain Golden was the wealthiest sea captain in Cape Crusade and Staten Island. He owned his own boat store called Captain Golden's Boats.

"OK. Do you think that will get people to get off their asses to go and slay that monster?" Christo said.

"I think so. Who couldn't use that extra money?" Rocky replied.

"That sounds like a plan," Travis said.

"OK. I will announce this first thing tomorrow morning here at 10:00 and post some flyers in here and around town. I will need your guy's help in doing so," Rocky replied.

"OK," Everybody said.

"Now let's grab a drink and toast to the demise of that abomination from hell!" Rocky said.

They all raised their glasses and toasted.

"Let's slay that fowl creature once and for all and send it to the fiery depths of hell where it belongs!" Christo exclaimed.

Travis and Milo drank with the Bloodhounds that Saturday night and went home feeling better about their chances of getting revenge on the Serpent that killed their friend. The next day rolled around and it was Sunday, August 6, 1904.

Marco woke up and made a cup of coffee. Then he stepped out into the breezy, coastal air and retrieved the newspaper. On the front page it read: "Another killer Silver Serpent in the Atlantic!"

Marco read some more and discovered that Captain Golden was offering a $10,000 reward to the slayers of the Silver Serpent. The newspaper announced that if anybody was interested, they should go to the Sandbar for more details on the generous bounty.

That sparked his interest, since he had been struggling with his bills lately, and he too wanted revenge on the creature that killed his friends. Marco jumped in his horse drawn buggy and rode over to the Sandbar. He walked inside and saw a boisterous mob of fishermen and whale hunters talking about the cash reward for the Silver Serpent.

Marco walked up to the Bloodhounds and introduced himself.

"How you doing fellas? My name is Marco Gumwood. I read in the newspaper about the reward for the Silver Serpent. That's what I came here to discuss," Marco boldly stated.

"I'm alright, Marco. How about yourself? I'm Rocky and these are my comrades, the Bloodhounds," Rocky replied.

"It's nice to meet you fellas. So how are we going to slay that gigantic sea monster?" Marco said.

"How are we going to slay it? I take it you want to ride along with us on this mission," Rocky replied.

"Sure, why not. There is strength in numbers, right?" Marco said.

"Yes, that is true. But it is no easy task when you are dealing with a Silver Serpent," Christo replied.

Just then Milo and Travis walked through the front doors of the Sandbar.

"I'm telling you that I know how to slay the Silver Serpent!" Rocky exclaimed.

"Yeah, me too!" Marco responded.

"How you fellas doing?" Travis asked.

"OK Travis. How you doing?" Rocky responded.

"Marco, this is Travis and Milo. They witnessed one of their friends being slayed and devoured yesterday by the Silver Serpent," Christo said.

"I'm sorry to hear that fellas. I witnessed the same thing a couple of days ago. The Silver Serpent devoured two of our friend's right in front of us. It was a horrific and gruesome scene. I can't get it out of my head," Marco replied.

Marco and Molly were still unaware of their other friends, Billy and Craig's recent bloody demise, courtesy of the Silver Serpent.

"OK, so that creature has slain and devoured some of our friends. Let's put our heads together and slay that abomination!" Travis exclaimed.

"How do we slay that beast?" Milo asked.

"A silver harpoon through its heart is the only way to slay it," Marco replied.

"How do you know that?" Rocky asked.

"An old fisherman named Walter told me. He has had firsthand experience in tangling with that monster, and he was on the crew of the boat that slayed the Silver Serpent's lover," Marco replied.

"Old man Walter. He's an old drunk that has been out at sea for too long. Some of the stuff he says is just the liquor talking," Christo said.

"Maybe. However, he sounded very sure of himself, and he has slayed one of those Silver Serpents before, and that's how he did it. With a silver harpoon through its cold heart. I believe him," Marco replied.

"Well if he said that he has slain one of those silver devils before, then maybe we just have to believe him. Let's gather some silver harpoons and give it our best shot," Rocky said.

"I'm in!" Travis yelled.

"Me too!" Milo exclaimed.

"Let's do this! Let's avenge the deaths of our lost friends and put the Silver Serpent to eternal rest!" Marco shouted.

"It's settled then. We shall journey out on our mission two days from now on Tuesday, August 8. That should give us enough time to gather all of our supplies that we will need for this expedition," Rocky said.

"Let's drink to this bounty mission and toast to our good luck, health, and fortune!" Christo replied.

"We all have to be prepared that some of us might not come back to land ever again, and we might not see our families ever again. That Silver Serpent is a freakishly powerful and devastating creature from the deepest and darkest depths of the Atlantic Ocean. It is battle hardened and wise for a beast and does not like to be meddled with. It is a cold-blooded killer and won't think twice about slaying and devouring any of us. Just be prepared for what we are about to encounter," Rocky said.

"OK. Let's say we do slay that thing. How are we going to split up the reward money?" Marco asked.

"We will divide it evenly so all of us receive our fair cut," Christo replied.

"Bartender, get us all some shots of whiskey and some ice-cold beers," Rocky demanded.

"OK, that's coming right up fellas," the bartender replied.

The excited crews of fishermen and whale hunters drank their shots and raised their beers in the air.

"To the death of the Silver Serpent!" They all shouted.

They drank their beers and discussed their plans and strategies for this treacherous sea mission.

Marco drank about six beers and then said his goodbyes to the Bloodhounds. He also gave Rocky his landline, just in case he needed to get in contact with him. Then he rode home. Travis and Milo drank all day and night with the Bloodhounds and got ready to go home pretty hammered at about midnight. They were all heavy drinkers, so they could hold their liquor.

"How would you fellas like to be members of the mighty and valiant Bloodhounds?" Rocky asked Travis and Milo.

"Sure. That would be an honor," Travis replied.

"I'm in," Milo said.

"OK, it's official. You gentlemen are now a part of the brave and bold Bloodhounds from Cape Crusade! Welcome to our family! It's an honor to have you gentlemen!" Christo exclaimed.

"OK. Let's meet here tomorrow at noon, so we can put our money together, and then go and purchase the supplies we're going to need for this expedition," Rocky said.

"Aye-aye Captain," the Bloodhounds replied.

The Bloodhounds went home heavily intoxicated to get some rest.

Chapter Seven
The Supplies

The next day it was Monday, August 7, 1904. The fiery, golden sun was shining, and it was a beautiful day in Cape Crusade. The salty, sea breeze was gusting through the harbor town. The Bloodhounds met up at the Sandbar to put their money together. Then they discussed the supplies that they needed.

"Good afternoon, Bloodhounds. Let's add up our money to see how much we have. We are going to need about 230 dollars for everything," Rocky said.

"OK guys. Let's empty out our pockets," Christo replied.

All the Bloodhounds emptied their pockets onto the table. After everyone was done shelling out their money for the expedition, there was a total of 225 dollars.

"OK, that should be enough to cover our expenses," Rocky said.

"Now let's go to the Purple Octopus to purchase our supplies," Christo replied.

The Bloodhounds gathered in their horse drawn buggies and rode to the Purple Octopus.

They arrived at the deep-sea warehouse and walked in.

"OK, we are going to need four silver harpoons," Rocky said.

The silver harpoons cost thirty dollars each. After they bought four of them, they had 105 dollars left for food, water, and beer.

They bought everything that they needed and returned to the Sandbar. Rocky ordered Christo to call Marco's landline and tell him to join the Bloodhounds at the Sandbar. Marco walked into the Sandbar at about 3:00 pm with his girlfriend Molly.

"How's it going gentlemen?" Marco said.

"OK Marco. We have all the supplies that we are going to need for this mission to slay the Silver Serpent," Rocky replied.

"If any of you have firearms, bring them tomorrow. We need as much firepower as possible to drill and pummel that creature with," Christo said.

The Bloodhounds ordered some beers to calm their excited nerves.

"This is my girlfriend, Molly," Marco said.

"It's nice to meet you Molly," Rocky replied.

"It's nice to meet you Molly," the other Bloodhounds said.

"It's nice to meet you guys as well," Molly said.

"Marco, would you like to be a member of the Bloodhounds?" Rocky asked.

"Of course I would. We are going on this mission together tomorrow," Marco replied.

"Well then congratulations Marco! You are now officially a crewmember of the Bloodhounds! We're brothers forever! Even in death!" Rocky said. The total number of Bloodhounds was eleven.

"Cheers!" The Bloodhounds yelled loudly.

Molly didn't like the sound of that one bit.
The Bloodhounds ordered some all you can eat fried sea bass and some pitchers of beer. They ate and drank like kings and huddled up for a last-minute meeting.

"OK Bloodhounds, we are going to meet at the docks at 6:00 am to load our supplies and launch. We will be traveling on our sacred vessel, *The Bloodhound*," Rocky said.

"Aye-aye Captain," the Bloodhounds replied.

Everybody drank their last beer and went home for some much needed rest.

Chapter Eight
The Silver Serpent Expedition

It was Tuesday, August 8, 1904. The big day of the Silver Serpent expedition. Marco awoke at 5:00 am next to his gorgeous girlfriend Molly and climbed out of bed. He walked to the kitchen and brewed a pot of coffee. Molly walked in after him.

"Are you sure that you're ready for this my love?" Molly asked.

"I'm as ready as I'll ever be my love," Marco replied.

"I'm worried about you. That Silver Serpent is so gigantic and ferocious. What if you don't come back?" Molly said in a very concerned tone.

"Don't worry about me baby. I'll come back to you no matter what. We are going to slay that beast once and for all," Marco replied.

"I am worried about you baby. I don't know what I'd do without you. I love you Marco," Molly said as she started to cry.

"Don't cry my love. The Bloodhounds know what they are doing and have good heads on their shoulders. I wouldn't be going with them if I didn't trust them," Marco replied.

"How can you trust them if you barely met them? You have never been out to sea with them. You just got drunk with them," Molly said.

"I know that baby, but the word around town is that these guys are professionals, and they are some of the best whale hunters around," Marco said.

"Yes, the best whale hunters around, but how do you know that they are the best serpent hunters my love?" Molly asked.

"The point is that they know how to find sea creatures and slay them. That is the objective of our mission," Marco said.

"Promise me that you will come back alive in one piece. I love you," Molly said.

"I promise sweetheart. I love you too," Marco replied.

Marco and Molly ate breakfast and drank their coffee before they rode over to the docks. Marco arrived at the Cape Crusade docks at 6:00 am sharp and searched for the boat called *The Bloodhound*. He laid his eyes on a magnificent vessel painted bright red and gold, with black, and it read; *The Bloodhound* on the sides of it with a logo of a snarling bloodhound with a bloody fish in his jaws.

Marco and Molly shared a deep and passionate kiss before they said their goodbyes. Then Marco made his way over to *The Bloodhound* and walked onboard with his leather bag; which contained some clothes, a canteen, and a colt model 1903 handgun. All the Bloodhound crew were already onboard, including Travis and Milo. Rocky was the first one to greet Marco.

"Good morning, Marco. Welcome aboard *The Bloodhound*. Place your belongings in the cabin for now," Rocky said.

"Good morning, Rocky. Are you ready for this mission my good man?" Marco asked.

"I was born ready. It's about time somebody put an end to that treacherous Silver Serpent," Rocky replied.

"Yeah, that prize money wouldn't hurt anybody either," Christo said.

"We could all use that prize money. I want the money and the bragging rights to say that we, the Bloodhounds, slayed the Silver Serpent," Travis said.

"Yeah, we will be famous heroes!" Milo exclaimed.

"Don't get too cocky just yet. First we have to find that creature, and then we have to slay it," Rocky replied.

"OK, is everybody onboard? Great. Let's start the engines and head out towards the deep-blue sea," Christo said.

The Bloodhounds waved goodbye to their loved ones and began their journey out into the depths of the mystical and nefarious Atlantic Ocean, to hunt and slay the legendary Silver Serpent. It was a gloomy and overcast day with the wind howling and dark gray clouds looming. There was also a slight mist in the air.

"I hope we don't run into any storms on this journey," Travis said.

"This weather does appear somewhat suspect," Rocky replied.

"We should be alright. It just looks like some mild rain clouds in the sky," Christo said.

"We can handle it. I don't think we will get caught up in any storm," Marco said.

"About how far out does the Silver Serpent roam?" Milo asked.

"We don't know that for sure, but he has been spotted around Boat-Wreck Lane and Hammerhead Hedge recently. That was where some of the attacks took place," Rocky said.

"I know. I was there," Marco replied.

"Yes, so was I," Travis said.

"That's where I saw it too," Milo said.

"Hammerhead Hedge was where we saw it slay and devour our friend Rusty," Travis replied.

"OK. So we know where it likes to hunt. We should definitely check those places out," Rocky replied.

"We have some key destinations to scope out. Where should we head first?" Christo said.

"Let's head towards Boat-Wreck Lane first. That's about sixty miles to the east," Rocky said.

"Aye-aye, Captain," Milo replied.

The Bloodhounds headed east towards the ominous Boat-Wreck Lane.

"Get all of the harpoons and firearms ready, just in case that devilish beast pops up out of the blue," Rocky ordered.

The Bloodhounds loaded their guns and took the gleaming, silver harpoons out of their cases.

"Sharpen those babies up. We need that silver to pierce through that Silver Serpent's black heart," Christo said.

The Bloodhounds had four silver harpoons and ten firearms consisting of; handguns, rifles, and shotguns. They were a good-sized sea crew eager to execute the king of the ocean, the Silver Serpent. The Bloodhounds had blood, vengeance, glory and fortune on their minds.

Chapter Nine
The Bloodhounds

The Bloodhounds arrived at Boat-Wreck Lane at about 8:00 on that cloudy and balmy morning. They saw some humpback whales gracefully swimming just under the ocean's glistening, emerald surface. Rocky lit up a fine Cuban cigar and made sure his guns were loaded.

"This was where the Silver Serpent attacked us and slayed my friends Nancy and Nate," Marco said.

"Did you see it coming, or did it surprise you?" Christo asked.

"It just popped up out of nowhere and nailed our boat's hull with tremendous force and impact," Marco replied.

"That thing is elusive and devastatingly powerful. We have to keep our eyes and ears open at all times," Rocky said.

The Bloodhounds threw some bloody chum into the water to try and attract the Silver Serpent.

"Damn, I'm hungry," Travis said.

"We have some sausage and egg biscuits, cereal, coffee, and orange juice in the cabin. Help yourself," Rocky replied.

"Thanks Captain. I'm gonna grab a quick bite," Travis said.

"What do we do if we see that monster?" Milo asked.

"We load the harpoons and fire them at its heart. We should also blast some bullets at its head and its heart to weaken it and slow it down," Christo said.

"That's right," Rocky replied.

"I think I'm gonna grab a quick bite too," Milo said.

Milo joined Travis in the cabin to eat some sausage and egg biscuits and drink some coffee. In the cabin there was a large refrigerator and a cedar table with some cedar chairs. Travis opened the fridge and saw that it was full of beer and deli sandwiches.

"Damn, that's a lot of beer and sandwiches," Travis said.

"That's always good. What kind of beer is it?" Milo asked.

"It's Yellow Crab and Stingray," Travis replied.

Those brands were the two most popular and enjoyed beers in the 1900's in Cape Crusade, and throughout Staten Island.

"It's too early to drink," Milo said.

"I know that. I know I'll want one later though," Travis said.

The two friends sat down at the table and ate some sausage and egg biscuits with some coffee and orange juice.

"Look over there! It's something colossal!" Christo exclaimed.

The massive creature that they spotted was Bo, the whale shark.

"Head that way to see what it is," Rocky said.

Julius took control of the helm and steered towards Bo. Julius was another Bloodhound's crewmember.

They got within about thirty yards of Bo and realized that he was a whale shark.

"That's not the Silver Serpent. It's a massive whale shark," Rocky said.

"Should we harpoon it?" Christo asked.

"No, let's leave it be. We need to save our harpoons and firepower for the Silver Serpent," Rocky answered.

Bo spotted *The Bloodhound* gliding towards him. He realized that they were whale hunters, and he swam away. Bo swam to Slick's cave to alert him of the boat at Boat-Wreck Lane.

"It's gone now. Do you think this chum will attract the Silver Serpent?" Julius asked.

"Maybe it will. It's worth a try," Rocky said as he puffed on his fine cigar.

Travis and Milo finished their breakfast and walked out of the cabin and onto the main deck.

"Have you guys seen anything yet?" Travis asked.

"Yeah, we just saw a whale shark the size of a submarine, but it got spooked and swam away," Christo replied.

"A whale shark, huh? I've never seen one of those in real life before," Travis said.

"Well you just missed it buddy," Rocky said with a chuckle.

The chum was all around the boat and it started to attract some impressive and menacing great white sharks.

"Look at those great whites! They are beautiful specimens," Marco said.

"That's good. I heard that Silver Serpents like to devour sharks," Rocky replied.

The great whites were swimming around in the chum and devouring the bloody chunks of fish and guts. There were a total of four sharks relishing the chum brunch.

Bo arrived at Slick's cave and made a sonar sound to notify Slick of his arrival. Slick heard Bo's signal and stuck his head outside the cave.

"What's up, Bo? Come on in," Slick said.

"How you doing Slick? Did I come at a bad time?" Bo replied.

"I'm alright buddy. No, it's fine. I just woke up about twenty minutes ago," Slick said.

Bo swam inside Slick's cave.

"I just came from Boat-Wreck Lane. There was a boat of whale hunters out there patrolling the waters," Bo replied.

"Really? How many hunters were on the boat?" Slick said.

"I'd say about nine or ten," Bo replied.

"They are probably looking for me. Maybe I should pay them a visit," Slick said.

"Do you think that is a good idea Slick? Those whale hunters are always armed to the teeth with harpoons and guns," Bo replied.

"I know they are. When have I ever let that stop me?" Slick said.

Slick was sharpening his razor-sharp claws on a huge rotating stone.

"I just want you to be careful Slick. You are my best friend and I don't want anything to happen to you," Bo said.

"Don't get all mushy on me Bo. I'm just kidding. I appreciate that Bo. You are my best friend also. This is our ocean and we call the shots here. Those whale hunters are gonna have to learn that one way or the other," Slick replied.

"Do you want to go scope it out over there at Boat-Wreck Lane?" Bo asked.

"Sure, let's go check it out and see what's happening," Slick answered.

The two enormous ocean creatures swam out of Slick's cave and headed towards Boat-Wreck Lane. It took them about fifteen minutes to get there. When they arrived, they saw that the Bloodhounds were still there. They also noticed the sharks that swam through the chummed waters and devoured pieces of bloody fish.

"Listen. Let's not swim too close to the surface, so we can remain out of their site," Slick said.

"OK," Bo replied.

"Those great whites sure do look tasty," Slick said.

"What do you want to do?" Bo asked.

"I'm gonna swim up under the sharks and grab one of them in my jaws," Slick replied.

"Are you sure the hunters won't see you?" Bo asked.

"I'll try to remain deep enough, so they can't see me. Then I'll dash up under the sharks and snatch one in my jaws," Slick said.

"OK. Be careful bud," Bo replied.

"OK. Here I go," Slick said.

Slick swam deeper and towards the great white sharks. When he positioned himself directly under the sharks, he struck at one and clamped it down in his deadly jaws. Slicks razor sharp teeth and claws ferociously tore through the shark's flesh. Slick slayed the shark and dragged it back towards Bo. The other sharks chased Slick and tried to bite him. Slick smacked the sharks with his spiked tail, and they swam away.

"Where did all the sharks go?" Rocky asked.

"I don't know. Maybe they got their fill of chum and swam off," Christo replied.

"Maybe. Or maybe something more formidable frightened them off," Rocky replied.

"Something more formidable like the Silver Serpent," Marco said.

"Maybe Marco. Let's hang around this area a little bit longer to see if anything pops up," Rocky replied.

Slick tore chunks of flesh off the shark with his freshly honed claws and teeth. His teeth were like battle swords and his claws were like scythe blades. He chomped down on the fresh, shark flesh and savored every delectable bite. Slick devoured the entire twelve foot great white shark in a New York minute.

"That was delicious!" Slick exclaimed.

"That boat is still there. I wonder how long they are going to stay there," Bo said.

"I don't know. Who cares? Let them roast under that scorching sun for hours," Slick replied.

"Are you gonna drill their boat?" Bo asked.

"I'm thinking about it. That would start a war, and they would definitely try to shoot me with harpoons and guns," Slick said.

"I know. That is risky business," Bo replied.

"What the hell. I'm gonna give them a dose of their own medicine," Slick said.

Slick torpedoed his body directly at the boat's hull and crashed into it with Godly force. The jolt from the violent blow shook the entire boat and two of the Bloodhounds fell overboard. The two Bloodhounds that went overboard were Jason and Yanick.

"Holy shit! What was that?" Rocky exclaimed.

"It's the Silver Serpent! Jason and Yanick fell overboard!" Christo yelled.

The Bloodhounds spotted a gargantuan, silver figure about twenty yards under the choppy water.

"That's him alright! He smashed into us just like that last time!" Marco said.

"Get the harpoons and guns ready!" Rocky ordered.

Julius and Gumby grabbed the four silver harpoons and prepared them to be fired. Gumby was another member of the Bloodhounds. The rest of the Bloodhounds grabbed their guns and loaded them as well.

"It's still too deep to hit it. We have to hope that he comes up to the surface," Christo said.

"Throw Jason and Yanick a rope so that they can climb aboard," Rocky ordered.

The Silver Serpent spotted the two overboard victims and recognized that as a feeding opportunity. Slick slashed through the water directly towards them.

"Holy shit! It's going after Jason and Yanick!" Rocky said.

"Prepare to fire the harpoons!" Christo exclaimed.

Rocky, Julius, Gumby, and Christo aimed the loaded harpoon guns at the fast-moving Silver Serpent. Slick swam up to the surface and savagely snatched the struggling Yanick with his steely jaws in a death grip.

"Aim for his heart and fire!" Rocky exclaimed.

The four Bloodhounds armed with the harpoon guns aimed at the center area between Slick's upper limbs and fired their harpoons. The other Bloodhounds fired their guns at Slick's head and upper body. Julius's silver harpoon struck Slick below his heart near his chest cavity, and Gumby's silver harpoon hit Slick just below his head. Rocky's silver harpoon was headed straight towards Slick's heart but Slick batted it away with his right upper limb. Christo's silver harpoon struck Slick right next to his left upper limb. Slick let out a savage and thunderous roar as he ripped the barbed harpoons out of his body with his upper limbs. The gunshots hit Slick all over his body as he dove back down into the ocean with Yanick's bleeding and shredded corpse in his jaws.

"Did we hit him?" Gumby asked.

"Yeah, but not in the heart," Rocky said.

"Pull the harpoons back in with the ropes," Christo ordered.

The Bloodhounds pulled the four silver harpoons back in the boat.

"Son of a bitch! That monstrous demon slayed Yanick!" Rocky exclaimed.

"We shot that monster with all of our guns and hit him with all four of the silver harpoons, and it still didn't slay him. Where did a beast like that come from? I believe God created all of the living creatures, but why would he create such a destructive death machine," Travis said.

"We need to hit him in the heart. That's the only way to slay it," Marco replied.

Jason grabbed the rope from the boat and climbed back aboard.

"Are you okay Jason?" Rocky asked.

"I think so. Damn, that creature killed Yanick!" Jason exclaimed.

"We know Jason. We saw everything," Christo replied.

"You saw everything? I had front row seats to that horrific event. That beast from hell grabbed Yanick with his razor-sharp teeth right in front of me. I'm lucky it didn't get me too!" Jason exclaimed.

"Yes, you are lucky it didn't get you. We are one Bloodhound less now without Yanick. Rest in peace brother Yanick. May God bless your soul," Rocky said.

"Did the Silver Serpent attack you at all?" Christo asked.

"Yeah, it hit me with its spiky tail in the ribs. I noticed a little bit of blood leaking out in the ocean," Jason replied.

"Let's check it out. Lift up your shirt," Rocky said.

Jason lifted his shirt up, and there was a six inch wide gash just under his right pectoral muscle. The gash was about two inches deep. Blood was oozing out of the wound.

"It got you alright. Damn, that looks painful," Marco said.

"Let's cover that up with some cloth. Get me some alcohol also," Rocky ordered.

Gumby brought him a fresh cloth and a bottle of New York whiskey. Rocky doused the cloth in the whiskey and then pressed it on Jason's wound. Then he wrapped it tightly with another cloth to stop the bleeding.

"Do you want us to take you back now, or can you hang in there with us?" Rocky asked.

"I'm okay. The wound doesn't hurt as bad after a couple shots of whiskey, and the bleeding seems to be stopping," Jason replied.

"You are a true and mighty warrior! A true Bloodhound!" Christo exclaimed.

"He is a true warrior and a true Bloodhound!" Rocky yelled.

"What do you want to do now?" Marco asked.

"Let's have a round of drinks. I think we could all use one," Rocky replied.

"Julius, get us all some shots of rum and a round of beers," Christo said.

Julius went to the cabin and grabbed a bottle of Jamaican white rum and some ice-cold beers from the fridge. He put all the bottles in a bucket and carried it out to the Bloodhounds.

"A toast to Yanick. Our fallen brother is gone, but never forgotten. May God protect his soul on its journey into the afterlife. Rest in peace Bloodhound," Rocky said.

"To Yanick!" The Bloodhounds yelled.

They all took their shots of rum and popped open their beer bottles.

"I can't believe we saw that malicious creature first hand with our own eyes. It's even more terrifying in real life. Did you see those glowing, ruby-red eyes it had? They glinted with fiery wrath and bloodlust," Christo said.

"I did. It was like all those myths, stories, and legends we heard growing up, came true right before our eyes," Rocky replied.

"That was insane. That thing is going to be harder to slay than we thought. We hit it with all of our harpoons and multiple shots to its head and upper body. That sinister monster just took it and dove back into the depths of the Atlantic," Travis said.

"We have to hit it in the heart!" Marco exclaimed.

"I think Marco is right. That stuff that old man Walter told him is probably true, since he and his crew slayed a Silver Serpent in their day," Rocky said.

"How do you know that it was Walter's crew that slayed a Silver Serpent? Milo asked.

"I don't know. That is the story, and I believe it," Rocky said.

"I believe it too. Why would that old man lie to me? Yes, he's a drunkard, but I still believed what he was saying," Marco said.

"Yeah, old man Walters is definitely known for storytelling," Rocky said.

"Yeah, that is true. That old dinosaur loves to drink and tell stories about his crew's glory days," Christo replied.

The Bloodhounds started to laugh a little bit, but they still felt morbid after losing one of their own, Yanick.

"Well, we need to hit that beast in the heart next time we see it. Our lives depend on it," Rocky said.

"Walter said that they slayed the Silver Serpent's lover only a couple of years ago," Marco replied.

"And you believed that? Did you get a good look at Walter? There is no way in hell he could have been out there battling the Silver Serpent a couple of years ago," Christo said.

"Why would he lie?" Marco replied.

"Because he's an old drunk," Christo answered.

"You can believe whatever you want to believe, but I believe Walter. I believe our best chance to destroy the Silver Serpent, is to pierce its cold, black heart with a silver harpoon," Marco said.

Chapter Ten
Slick's Wrath

Slick decided to swim to Oliver's part of the ocean as he chewed and swallowed the last pieces of Yanick's sinewy corpse. Oliver lived out towards Squid Alley. That was about five miles east of Slick's cave.

Slick arrived at Oliver's place of residence and sent his hydro-sonar signal that announced his arrival. Oliver heard it and swam out of the towering stocks of seaweed and kelp to greet Slick.

"How you doing Oliver?" Slick said.

"I'm alright Slick. Just taking a midday snooze," Oliver replied.

"Did I wake you up? Sorry bud," Slick said.

"Yeah, but it's alright. I didn't want to sleep too long anyway," Oliver replied.

"OK. I just came from Boat-Wreck Lane. It was total mayhem over there," Slick said.

"What happened now, Slick?" Oliver replied.

"I attacked some whale hunters and devoured one of them. The others fired harpoons and guns at me," Slick said.

"Are you okay? Did they hit you?" Oliver replied.

"Yeah, I'm okay. They hit me below my head and in the upper body with the harpoons, and their gunshots hit me in the upper body and head area, but they did not go too deep. I have some minor pain and bleeding, that's all. Thank the great Sea God for my scaly armor," Slick said.

"Damn, that sounds pretty rough man. Do you want some special seaweed to wrap around those cuts?" Oliver replied.

"Sure man. Give me some," Slick said.

Oliver handed Slick some purple and yellow seaweed to wrap around his war wounds.

"There you go brother. That seaweed has special healing powers in it," Oliver replied.

"Thanks buddy. I know it does. It always helps," Slick said.

"What do you want to do now?" Oliver asked.

"Let's go destroy those whale hunters," Slick replied.

"Are you serious? Don't you want to heal up first?" Oliver said.

"No, I'm okay. I'm ready to slay those miserable humans once and for all," Slick replied.

"OK. I'm with you man. Let's do this," Oliver said.

The two colossal sea creatures swam back towards Boat-Wreck Lane. The Bloodhounds were still there.

"OK Oliver. Let's collide into that boat and slay whatever falls overboard," Slick ordered.

"OK Slick. I'm ready buddy. Let's go," Oliver replied.

The Bloodhounds were still drinking and catching a good buzz. The onerous gray clouds were floating across the night's dark sky like smoky spirits. It was about 7:30. Slick and Oliver accelerated rapidly towards the boat's hull and rammed it violently with their massive bodies.

The thunderous blow rocked the boat and the Bloodhounds to their core. Rocky, Travis, and Milo fell overboard.

"Get the harpoons! It's the Silver Serpent!" Marco exclaimed.

Gumby and Christo jumped up and grabbed the silver harpoons. The rest of the Bloodhounds grabbed their guns.

"Shoot that beast now!" Gumby yelled.

"Throw Rocky and them some life preservers and some ropes!" Julius exclaimed.

Julius ran to the cabin and grabbed his rifles.

"Fire the harpoons at its heart!" Marco exclaimed.

Jason threw the life preservers and the ropes to the overboard Bloodhounds. The Silver Serpent grabbed Rocky with the claws of his upper limbs, and crunched down on his head with his toothy jaws making it explode in his mouth like an oversize blood orange. Then he dove back down into the ocean. Oliver wrapped his tentacles around Travis and dragged him down into the dark bluish-black waters to drown him. Slick finished chewing on Rocky's head and then ripped his heart out of his chest and left his deformed corpse bleeding in the nebulous water. Slick swam towards Milo's struggling body just as he grabbed for the life preserver ropes. Slick snatched Milo with his left upper limb and sliced him up the middle from groin to the top of his skull with his right upper limb. Gumby and Christo fired the harpoons at Slick's heart, but Slick was moving too fast for them to hit their target. The harpoons bounced off the steely spikes on Slick's back. Gumby and Christo retrieved the silver harpoons easily since they had not stuck into Slick's flesh.

The Bloodhounds were firing their guns at Slick's rapidly moving body underwater. Slick devoured Milo's left half and left his right half floating in the bloody, black water, for now. Then he called Oliver over to come up with a game plan.

"What did you do with that dead body?" Slick asked.

"I left it over there by the first human that you slayed," Oliver replied.

"OK. Let's hit them with all we got one more time and try to slay as many of them as we can," Slick said.

"OK buddy. I'm with you," Oliver replied.

The two sea creatures swam explosively towards *The Bloodhound* and murderously bashed it again, even harder this time. That created a leaking hole in the hull. Gumby, Christo, Julius, and Marco fell overboard this time. Jason grabbed a silver harpoon and prepared it to fire at the Silver Serpent.

"Holy shit! Our boat is critically damaged! We're sinking!" Randy yelled. Randy was another member of the Bloodhounds.

"Throw the poor bastards some life preservers for God's sake!" Jason exclaimed.

Bugsy grabbed the life preservers and threw them to the overboard Bloodhounds. Bugsy was another member of the Bloodhounds.

Slick slashed his way through the bloody water and snapped down savagely on Gumby's torso with his blood and guts stained teeth.

"AHHH, it's got me! Shoot that damn thing!" Gumby yelled out in excruciating pain.

Oliver grabbed Julius with his long tentacles and pulled him down further into the chilly depths of the Atlantic. After drowning Julius, Oliver went after Christo and wrapped his tentacles around his legs and torso and ripped him in half at the waist.

"That's the spirit Oliver! Let's slay them all!" Slick exclaimed.

Slick sped after Marco like a missile, just as Marco was pulling himself up the side of the boat with the life preserver rope.

"Shoot it!" Marco yelled.

Randy reached for another silver harpoon to try and fire it at the Silver Serpent's heart. Bugsy was firing round after round from his rifle at the Silver Serpent's head. Randy grabbed the silver harpoon and stood right next to Jason. Slick grasped Marco in his jaws and crunched down with devastating power and crushed all of his ribs at once.

"Fire!" Jason yelled.

Jason and Randy fired the silver harpoon at the Silver Serpent's heart. Slick blocked one harpoon with his claws, and the second one hit him just above his heart. It hurt Slick, but he knew that it did not hit his heart. Slick ripped Marco's guts out of his stomach with his teeth and devoured his entire body within a matter of seconds. Then he swam over to Gumby's and Christo's bodies to devour the rest of their fresh, bleeding cadavers.

"I think there are still two of them left. What do you want to do Slick?" Oliver said.

"Their boat is sinking fast. It's just a matter of minutes before they are swimming in the ocean with us. Let's wait for that to happen and then finish them off. My head and upper body heart too much from all of those harpoons and gunshots to ram it again," Slick replied.

"OK, you're the boss," Oliver replied.

"In the meantime, go fetch me those first victims, so I can devour them before the sharks get to them," Slick ordered.

"You got it," Oliver replied.

Oliver swam over to Rocky's and Travis's bloody corpses and wrapped his tentacles around them. Then he towed the gash riddled cadavers back to Slick..

"Thanks Oliver," Slick said.

"No problem buddy," Oliver replied.

"Are you sure you don't want any? These humans are highly nutritious and really tasty, you know," Slick said.

"I guess it won't kill me to try a piece," Oliver replied.

Slick tore off one of Travis's legs and passed it to Oliver.

"Of course it won't Oliver. It'll make you stronger though. Try it buddy," Slick said.

Oliver took the leg and chewed on it with his thousands of small but sharp teeth.

"Not bad buddy. It tastes kind of like seal but more gamy," Oliver replied.

"You think so. I think it tastes more like marlin," Slick said.

Slick devoured the rest of Rocky's gruesome body and began to work on Travis.

"Do you mind? Or do you want to devour this human?" Slick asked.

"I'll devour it. These humans taste pretty good after all," Oliver replied.

"I told you so. They invigorate us and are good for our diet also. Here you go Oliver. Feast on this whale hunter,"

Slick passed Travis's corpse to Oliver.

The sinking and critically damaged *Bloodhound* was almost completely underwater. Jason and Randy stood on top of the bow, and each held a silver harpoon.

"Look. They are almost completely underwater," Oliver said.

"I know. It's just a matter of time before they are struggling helplessly in the water with us. Let's wait for that, so they don't have another chance to fire those harpoons at us. They are in our domain now," Slick replied.

"That's very strategic thinking Slick. I like the way your mind works," Oliver said.

Sure enough. Five minutes went by, and the only remaining Bloodhounds were grabbing on to floating objects to try and stay above water.

"This is a golden opportunity to strike, Oliver! Are you ready buddy?" Slick said.

"You know it partner! Let's finish them off!" Oliver exclaimed.

Jason and Randy sat on top of a floating table holding on to the last two silver harpoons. Everything else was sinking to the bottom of the ocean.

"Be ready for anything Jason. That monster could pop up from anywhere at any time," Randy said.

"OK, you be ready too. If that beast does pop up, one of us must pierce its heart with our silver harpoons! Our lives depend on it," Jason replied.

"OK. Aim steady," Randy said.

"OK man," Jason replied.

Slick and Oliver swam over to the floating table and hit them from underneath. The Bloodhounds fell into the Atlantic. They fired their last silver harpoons at Slick but he dodged them. Slick grabbed Jason in his jaws and bit down violently in Jason's chest and neck area. Blood gushed out all over Slick's face and head. Oliver wrapped his tentacles around Randy's neck and choked him. Randy felt Oliver's long, powerful tentacles squeezing the life out of him as everything went black. Then he dragged Randy down into the inscrutable depths of the Atlantic Ocean and ripped his head from his body.

Slick tossed Jason up in the air like a rag doll and opened his deadly jaws wide to catch Jason's fall with his mouth. He snapped his jaws shut on Jason's body with a loud and juicy crunch. Jason felt a brief second of excruciating pain and then felt nothing at all as Slick made human stew out of him. Just like that, all the notorious Bloodhounds were dead and gone at the claws and tentacles of the Atlantic Ocean's most dynamic duo, Slick and Oliver.

"OK. That's all of them. Let's go home," Slick said.

"What do you want to do with this body?" Oliver asked.

"Give it to me. I'll finish devouring it at my cave," Slick replied.

"OK bud. Here you go," Oliver said.

Oliver passed Randy's headless body over to Slick.

"Thanks a lot for your help buddy. You are a true friend," Slick replied.

"Anytime pal. It was fun. You know I always got your back. It turned out that that was more fun than I'd thought it be and humans taste better than I imagined. I'll see you later boss," Oliver said.

"I'll see you later brother," Slick replied.

Oliver swam back to his home at Squid Alley and Slick swam back toward his cave with Randy's marred carnage skewered on his scythe-like claws.

Chapter Eleven
The Knight Sharks

The next day it was Wednesday, August 9, 1904. Cape Crusade was like a ghost town with a somber silence. Molly woke up and decided to head over to the Sandbar. She arrived and walked through the door.

Inside there were some whale hunters and fishermen as usual, but it was more silent. Molly saw Walter sitting at a table by himself drinking some Jameson Irish Whiskey.

"Hi, Walter. How are you doing?" Molly asked.

"Do I know you dear?" Walter asked.

"Yes, we met the other day. My boyfriend and I introduced ourselves to you, and we talked for a while about the Silver Serpent," Molly replied.

"Oh yes dear, I'm sorry. My memory slips from time to time," Walter said.

"It's okay. Have you seen any of the Bloodhounds around? They went out on an expedition yesterday and nobody has come back yet. I'm getting worried. Marco, my boyfriend, was with them," Molly replied.

"What was he doing going on an expedition with those maniacs? Those fellas are plum crazy!" Walter exclaimed.

"They were going after the Silver Serpent to try and kill it. Didn't you hear about that?" Molly asked.

"Oh, that's right. They were going after the Silver Serpent. I tried to talk them out of it. I told them it was too dangerous," Walter replied.

"Oh my God! Do you think something happened to them?" Molly gasped.

"Most of the people who go after the Silver Serpent never come back. You have to prepare yourself for that reality, my dear," Walter said.

"They could still be out at sea though, right? Don't these things take a couple of days sometimes?" Molly asked.

"Yes, they could still be out there, or they could be dead," Walter replied.

"Don't say that Walter! How could you say that? That's my boyfriend you are talking about! I love him," Molly exclaimed.

"Calm down sweetheart. I didn't mean to upset you. I'm just trying to prepare you for all the possible outcomes. My crew and I were the last ones to slay a Silver Serpent. We slayed a female and her unborn offspring. That really pissed off the male Silver Serpent. He is still out there," Walter replied.

"Yes, you told me that story already," Molly said.

"My crewmates and I were the best ocean hunters that the coastal northeast has ever seen. We had enough heart and brains to slay a Silver Serpent," Walter said proudly.

"We need to go out there and look for them," Molly said.

"I'm too old to go out on any more sea adventures. My time is spent on the docks and in the bars these days," Walter replied.

"Please Walter. You are the only one that knows where it is and how to kill it," Molly said.

"Give it another day. If they don't come back by tomorrow, I will see what I can do to help you," Walter replied.

"OK. I can do that. Thank you so much Walter," Molly said.

Molly walked out of the Sandbar and into her horse drawn buggy and rode home. Another day went by and it was Friday, August 11, 1904 and still no sign of Marco or the Bloodhounds. Molly deduced to return to the Sandbar to find Walter. She walked inside and found Walter having some fried oysters with a cold beer.

"Hello Walter. Marco never came home last night. I think something has happened to him and the Bloodhounds," Molly said.

"OK dear. I will have my son-in-law research this matter for you. His name is Clayton, and he is sitting right over there," Walter said.

Walter pointed to a brawny man with black hair and a black beard, sitting at the bar.

"What can Clayton do for me?" Molly replied.

"He and his crew are going to go out to Boat-Wreck Lane to fish for sharks and tuna. He told me that that was where the

Bloodhounds were going to hunt for the Silver Serpent. He can go look for their boat and any sign of them," Walter said.

"OK that's great. Can I go with him?" Molly replied.

"I don't know if that's such a great idea. What if he and his crew run into the Silver Serpent? Do you really want to be there if that happens?" Walter said.

"I suppose not. I've already seen that monster once in my life, and that was enough. I don't think I could handle another encounter with that ghastly creature," Molly replied.

"That was a wise decision on your part. Just sit tight and wait to see what news Clayton brings back for us," Walter said.

"OK Walter. Thank you," Molly said.

"Come on. Let me introduce you to Clayton," Walter replied.

Walter and Molly got up from their table and walked towards Clayton.

"Clayton, this is Molly. Molly, this is Clayton," Walter announced.

"Hello, Molly. How are you doing?" Clayton said.

"Hi, Clayton. It's nice to meet you," Molly replied.

"What can I do for you?" Clayton asked.

"My boyfriend went on an expedition with the Bloodhounds three days ago and hasn't come back. They went to hunt the Silver Serpent," Molly replied.

"Oh dear. That doesn't sound good. What's his name?" Clayton said.

"His name is Marco. I'm worried that something might have happened to him, because it's been three days since I've last seen him," Molly said.

"If it's been that long, the chances are that something has happened to him. I'm going to go to Boat-Wreck Lane to fish for sharks and tuna. I will look for any sign of Marco and the Bloodhounds and report it to you ASAP," Clayton replied.

"OK. Thank you very much Clayton," Molly said.

"No problem. I overheard the Bloodhounds saying that that was one of the spots they were going to hunt for the Silver Serpent. I was mainly going there to fish for sharks and tuna, but since you told me about your situation, I want to help you," Clayton replied.

"Thanks again Clayton. I really appreciate it," Molly said.

"C'mon Knight Sharks! Let's go do some real fishing!" Clayton exclaimed. The Knight Sharks cheered and raised their drinks in the air.

The Knight Sharks guzzled their last drinks and marched vivaciously out the door. Then they headed toward the boat launch. It was just down the street from the Sandbar. Clayton's crew was called the Knight Sharks and their boat was called *The Knight Shark*. They were made up of seven, highly-intelligent and skilled shark and tuna fishermen. They earned their name, the Knight Sharks, because they all loved medieval folklore about the heroic, valiant knights that battled in wars and slayed dragons. And because they also loved sharks and shark fishing. The Knight Sharks loaded all of their gear that included; two silver harpoons, some guns, and plenty of beer, hard liquor, water, and food onto their boat and headed out towards the Boat-Wreck Lane.

It was about 2:00 in the afternoon. The sky was gunmetal gray and gloomy with the fresh smell of the Atlantic in the air. That summer day also had fitful winds that made the sea come to life. The Knight Shark's crewmembers included; Augustus, Gregory, Polly, Rodney, Ringo, Zeus, and the Captain, Clayton. Their massive boat was loaded with an abundance of ice-cold beer, whiskey, rum, water, and food. It was painted royal-blue, silver, and burgundy and had *The Knight Shark* spelled out in big blue letters with a silver shark in a knight's armor, underneath. The rest of the boat was painted burgundy. Although these fishermen had a lot of experience in tuna and shark fishing, they did not have any experience in dealing with a Silver Serpent. They still didn't know if they believed the stories they had heard about it, but they brought along some silver harpoons just in case those stories were true.

The Knight Shark traveled ruggedly against the gusty winds and choppy sea and finally arrived at the portentous Boat-Wreck Lane. Clayton called for the Knight Sharks to huddle up. All of them obeyed command.

Zeus and Gregory were ordered to throw the tuna lines out. Polly and Rodney were commanded to throw the shark lines out. Augustus, was told to accompany Clayton and help him load the silver harpoons and guns.

Everybody hopped to their tasks. After all the fishing lines were out and all the silver harpoons and guns were loaded. It was time for a drink.

"It's five o'clock somewhere. Somebody, throw me a cold one," Zeus said.

"I'll go get some. Anybody else want one?" Rodney replied.

"Yeah, get me one too," Gregory replied.

"I'm okay," Augustus said.

"I'm fine for now," Clayton replied.

"Do you want anything Polly?" Rodney asked.

"Yeah, bring me a cup of the strongest whiskey on this boat," Polly replied.

"You got it brother. What about you Ringo?" Rodney said.

"Yeah, grab me a cold beer," Ringo replied.

Rodney grabbed four beers for Zeus, Gregory, Ringo, and himself and brought out a bottle of New York Whiskey with a blue cup on top of it.

"Here you go Knight Sharks. Cheers to a successful fishing trip!" Rodney cheerfully announced. Everybody grabbed their drinks except for Augustus and Clayton.

"Cheers!" Zeus exclaimed.

"Cheers to a successful fishing trip!" Polly said.

Clayton was watching the shark and tuna lines like a vigilant hawk.

"Do you think we will see any sign of the Bloodhounds or the Silver Serpent?" Augustus asked inquisitively.

"I hope we see some signs of the Bloodhounds. I'm not too eager to see the Silver Serpent. If it does exist," Gregory replied.

The winds were howling and the boat was going up and down on the powerful, rolling swells. Zeus finished his beer in just a few guzzles and grabbed another one. At that moment one of the shark rods received a vicious tug on it. Polly set down his cup of whiskey and grabbed the shark rod. He jerked it back forcefully to set the hook.

"Holy smokes! This feels like a real whopper!" Polly exclaimed.

"Is the hook set Polly?" Clayton asked.

"It sure feels like it!" Polly exclaimed.

"OK, take it easy. Keep the rod up and let the shark tire itself out," Clayton said.

"Aye-aye Captain," Polly replied.

The hook was set and the glorious fight with the shark was on.

"Whoa! Reel that sucker in!" Gregory exclaimed. The rod was bent violently, and Polly was struggling to reel the shark in. The Silver Serpent happened to be hunting for sharks also, that afternoon, around Boat-Wreck Lane. He noticed the boat and the shark that was being reeled in. He decided to snatch the shark from the fisherman's line. Slick swam up to the ten foot lemon shark on the hook and chomped it in half. Then he swam away with the tail end of the shark in his jaws. All of a sudden, Polly felt a huge release of tension at the end of his line.

"What the hell? I think it slipped off the hook," Polly said.

"Are you serious? What the hell happened?" Clayton replied.

Polly continued to reel in his line. He finally reeled it all the way in and was shocked at what he saw next. All that was left at the end of Polly's line was the lemon shark's head and half of its upper body. Clayton could see that something was sticking out of the shark's stomach. It looked to be mangled human body parts.

"Reel that shark in. There is something in its stomach," Clayton said. Then they spotted an enormous, glimmering, silver figure in the water that swam by just underneath the boat. The mammoth object was gleaming like a silver torpedo with glistening emeralds and sapphires.

"Do you see what I see?" Polly asked.

"Yes, that's the Silver Serpent! Clayton exclaimed.

The rest of the Knight Sharks pushed each other out of the way to catch a glimpse of the elusive and mystical, Silver Serpent. They had never seen one in their lives.

"Holy smokes! That creature really does exist! It is gigantic!" Ringo exclaimed. The Silver Serpent swam deeper under the water, so that the Knight Sharks would lose sight of him. Slick deduced to swim back to his cave, because he had had his fill of shark and really wasn't that hungry anymore. Besides, he didn't feel like battling humans tonight, and he wanted to remain low key and unseen. Polly reeled his line all the way to the side of the boat, and Zeus gaffed the top half of the shark's body onto the boat. The shark had a human head, and an arm inside of its partially ripped stomach.

"Sweet Jesus! It's human body parts!" Augustus exclaimed.

"Now we know what caused the damage to that shark you just reeled in. The Silver Serpent did it, and he wants us to know that he did it. That is why it swam by us," Clayton said.

"Do you think that could be one of the Bloodhound's body parts in the shark's stomach?" Zeus asked.

"I don't know. Why don't you check him for some id?" Gregory said sarcastically.

"Don't be a wise guy," Zeus said boldly.

"It's just a severed head and an arm," Augustus said.

"Keep your eye out for that Silver Serpent. We have seen it already. We could see it again. It could pop out from anywhere at any time," Clayton stated.

"What a minute. I recognize that patch on the arm. That's the Bloodhound's patch," Polly said.

The Bloodhounds sported patches of a Bloodhound on their right arm's sleeve to represent their loyalty to their organization. That arm still had pieces of shirt sleeve stuck to it, and the patch was still visible.

"I'll be damned! You are right Polly!" Clayton exclaimed.

"Well, now we know what happened to them. They were devoured by bloody sharks," Rodney said.

"That could be the case, but we still have to keep an open mind to this entire situation. The Silver Serpent most likely destroyed their boat, devoured most of them, and left some of their body parts for the sharks to finish off. What else could have possibly destroyed their boat like that?" Clayton said.

"You are right Captain. That is a logical explanation as well," Zeus replied.

"Do you recognize the head? It is severely mangled," Gregory said.

"No. It is too chewed up," Polly replied.

"Wow! This is incredible! Get us all another round of beers, Zeus. I have to calculate our next move," Clayton said.

Zeus dug into one of their ice boxes and grabbed seven cold beers for the whole crew.

"What should we do next Captain? Should we continue fishing or should we go after the Silver Serpent?" Augustus asked.

"Or should we report this latest news to Molly to give her some closure?" Gregory replied.

"I don't know yet. These are all optional actions that we could take," Clayton said. Clayton took a healthy guzzle from his beer. The Knight Sharks did the same.

"What do you fellas want to do?" Polly asked.

"I say we go after that damned Silver Serpent," Zeus said.

"I say we return to land to report what we have seen to Molly and Cape Crusade," Gregory replied.

"I say we fish for sharks and tuna and be prepared with our silver harpoons in case we do see the Silver Serpent," Polly said.

"I'm with Polly," Augustus replied.

"I say we continue drinking our beer and fishing," Rodney added.

"What do you want to do Captain?" Zeus asked.

"I say we continue fishing and keep our eyes peeled for the Silver Serpent," Clayton said.

"OK. It's settled. Let's check our lines," Polly replied.

"Sounds good to me," Rodney said.

The Bloodhounds took orders from their Captain, but their opinions were also valued and included.

"Rig' em up fellas! Let's drink some beer and catch some sharks and tuna!" Clayton said enthusiastically..
"What should we do with the body parts and the top half of this lemon shark?" Zeus asked.

"We'll keep them as evidence and proof that the Silver Serpent caused the Bloodhound's unfortunate demise. Throw them on ice," Clayton replied. Then they grabbed some more beers and sparked up some cigars and pipes. The balmy and windy day turned into a calmer day with the sun peaking out of the clouds, after their lines were back in the water. It was quiet and tranquil for the moment.

"OK Knight Sharks, let's be ready for some shark and tuna action," Clayton replied.

"We should also be ready for some Silver Serpent action. It could be that that creature is responsible for this entire situation, and it could still be lurking around these waters with blood on its tongue," Augustus said soberly.

"That is right. Let's stay on our toes and keep our eyes and ears open," Clayton ordered.

"Aye-aye Captain. Who wants another beer?" Zeus replied.

"Just get everybody another beer, you sea slug," Polly said. The Knight Sharks laughed.

Zeus fetched another round of ice-cold Stingray beers for the Knight Sharks. The orange sun was setting in the western, indigo sky and the darkness was creeping in. The Knight Sharks continued drinking beer and smoking their cigars and pipes with their eyes glued to their fishing lines and the sable, ocean's surface.

Slick arrived at his cave and laid down on his cushy bed of kelp. He ate some emerald seaweed to relax and help him sleep. He wondered how long that boat would stay there. Then he stopped caring and dozed off. The Knight Sharks were on edge and curious as to what the Silver Serpent's next move might be.

They continued to drink heavily and fish. They had not caught anything all day besides that upper half of that lemon shark and some human body parts.

"Get me a shot of rum!" Polly exclaimed. By this time the Knight Sharks were getting good and drunk. They were all good-sized men, so they all had a high tolerance for alcohol.

"We haven't seen the Silver Serpent for hours now, and we haven't caught any damn sharks or tuna," Augustus said.

"Tell me about it. I think the Silver Serpent is lying low right now. Maybe sometimes, he chooses not to be seen," Clayton replied.

"Maybe it knows we are still here and is waiting for his opportunity to strike," Zeus said.

"Only God knows. God, please protect us. It would be really something extraordinary if we saw it again," Gregory replied.

"It's extremely rare to catch a glimpse of that monstrous sea creature," Rodney said.

"I had a feeling that the legend was true, and now I know it was the Silver Serpent that slayed the Bloodhounds," Polly replied.

Just then there were strikes on a tuna rod and a shark rod simultaneously. Zeus grabbed the tuna rod, and Augustus grabbed the shark rod. They both pulled back forcefully and set the hook. The battles were on.

Augustus and Zeus were both struggling mightily, but both landed their game right up onto the boat's deck. Augustus caught an 8-foot bull shark, and Zeus caught a 200 pound Atlantic bluefin tuna. Both were admirable and impressive catches. Polly gutted them, and threw them on ice.

"That's excellent! Those are two terrific catches. I say we end our day on that note and head back to land. We are all drunk and could use some rest," Clayton said.

"Aye-aye Captain." Zeus exclaimed.

"What about the Silver Serpent?" Rodney asked.

"What about it? We fished here all day and only saw it once. We did not come here to slay it. The silver harpoons were just a safety precaution if it had attacked us. We came out here to fish and search for any sign of the Bloodhounds. That's what we did. Let's call it a day," Clayton replied.

"I agree with the Captain," Polly said.

"Maybe we will see it again another day. It is late already and I'm tired as a boxer in the twelfth round," Augustus replied.

The Knight Sharks reeled in their lines and prepared to head back to shore. They all took shots of rum and whiskey and popped open some beers for the trip back home. They cheered to a safe, informative, and successful fishing trip.

Chapter Twelve
The Latest News

The Knight Sharks arrived at the docks safely and heavily intoxicated that Friday evening. They docked their boat and left the fish they caught and the human body parts in separate ice boxes in the cabin and locked it up. They rode home in their horse drawn buggies. The next day rolled around and it was Saturday, August 12, 1904.

The Knight Sharks woke up late because of their hangovers and rode over to the Sandbar. Molly rode over there also to get the latest news. She walked into the beloved bar and grill.

"Hello, Clayton. How was the fishing trip? Did you find out anything regarding Marco and the Bloodhounds?" Molly said.

"Good afternoon, Molly. Yes, unfortunately we did find some signs of the Bloodhounds. We found a human head and arm in a shark's stomach. The arm had a Bloodhounds patch on it. We still have the body parts on ice in our boat, if you don't believe me. I believe that they were all slain by the Silver Serpent," Clayton replied.

"Oh my God! I can't believe it! Marco is dead!" Molly exclaimed. She burst into hysterical tears.

"I'm so sorry for your loss Molly," Clayton said.

"How do you know that the Silver Serpent killed them?" Molly asked.

"I don't know for sure, but it's pretty safe to bet that the Silver Serpent did them in, because there was no sign of their boat. Only a Silver Serpent could have destroyed their boat like that. The shark we caught was bitten in half by something while we were reeling it in. Only the Silver Serpent could have done something like that. After we caught that mangled shark, the Silver Serpent swam passed us, just underneath our boat. We were really lucky it didn't attack us," Clayton replied.

"That is insane! That monster cannot just continue to go on slaying and devouring innocent people. It has to be stopped!" Molly said.

"We are trying ma'am. It is no easy task to slay a Silver Serpent," Zeus replied.

"Well you should try harder!" Molly exclaimed. She stormed out of the door crying.

"Geez. She took that pretty hard. Poor thing," Augustus said.

"What do you expect? She lost a loved one," Gregory replied. The Knight Sharks ordered some fried fish and shrimp with some ice-cold beers. Despite being hung-over, the Knight Sharks could continue drinking the next day.

"What should we do about that Silver Serpent? He is slaying too many of our town's people," Polly said.

"We are shark and tuna fishermen. We are not Silver Serpent hunters," Zeus replied.

"That's true, but do you just want to stand idle while that beast continues to slay and devour people from our own town?" Rodney said.

"We could go out there and try to slay it, but if things go wrong, we're all dead meat," Augustus replied.

"That ocean is his territory and he knows it and protects it well. They say that only a silver harpoon through its heart can slay it. That is an extremely difficult task, considering how colossal and elusive he is and how rapidly he cuts through the water," Clayton said.

"Didn't Walter and his crew slay a female Silver Serpent with her offspring in her belly?" Polly asked.

"Yeah, that's the story," Gregory replied.

"Then that means that it can be slayed," Rodney said.

"There is a difference between slaying a pregnant female and the alpha male of the Atlantic Ocean. The Silver Serpent that is out there is a finely tuned and intelligent killing machine. It calculates its moves, and has a taste for human blood and a mind for revenge. It only knows death and destruction," Clayton replied.

"That is true. It is one tough son of a bitch," Augustus said.

The Knight Sharks all ordered another round of beers. The fried fish and shrimp were being devoured in large quantities with tartar and cocktail sauce. The seafood at the Sandbar was so delicious, because it was so fresh. It had usually been caught a day or two before it was served. And sometimes, it was served that same day it was caught.

Each day the Sandbar served a different kind of fish as its special for the day. Today the special was fried spotted sea trout.

"We should inform Bruno of what we saw on our last fishing trip," Zeus said.

"That's a great idea. That way he can help us spread the news about the Bloodhound's demise and the existence of the Silver Serpent," Clayton said. Bruno was the proprietor of the Sandbar. He was a sixty year old man with historical ties to Cape Crusade.

"How you doing, Bruno? Join us, because there is something we need to tell you," Zeus announced.

Bruno was talking to his wife and son at the bar.

"What's going on, Clayton? I'll be right over," Bruno replied. Bruno excused himself from his family and walked over to the Knight Shark's table.

"How you doing, Bruno?" Clayton asked.

"I'm okay. How you doing, Clayton?" Bruno replied.

"I'm just dandy. I have some news to report to you," Clayton said.

"Oh yeah? What kind of news?" Bruno replied.

"We came in last night from a fishing trip. We saw some body parts from a dead Bloodhound in the belly of a shark we caught. That led us to believe that the Bloodhounds are dead. We also caught a brief glance at that monstrous Silver Serpent. It swam by us, just underneath our boat," Clayton replied.

"How did you see that?" Bruno asked.

"The shark that we caught had the body parts still in its stomach. As a matter of fact, when we were reeling in that shark, something bit in half. Polly reeled in its head and what was left of its upper body. It had to have been the Silver Serpent that chomped the shark in two. We still have the body parts on our boat," Clayton replied.

"Lord have mercy! You witnessed all of that for yourselves?" Bruno exclaimed.

"My crew and I all witnessed those events for ourselves. You can trust me, as you know me as a man of my word," Clayton replied.

"I think that we should spread the word to be on the lookout for that monster," Polly suggested.

"What do you want me to do?" Bruno asked.

"I think that you should announce to any fishermen and whale hunters that the Silver Serpent has been slaying and devouring people around Boat-Wreck Lane and Hammerhead Hedge. And it has also been destroying and sinking their boats. You could also mention that it has been spotted by us in those areas. That way they can be cautious when they are in those areas and won't be unprepared," Clayton replied.

"OK. I can do that. I'll make some flyers tonight and post them up around the bar tomorrow," Bruno said.

"That's a great idea," Clayton said.

"I also have a contact with the Cape Crusade Morning Star. I can relay this news to them, so they can print it in the newspapers," Bruno replied.

"That's an even better idea," Augustus said.

"OK. I'll do that first thing tomorrow morning," Bruno said.

"Thanks a lot Bruno. You are a real pal," Clayton replied.

"No problem. I want to keep this town as safe as possible. That Silver Serpent has been costing me money, because he has been eliminating my customers. I'm glad he didn't get you and your crew," Bruno said.

"There has to be some way to slay that Silver Serpent," Zeus announced.

"Can I get you guys another round of beers or some more food?' Bruno asked.

"Sure buddy. We'll take another round of beers and some more fish and shrimp," Clayton replied.

"That's coming right up," Bruno said. The Knight Sharks ate their delectable food and drank their frosty beers. They felt a bit of relief now that Bruno was going to help them spread the word about the Silver Serpent.

Chapter Thirteen
The Silver Serpent Strikes

A day had passed and it was Monday, August 14, 1904. Bruno woke up early and walked over to the Cape Crusade Morning Star. That was the local newspaper station. He walked through the doors and contacted Barney. Barney was an editor for the Cape Crusade Morning Star. He told Barney the latest news on the Silver Serpent and the Bloodhounds. Barney wanted to see the body parts for himself, so Bruno contacted Clayton. Clayton told them to meet him at the boat docks, so he could show them. Once he showed them, Barney took photos of the half eaten lemon shark and the chewed-up human head and that arm with the Bloodhounds patch on it. Barney immediately published those graphic photos, and the story that went along with them, in the Morning Star.

The headlines on the front-page of the Cape Crusade Morning Star, read; "The Silver Serpent Strikes!" The newspapers were selling like hot cakes because people could not resist learning more about the legend of the Silver Serpent and the destruction he'd caused, the half eaten lemon shark, and the demise of the notorious Bloodhounds. It struck fear in them and excited them at the same time.

Bruno also posted flyers in his bar that read; "The Silver Serpent is out there!" People from all over Cape Crusade and Staten Island, were now finding out that this mythological, mystical, and legendary creature, was real. And that the danger was all too real. Newspapers sold for a nickel back then and even then, the newspaper stations everywhere were making a nice chunk of change with this latest, mind-blowing story.

The story told the readers about the Silver Serpent's latest killings and how one of the Knight Sharks named Polly caught a half-eaten lemon shark with body parts that belonged to a fallen Bloodhound. The article said that the shark was ripped in half by the Silver Serpent while it was being reeled in by Polly. No sign of the Bloodhounds boat was found. Only those body parts found in the shark's belly.

The article also mentioned that the Silver Serpent was spotted by the Knight Sharks, shortly after they discovered the human body parts in the partly devoured shark. That led the readers to believe that the Bloodhound's boat was attacked and destroyed by the Silver Serpent, and it devoured most of the Bloodhounds and left some human carnage left over for the sharks.

People all over Staten Island were shocked despite some non-believers. Some refused to believe that story because they had never seen the Silver Serpent for themselves, and they only believed what they could see. Most people believed it though, due to all the recent missing people and boats, but they were too scared to venture out there and find out for themselves, firsthand.

The purpose of the article was to warn people of the danger and threat that the Silver Serpent posed, and perhaps inspire someone to venture out into the deep blue sea and attempt to slay it. It accomplished both of those goals. Barney also mentioned that Captain Golden's $10,000 reward to the slayers of the Silver Serpent, still stood. Back in the Atlantic Ocean the Silver Serpent was going for his afternoon swim around Boat-Wreck Lane. He decided to go by Bo's residence to see what he was up to. Bo was sleeping when Slick arrived. Slick signaled for Bo to come out with his hydro-sonic sonar signal. Bo heard the signal and swam outside his cave.

"Say, killer. How you doing?" Bo said.

"Say, tentacles. I'm doing great man. I'm just going for my afternoon swim. Why don't you come along?" Slick replied.

"OK. I was just getting up anyway," Bo said.

Bo and Slick lurked around Boat-Wreck-Lane and hunted for fish and sharks to devour. There was none in that area, so they deduced to swim towards Hammerhead Hedge. They glided smoothly just below the surface, so that they could feel the welcoming warmth from the sizzling sun's rays. It was a typical summer day out in the Atlantic Ocean with lots of sea-life engaging in their daily routines.

The seagulls dove down like arrows at the leftover bait that the fishing boats threw overboard. The sharks were roaming through the water like fighter pilots seeking a target. The zeppelin shaped whales were blowing torrential mists of spray through their mighty blowholes just above the ocean's glittering surface. Seals and fish were being chased by great white and mako sharks. The two sea monsters arrived at Hammerhead Hedge, and they spotted Hank the hammerhead with his shark goons.

"How's it going, Hank?" Slick asked.

"What's up, Hank?" Bo said.

"I'm okay. How you fellas doing?" Hank replied.

"Just great," Slick said.

"I'm feeling pretty good," Bo said.

"What's going on in these parts of the ocean?" Slick asked.

"The same old tale of woe. Things have been dead around here lately. A lot of blue fish and sea bass have migrated to other parts of the Atlantic to avoid being devoured," Hank replied.

"Where are you sea creatures catching your meals these days?" Slick asked.

"Sometimes we catch some here, but most of the time we have to travel to Boat-Wreck Lane and Squid Alley to fill our bellies," Hank replied.

"I hear Squid Alley has a lot of sea-life these days. Let's go check it out. It's only about a fifteen minute swim from here," Slick said.

"That sounds good to me. What do my comrades say?" Hank replied.

"Let's hunt and feast," Hank's shark goons responded.

"Let's head out then," Bo said.

The two sea monsters headed towards Squid Alley with Hank and his goons. There were a total of six sharks in Hank's crew. They arrived at Squid Alley and saw that there was a lot of activity going on. There were huge manta rays and lots of barracuda and other fish swimming around.

"It looks like a real seafood buffet here!" Slick said.

"Yes sir! We hit the jackpot here my friends!" Bo exclaimed.

"You betcha! This is a real score right here buddy!" Hank said.

The two sea monsters and the shark's eyes lit up like fires when they saw all the potential prey swimming right in front of them. A mechanism went off in their brain that transformed them into bloodthirsty killing machines.

"I'm going after the manta rays," Slick said.

"I'm going after the barracudas," Hank replied.

"I'm going after the sea bass," Bo said.

They shot out like cannons after their desired prey. Slick was poked in the eye by the tail-end of the first manta ray he went after, and it stung him severely.

"Damnit, that hurt! I better not be blind in that eye!" Slick exclaimed. The Stingray's venom burned Slick's left eye tremendously, and he was temporarily blind from that eye. Then Slick grabbed the manta ray's spear-like stinger in his jaws and brutally ripped it from its body. He spat that out and then grabbed the manta ray's head with his upper limbs and drove his claws through its eyeballs. Then he chomped down on the head and pierced its brain with his teeth and slayed it instantly. After that, Slick's left eyesight began to come back, and he began to enjoy his meal. Silver Serpent's were incredibly fast healers, and they had an extremely high tolerance for pain.

Another manta ray saw what Slick had done to his companion and came at him with his lengthy, raised stinger like a gigantic, spired lance. Slick grabbed the stinger with his jaws and bent it in half with his left upper limb and disabled it. Slick slashed at the manta ray with his claws and shredded it into four separate pieces. He quickly had another fresh meal right in front of his glowing, blood-red eyes. Hank and his goons went after a school of barracuda. The barracuda were lightning fast, so the hammerhead sharks only caught a couple of them.

Although Bo's meals mainly consisted of krill, he occasionally liked to devour fresh fish. His favorite was sea bass. He opened his gigantic mouth wide and swallowed about ten sea bass in one gulp.

"AHH, that was delicious," Bo said to himself.

Just then, a school of bull sharks approached Hank and his crew.

"What's going on, Hank?" Tommy asked. Tommy was the leader of the bull shark squad.

"We're just here trying to grab a bite to eat," Hank replied.

"You'll save some for us, won't you?" Tommy said.

"Sure. No problem Tommy. There's enough here for all of us," Hank replied.

Slick finished devouring his second manta ray when he spotted some tarpon about forty yards in front of him.

"Hank, do you see those tarpon? Let's go get some," Slick said.

"Yes, that's an excellent idea," Hank replied. Slick and the hammerhead sharks went after the lean, silvery tarpon.

Tommy and his bull sharks followed their lead. The tarpon spotted them coming and tried to escape with their lives. They were very fast, and some of them got away. Most of them were trapped in the toothy jaws of Slick and the sharks, and they became another quick meal.

"Man, I'm full. That was a plethora of fresh seafood," Hank said.

Tommy and his crew devoured their fair share of Tarpon as well, and they left happily with full, shark bellies.

"It sure was. I can coast home satisfied on a full belly," Slick replied.

"I'm still hungry. I think I see some krill up ahead," Bo said.

"Go get'em Bo. You are mighty whale shark, so you need all the nutrition you can get," Slick replied.

"We're going to jet. It was an honor hunting with you, fellow sea creatures. Take care," Hank said.

"Likewise Hank. See you later," Slick replied.

"Take care Hank. Stay out of those wicked fishermen boats," Bo said.

Hank chuckled. Hank and his crew headed back home to Hammerhead Hedge.

"What do you want to do Slick?" Bo asked.

"I don't know. I'm not tired yet. Let's roam around and explore for a while," Slick replied.

"OK. Where should we explore?" Bo said.

"I don't care. Wherever the current takes us," Slick replied.

"OK. Lead the way. Are you still hungry?" Bo said.

"Yeah, I could go for some dessert. Let's see what lies ahead of us," Slick replied.

The two sea monsters cruised north towards an old sunken ship called *Old Bluebeard*. *Old Bluebeard* had lots of different sea life, and it attracted humans, because they wanted to search it for sunken pirate's treasure.

Slick figured he would look for some dessert while he was there. The two glorious sea beasts arrived there and saw some enormous Atlantic Goliath grouper and some human scuba divers that investigated the sunken ship.

"Look Bo. There are some scuba divers over there," Slick said.

"Yeah, I see them. There are some giant grouper here also. Which ones are you gonna devour?" Bo replied.

"I think I'll devour some humans to mix it up a little bit. What about you Bo?" Slick said.

"That's a no-brainer. I'm gonna devour some of those plump, juicy grouper," Bo replied.

"OK. Let's go get some!" Slick exclaimed.

"Yeah buddy!" Bo replied.

Slick and Bo swam toward the humans and the grouper that surrounded the sunken ship. They tried to be as stealthy as possible despite their colossal size. There were three humans and five grouper swimming around the proximity of *Old Bluebeard.*

Slick swam up to the scuba divers and struck at one with his slithery upper body and spiky head. He trapped the first human in his deadly jaws. Another scuba diver aimed his spear gun and shot Slick in the belly. Slick felt a sharp sting in his belly. The third scuba diver panicked and went into convulsions. Slick's jaws snapped down with ferocity on that first human, before he could shoot him with his spear gun. Slick's teeth went through the scuba diver's heart and lungs like steak-knives slicing through filet mignon. Clouds of candy apple-red blood filled the ocean's navy-blue water. Slick left that body there, and went after the scuba diver that shot him with the spear gun. That human attempted to escape, but Slick sliced him open with one slash of his right upper limb. Slick tore open the diver's belly and ripped out his guts and organs.

Slick spotted the third human that was sinking to the ocean floor. That was the one having violent convulsions. Slick wondered why that human was just sinking instead of trying to escape with his life. He figured something was wrong with that human. Feeling no mercy, Slick darted at that human and bit his head clean off the shoulders. That human never saw what hit him and probably only felt a millisecond of pain. Slick devoured the head and the rest of the corpses floating around that bloody area.

Bo opened his mouth wide and plunged himself towards the school of grouper. He swallowed four out five of them with one mighty gulp. The two sea monsters definitely got their fill of dessert.

"AHH, that was simply delectable," Slick said.

"Yeah, those grouper tasted really succulent. How did those scuba divers taste?" Bo replied.

"They were kind of bony, but that last scuba diver was kind of plump," Slick said.

"What do you want to do now?" Bo asked.

"Let's head back home. We have had our fair share of meals for the day. I'm stuffed," Slick replied.

"We sure did buddy. We ate like kings today," Bo said.

"Yup. That's because we are the kings of this ocean. Let's go home now," Slick replied.

"OK, sounds good. Let's go brother," Bo said.

Chapter Fourteen
Tiffany and Heather

Polly picked Clayton up at his house, and they headed over to the Sandbar the next afternoon to have some cold beers and some fresh, fried black drum. The day was Tuesday, August 15, 1904. Bruno was there making sure that the bar was running smoothly.

"How's it going, Bruno?" Clayton asked.

"I'm staying busy with all this Silver Serpent talk. People can't get enough of this latest story," Bruno replied.

"Yeah I bet. People are finally starting to believe the legend," Polly said.

"I heard that Captain Golden is offering a $10,000 reward for the Silver Serpent's head. Does that deal still stand?" Clayton said.
"Yes it does," Bruno replied.

Clayton and Polly ordered some ice-cold beers and some all you can eat fried black drum. The fried fish was so fresh, that the flaky, white fillets were falling apart. It was a scorching day outside, so the beers tasted especially refreshing.

"Has anybody seen Captain Golden to confirm that bounty?" Polly said.

"Yes, he was here a couple of days ago, and he assured me that he would pay $10,000 to the crew that slayed the Silver Serpent," Bruno replied.

"Does anybody have the balls to try and slay the Silver Serpent? That is the question," Clayton said.

"At least a handful of people will, I'm sure. I say that we try and go after it also. If we slay that serpent, we can use that money to buy new fishing equipment," Polly replied.

"Yeah, I guess we could try it. What do we have to lose besides our lives?" Clayton said.

"That's true," Polly replied.

"We'll have to really ponder this decision. We should definitely take our silver harpoons with us the next time we go out fishing," Clayton said.

"Yeah, just in case we do see that monster, we will be prepared," Polly replied.

Just then, two gorgeous, luscious women walked into the Sandbar. Clayton and Polly noticed them immediately. They were vivacious and curvaceous with spunky personalities. One lady was a beautiful blonde and the other one was a sexy, raven-haired brunette. The brunette winked at Polly and smiled.

Then they sat down at a table.

"Clayton, that brunette just winked at me. Let's go talk to her and her friend," Polly said.

"OK. Let's see what kind of charm you have," Clayton replied. "Excuse us, Bruno. We're gonna go talk to those hot babes that just walked in," Polly said.

"Go ahead gentlemen. Give them some of that old Cape Crusade charm," Bruno replied.

Clayton and Polly walked over to the table that the women were seated at.

"Hello. How are you lovely ladies doing today?" Polly said.

"Hi, I'm great. How are you?" The brunette replied.

"Hi, I'm Heather. What is your name?" The blonde said.

"Hi, I'm Clayton. It's nice to meet you Heather," Clayton replied.

"I'm Tiffany. It's nice to meet you guys," Tiffany said. Tiffany was the brunette.

"It's nice to meet you as well. I'm Polly," Polly replied.

"May I buy you ladies some drinks?" Clayton asked.

"That is so sweet of you. Sure. I'll take a Long Island iced-tea," Heather replied.

"That is very kind of you. Sure. I'll have a cold Stingray beer," Tiffany said.

"OK. I can handle that," Clayton replied.

"Awe, thanks sweetheart. You're a real gentleman," Heather said.

"Why don't you gentlemen join us? Have a seat," Tiffany said.

"OK. That sounds great," Polly replied.

Clayton beckoned one of the waiters. A waiter named Clyde came to their table.

"Hi, I'm Clyde. What can I get you for you ladies and gents today?" Clyde asked.

"Hello, Clyde. We'll take three Stingray beers and one Long Island iced-tea," Clayton replied.

"Can I get you all anything to eat?" Clyde asked.

"Are you ladies hungry? The fried black drum is excellent today," Polly said.

"Sure. We'd love some plates of all you can eat fried black drum," Tiffany replied.

"Are you gentlemen hungry also?" Heather asked.

"Yes, we already ordered the all you can eat fried fish plates. Our plates are over there on the bar. Let me go grab them, so we can get some more," Clayton replied.

Clayton walked over to the bar and fetched his and Polly's plates of black drum with lemons, tartar sauce and ketchup. The fried fish always came with crispy, golden, French fries on the side. Clyde returned with the ladies' plates.

"Can you bring us some more lemons and tartar sauce?" Polly requested.

"Sure, that's coming right up. Is there anything else I can get you?" Clyde replied.

"That's fine for now, Clyde. Thank you. Cheers to this delicious fish, cold beer, and these lovely ladies!" Clayton said.

"Cheers!" The table replied.

"Awe, you're such a sweetheart," Heather said.

"Where are you ladies from?" Polly asked.

"We are from Cape Carnivore," Tiffany replied.

"That's the harbor town in Long Island, right? What brings you to Cape Crusade?" Clayton asked.

"Yes, it is. We heard that this place has the best all you can eat fried fish in Staten Island," Heather said.

"We also heard about that Silver Serpent story," Tiffany replied.

"Wow. That kind of news spreads like wildfire," Polly said.

"It sure does. It's all over the papers," Heather replied.

"A story as big as that travels quickly," Tiffany said.

"What exactly did you read about it?" Clayton asked.

"We read that the Silver Serpent slayed a notorious group of whale hunters called the Bloodhounds," Heather replied.

"And that another group of fishermen called the Knight Sharks caught a half-eaten shark with parts of one of the Bloodhounds in its stomach. That is so horrific," Tiffany said.

"We also read that the Knight Sharks spotted the Silver Serpent on that fishing trip," Heather replied.

"That was all true. You are sitting down with the men that reeled in that shark and caught a glimpse of the Silver Serpent. We reported that news," Polly replied.

"Are you telling us that you guys are the Knight Sharks?" Heather asked.

"In the flesh. We are both members of the Knight Sharks. There are five more of us, but they are somewhere else right now." Clayton answered.

"Wait a minute. How do we know that you guys are Knight Sharks? Prove it," Heather said.

"OK," Clayton replied.

Clayton lifted his right sleeve and revealed a blue and silver tattoo of a shark suited in knight's armor, and above it read; Knight Sharks. Polly did the same.

"Wow! You guys are really the notorious Knight Sharks! What was it like catching that shark and seeing those human body parts?" Tiffany said.

"It was pretty shocking to see that carnage. I believe that God works in mysterious ways, because those body parts were evidence of the Bloodhound's demise," Clayton replied.

"How do you know that the Silver Serpent slayed the Bloodhounds if the body parts were found in a shark's stomach?" Heather asked.

"Because there was no sign of the Bloodhound's boat. Sharks could not have sunk that boat, but the Silver Serpent could have. Plus, it swam right underneath our boat. We're lucky it didn't attack and slay us," Polly replied.

"Holy shit! That sounds like one hell of a story," Tiffany said.

"I know it was the Silver Serpent that did this, because the Bloodhounds were not the first group of whale hunters or fishermen to be attacked or go missing around these perilous waters," Clayton replied.

"That is so frightening and bizarre. Are you guys going to go out there again and attempt to slay it?" Heather asked.

"My comrade and I here were just talking about that. We need to talk to the other Knight Sharks first, but we will definitely take our silver harpoons with us on our next fishing trip," Clayton said.

"You guys are very courageous. It takes a lot of balls to go out in that fierce creature's territory and face it head on," Tiffany commented.

"You can say that again," Polly said.

"Let's change the subject for a little bit and talk about something more pleasant," Heather suggested.

"OK. That's fine with me," Clayton replied.

They all ordered another round of beers and some shots of fine Jamaican rum. Time was flying by, and they were all having a ball and getting tipsy.

"Why don't we take this party back to my place?" Clayton suggested.

"OK. That sounds fabulous," Heather replied.

"Where do you live?" Tiffany asked.

"I live just up the road from here. I have a house overlooking the beach. It's walking distance from here," Clayton replied.

"That sounds wonderful. Okay, let's go," Tiffany said.

"I recommend that we walk since we have all been drinking like sailors," Clayton said. "

It's just up the road. It's a ten minute walk from here," Polly replied.

"OK, party animals. Let's go! I'll see you later Bruno," Clayton said.

"See you later Clayton. Be safe brother," Bruno replied.

The two Knight Sharks walked out of the bar with their attractive new lady friends. It was about 7:00 in the cool evening, and the crimson sun was setting amongst the lavender horizon with the fresh smell of the Atlantic Ocean in the coastal air. Polly led his gray and black Clydesdale and the ladies' brown and white Belgian horse into the Sandbar's stables and locked the gate with his keys. Then the group strolled towards Clayton's beach house and arrived ten minutes later.

"Come on in ladies. Make yourselves at home," Clayton said.

"Wow, this house is really spectacular," Heather replied.

"Thank you Heather. I do my best to keep it looking sharp," Clayton said.

"Do you have any kids?" Tiffany asked.

"Yes. I have a son that is thirteen years old. His name is Simon. He's spending the night at a friend's house tonight," Clayton replied.

"Oh, that's nice. I have a ten year old daughter myself. Her name is Ariel," Tiffany replied.

"That is grand. Kids are a true blessing," Clayton said.

"I don't have any kids. I always wanted some though," Heather replied.

"You are still young. You have plenty of time," Clayton said.

"I have an eight year old son and a five year old daughter. Their names are Joshua and Priscilla. What may I get you lovely ladies to drink?" Polly replied.

"I'll take a shot of whiskey and a cold beer, please," Heather said.

"I'll have the same," Tiffany replied.

"Get the same for me too, Polly," Clayton said.

"OK. I'll be a gentleman and fetch everyone's drinks," Polly replied.

"Thanks Polly. You are so sweet," Tiffany said.

"No problem. I know the bar in this house like the back of my hand," Polly replied.

Polly walked over to the bar in the next room in Clayton's house and grabbed a bottle of Irish whiskey, four cold beers, and four shot glasses, and placed them on a tray.

"Here you go ladies and gentlemen. Your drinks are served," Polly said. Polly handed everybody their beers and then poured them each a shot of whiskey.

"Thanks Polly," Heather said.

"Thank you Polly," Tiffany said.

"Thanks buddy," Clayton said.

"You're all very welcome. It's an honor and a pleasure to be with all of you special people on this wonderful evening. May God bless us and our loved ones, always," Polly replied.

"Why don't we go in the backyard, so we can enjoy the crisp night air and cool ocean breeze?" Clayton suggested.

"OK. That sounds great," Heather replied.

"That sounds lovely," Tiffany said.

"Let's go," Polly said.

The two couples walked outside the door and onto the backyard patio. The patio overlooked the pristine Cape Crusade Beach. The stars were sparkling like platinum fireflies amongst the onyx sky as the rolling waves came crashing in.

"I'm really glad you lovely ladies decided to join us here tonight," Clayton said.

"I'll second that," Polly replied.

"I'm glad we came also. It's always nice to make new friends. The view from this location is absolutely gorgeous," Heather said.

"Yes. This patio overlooking the Cape Crusade Beach is breathtaking," Tiffany replied.

"Thank you. It's my own piece of paradise. I'm glad you ladies are enjoying it. This is where I come to keep my sanity sometimes. The serenity really puts me at ease and clears my mind," Clayton said.

"I don't blame you," Heather replied.

"You look absolutely stunning tonight, Tiffany. Especially underneath the moon and stars," Polly said.

"Thank you Polly. You look very handsome as well," Tiffany replied.

"Thanks doll," Polly said.

Polly placed his arm around Tiffany. Tiffany embraced his hand and leaned her head on his shoulder. Polly leaned over and kissed her. Tiffany kissed back. Clayton took Heather's hand and led her to some patio chairs. She took his hand, and they sat down on the patio chairs with their drinks.

"Would you like to take this inside?" Polly asked.

"Sure," Tiffany replied. The couple walked inside Clayton's house and into the guest bedroom. They took off their clothes and jumped on the bed together. Polly kissed Tiffany on her neck and fondled her silky, perky breasts. Then the intoxicated couple engaged in hot and steamy sex.

Outside on the patio; Clayton was making his move on Heather. He started to kiss her sultry lips under the romantic moonlight.

"Would you like to go to my bedroom?" Clayton asked.

"That sounds nice," Heather replied.

The couple got up from their patio chairs and strolled inside Clayton's house and into his master bedroom. Clayton kissed Heather while he undressed her. They were both naked, and they jumped onto Clayton's bed. Heather straddled Clayton and rode him vigorously and passionately as he thrust inside of her creamy, velvety vagina. Both couples made deep and passionate love to each other for about twenty minutes, before they all climaxed. Then they kissed each other fondly and fell asleep comfortably in each other's arms.

The next day at Clayton's house everyone woke up with minor hangovers.

"Good morning, Heather. How did you sleep?" Clayton said.

"Good morning. I slept heavenly. How did you sleep?" Heather replied.

"I slept like a baby," Clayton said.

Clayton leaned over and kissed Heather's pouty lips.

"Would you like anything for breakfast or some coffee?" Clayton asked.

"Sure. That sounds delightful," Heather replied.

"OK. Let's go to the kitchen," Clayton said.

"OK," Heather replied. The couple walked into the kitchen. Over in the guest bedroom, Polly and Tiffany were just waking up.

"Good morning, Tiffany," Polly said.

"Good morning, Polly," Tiffany replied.

"Last night was a blast. Thank you for being such amazing company," Polly said.

"Yes it was. I had a fabulous time," Tiffany replied.

Polly leaned over and French kissed Tiffany's sweet lips. She was completely naked besides a t-shirt Polly had lent her to sleep in. Polly could see her hard, pink nipples through the shirt. Even though it was in the morning, Tiffany still looked very sultry and desirable. Polly started to touch Tiffany in her erotic zone, and that turned her on. Then he kissed her down there, and that really got her juices flowing. Tiffany returned the favor to Polly's delight. After all of that, they climbed on each other and made hot and steamy love again before breakfast.

"AHH, that felt so good," Polly said.

"It sure did. It's even better in the morning, I always say," Tiffany replied with a cute giggle.

"Would you like to grab some breakfast and coffee?" Polly asked.

"Yes, that sounds delicious," Tiffany replied.

Polly and Tiffany climbed out of bed, got dressed, and walked to the kitchen. Clayton and Heather were already there, drinking coffee and orange juice.

"Good morning," Polly said.

"Good morning, Polly and Tiffany. May I offer you two some scrambled eggs with bacon and some coffee?" Clayton replied.

"Good morning, Clayton and Heather," Tiffany said.

"Sure, that sounds tasty," Polly replied.

"Good morning, Tiffany and Polly," Heather said.

Clayton poured them each a cup of coffee and threw some more eggs and bacon in the frying pan. It was 12:00 pm on Wednesday, August 16, 1904.

"Breakfast is served," Clayton said proudly. Clayton served some scrambled eggs with crispy bacon and toast for everyone at the table.

"Thanks Clayton. This looks delicious sweetie," Heather replied.

"Thanks Clayton. You are a wonderful host," Tiffany said.

"Thanks buddy. You're a real pal," Polly said.

"You're all very welcome, and are always welcome here. Thank you all for blessing me with your company. Now, dig in and enjoy," Clayton replied.

Everyone enjoyed their fresh, homemade breakfast and drank their hot, creamy coffee.

"That was delicious. I think we better get back to Cape Carnivore," Heather said.

"Yes, I have to get back home to check on my daughter," Tiffany replied.

"OK. We'll walk you ladies back to the Sandbar, so we can pick up our horse and buggies," Polly said.

"OK. Let's go," Tiffany said. The two couples walked out of Clayton's beach house and back to the Sandbar.

"It was a pleasure meeting you lovely ladies. I hope that we can see each other again soon. If you ever need to find us, just come to the Sandbar and ask for us, or leave a message for us. If we're not there, we're always around the docks or out fishing at sea. We'll give you our landlines just in case you want to call us. I'm looking forward to seeing you again in the future. Take care and keep in touch. Goodbye for now," Clayton said.

"It was so nice to meet you guys as well. You two are real gentlemen. We will definitely come back to the Sandbar to find you guys. We'll give you our landlines just in case you want to get a hold of us," Heather replied.

"It was so much fun hanging out with you guys. You guys really know how to treat ladies and show us a fabulous time. We will definitely be back to see how you guys are doing," Tiffany said.

"Great, I'm so glad to hear that. I hope to see you lovely ladies soon. You two are really something special. Take care and keep in touch," Polly replied. Polly and Clayton leaned over and kissed their new lady friends, goodbye. Then Polly unlocked the stable and collected the horses. Polly collected some paper and a pencil from his buggy, so the four could write their names and landlines on them, to exchange. Heather and Tiffany climbed into Heather's horse drawn buggy and rode back to their harbor town of Cape Carnivore, in Long Island, New York. Polly and Clayton hopped into his buggy, and he dropped Clayton off and rode home still dreaming of Tiffany's sweet kisses.

Chapter Fifteen
The Knight Shark's Expedition

The next day it was Thursday, August 17, 1904. Clayton woke up at 11:00 am and brewed a pot of coffee. He walked outside and climbed into his trusty, horse drawn buggy. Clayton rode over to the Sandbar and arrived there at 12:00 pm sharp. The other Knight Sharks had just arrived as well. They all parked their horse drawn buggies and walked inside the Sandbar. Bruno was sitting at the bar with his good friend, Mike.

"Good afternoon. How's it going Bruno?" Clayton said.

"Good afternoon. All is well. How are you sand crabs doing?" Bruno replied.

"We are doing well. We came here to have a meeting and go over the last-minute details for our Silver Serpent expedition," Clayton said.

"Great. Go ahead. Make yourselves comfortable," Bruno replied. The Knight Sharks grabbed a table for themselves and took their seats.

A waiter named Jack attended their table.

"What can I get for you gentlemen today?" Jack asked.

"Grab us all a round of beers and some fried fish," Clayton replied.

"Yes sir. I will be right back with your drinks," Jack said. Jack brought them all some ice-cold Yellow Crab beers and told them that the fried fish would be right out.

"OK Knight Sharks. We are getting ready to venture out on a Silver Serpent hunting expedition," Clayton stated.

"I knew it. Do you guys really want to go through with this? We could end up in the belly of the beast, literally," Zeus replied.

"Damnit Zeus! We are going through with this and that's final! That is a decision that our crew made together, so I don't want to hear any more out of your trap. Sit down, shut-up, and listen," Clayton said.

"We are all set to go. We just need to pick up some last-minute supplies such as food, water, beer, liquor, and three more silver harpoons. We are going to take five silver harpoons with us this time rather than two silver harpoons like we had with us last time," Polly said.

"OK, that sounds sensible," Ringo replied.

"Augustus and Rodney are going to go to the Purple Octopus to grab these last-minute supplies. After they've bought them, they'll meet us at the boat launch, so we can head out to sea," Clayton said.

"Aye-aye Captain. We will get that done as soon as we finish our lunch," Augustus replied.

Jack brought the Knight Sharks their plates of all you can eat fried fish and fries. Today's special was fried Atlantic cod.

"OK Augustus. I appreciate it. Here is $250 to buy all the supplies," Clayton said. Clayton handed Augustus $250 in cash. The Knight Sharks drank a couple of beers and ate their fill of fried Atlantic cod.

Augustus and Rodney rode out to the Purple Octopus in Rodney's horse drawn buggy. The rest of the Knight Sharks rode out to the boat launch and waited for Augustus and Rodney to return with the supplies. It was about 2:00 in the sunny and serene afternoon in Cape Crusade when Rodney and Augustus returned with the supplies. They bought food, beer, water, liquor, and three more silver harpoons. Now they had a total of five silver harpoons.

"OK, let's get all of this stuff loaded onto the boat," Clayton ordered.

The Knight Sharks loaded all the supplies onto *The Knight Shark*.

"Make sure to bring your guns if you have any," Polly replied. The Knight Sharks brought their guns on the boat as well.

"OK Knight Sharks. Let's head out to the deep-blue sea," Clayton ordered.

It was about 3:00 in the afternoon when the Knight Sharks headed out into the depths of the Atlantic Ocean with Clayton at the helm. They decided to go to Boat-Wreck Lane first, since that was where they saw the Silver Serpent on their last fishing trip.

"Are we going to fish for sharks and tuna also on this expedition?" Polly asked.

"Sure. We can throw some lines out while we wait to see the Silver Serpent," Clayton replied.

"That sounds like a great idea Captain," Rodney said.

The journey to Boat-Wreck Lane took the Knight Sharks a couple of hours to arrive there.

"OK, we are here. Let's drop the anchor and grab some cold ones," Clayton said.

"Anybody else want one?" Augustus replied.

"Sure. Grab me one too," Zeus said.

"Just grab everyone a beer," Clayton replied. Augustus walked into the boat's cabin, opened the icebox and grabbed the crew some cold ones. He walked outside the cabin and distributed the beers.

"OK. Load the silver harpoons and guns and rig up the fishing lines," Clayton ordered.

"Aye-aye Captain," Gregory replied.

"Aye-aye Captain," Polly said.

Polly and Gregory loaded up the silver harpoon guns and firearms while Rodney and Zeus rigged up the fishing lines. Augustus and Ringo dropped the anchor and made sure the deck was clear of anything hazardous.

"Everything is all loaded and ready to fire, Captain," Polly replied.

"The lines are ready to be thrown out, Captain," Rodney stated.

"Great. Drop those lines in the water," Clayton said.

Zeus dropped two lines rigged with bonito on the hook, while Rodney dropped two more lines rigged with squid into the sparkling blue water. The Knight Sharks toasted their beers to a successful and safe fishing trip and hunting expedition. Then they prayed to God and asked Him to protect them with His shield of righteousness and loyal love. Back at Slick's cave, he was just waking up from an afternoon nap. He decided to swim over to Oliver's cave to see what he was up to. Slick arrived at Oliver's cave and signaled for him to come out.

"Say, Slick. What's going on?" Oliver said.

"How's it going, you crazy cephalopod? I was in the area, so I thought I'd stop by and say hello," Slick replied.

"Have you devoured anything today?" Oliver asked.

"No, I haven't. Would you like to go hunt for something to devour?" Slick replied.

"Sure buddy. We can do that," Oliver said.

"Where would you like to go?" Slick asked.

"Let's try Boat-Wreck Lane. There has been a lot of activity there lately," Oliver replied.

"OK, that sounds good," Slick said.

The two sea monsters swam out towards the notorious Boat-Wreck Lane. As they arrived, they spotted the Knight Sharks.

"It looks like we have company," Slick said.

"Yeah, it's those bull headed fishermen again. They don't know when to quit. What should we do?" Oliver replied.

"Let's hang around and look for some sharks or tuna to devour. They usually like to congregate in this area. Let's try to remain low key and out of sight of that sea-crew, for now," Slick replied.

"OK, that sounds like a sensible plan," Oliver said.

Slick spotted some bull sharks hunting around some coral reef.

"Look at those bull sharks. There are four of them," Slick said.

"Yeah, I see them. They are huge," Oliver replied.

"I know. Let's go feast on their tasty flesh," Slick said.

"OK. You lead and I'll follow," Oliver replied.

"You got it. Watch my back," Slick said.

Slick and Oliver swam as stealthily as possible towards the shiver of bull sharks. They got within twenty yards from the bull sharks. Slick torpedoed himself towards the largest bull shark there and snapped his jaws down savagely on the shark's head. The bull shark tried to wriggle himself free, but Slick's jaws were like steel traps clamping down on the shark's head. Slick used one of his upper limbs and slashed the shark's belly open. Blood and guts poured out of the shark's body with its head still clamped in Slick's lethal jaws. Slick tore chunks of flesh off the shark and devoured them. The other bull sharks attacked Slick. Slick battled the other three bull sharks and tried to slash and bite his way to victory. One of the bulky bull sharks bit down ferociously just above Slick's spiked tail. That hurt Slick and caused him to bleed out of a deep wound. Oliver saw this and joined in the melee to aid Slick. Oliver wrapped his formidable tentacles around the shark that bit Slick's tail area and tried to snag him away. The bull shark was very powerful and was not budging. That gave Slick an opportunity to slice the shark's gill area with his lower limbs. Slick slashed the bull shark's gills with his left lower limb. The other two bull sharks went after Oliver, and one of them grabbed one of Oliver's tentacles in its mouth. Slick dashed at that bull shark and snapped his head off with one clean snap of his jaws. The other bull shark swam away frantically. Slick and Oliver suffered some battle wounds, but at least now, they had three dead bull sharks to feast on.

"Wow! These sharks are huge! We have quite the feast here for ourselves," Slick said.

"Damn straight! These sharks have lots of fresh, juicy meat on them," Oliver replied. Slick and Oliver devoured piece after piece from the dead, bloody, and shredded bull sharks. The two, bloodthirsty sea monsters devoured all three bull sharks with ravenous, and savory satisfaction.

"What do you want to do now?" Oliver asked.

"Let's go have some fun with those fishermen," Slick replied.

"Are you sure about that? They are probably armed with harpoons and guns," Oliver said.

"They usually are. So what? We can take them out," Slick replied.

"OK. I'm with you brother," Oliver said.

"Great. Let's go smash that boat with Godly force," Slick replied.

The two sea monsters swam as fast as they could towards *The Knight Shark* and slammed into the hull with reckless abandon. The thunderous jolt rattled the Knight Sharks to their core and two of them fell overboard. The two that fall over board were Gregory and Polly.

"Holy shit! It's the Silver Serpent!" Zeus exclaimed.

Clayton got a good look at the ginormous Silver Serpent that swam right underneath their boat with a humongous, purplish-blue Octopus.

"It's the Silver Serpent and a giant octopus! Grab the harpoons and guns!" Clayton exclaimed.

"What about Gregory and Polly?" Rodney asked.

"Throw them the ropes with the life preservers!" Clayton replied.

Augustus and Ringo rushed to the cabin and gathered the harpoons and guns while Rodney threw the life preservers to the overboard Knight Sharks.

"Help us!" Polly exclaimed.

"Help! I don't want to die!" Gregory exclaimed.

"Grab the life preservers!" Clayton replied.

Polly and Gregory saw the life preservers about ten yards away from them.

"Quick. Let's grab the life preservers before that foul creature slays us!" Polly exclaimed. Polly and Gregory swam for their lives toward the life preservers. Just as they were swimming frantically to the life preservers, Slick grasped Polly with his two upper limbs and dragged him down into deeper waters. Oliver grabbed Gregory with his long, lethal tentacles and wrapped them around his neck and waist. Then Oliver proceeded to tow Gregory down into the inauspicious depths of the merciless Atlantic. Slick and Oliver met up about fifty yards below the surface with their two victims. Polly and Gregory were panicking and struggling to break free, but they were being held tightly by ferocious claws and tentacles. They were also running out of precious oxygen. They violently squirmed and twitched like insects in a spider's web as their lives flashed before their eyes. Just before Polly could take his last breath, Slick bit his head off and ripped his arms from his body. Gregory witnessed that in a pure state of utter fear and panic. Slick devoured Polly's head and arms while he was holding on to the rest of the body. Gregory felt like his heart and lungs were going to explode, and then he ran out of breath and died.

"Go ahead Oliver. Devour that bastard. We should always devour what we have slain. It's the code of the sea," Slick said.

"OK. I am really hungry, after all," Oliver replied.

Oliver chewed on the drowned Knight Shark, Gregory, with his thousands of small, but, razor-sharp teeth. Slick crunched his bloody jaws down on the rest of Polly's marred corpse and tore it up beyond recognition. He let the bloody flavor of the flesh dance on his tingling taste buds before he chewed and swallowed it down.

"Pretty good huh?" Slick asked.

"Not bad. These humans get tastier and tastier every time you devour one of them," Oliver replied.

Oliver chewed piece after piece of Gregory's cadaver and swallowed them. The two sea monsters finished devouring the two Knight Sharks with ease and satisfaction.

"AHH, that was delicious. I'm still kind of hungry though," Slick said.

"Yes it was. I'm still hungry too. What do you want to do? Oliver replied.

"Let's crash into that blasted boat again," Slick said.

"OK, I'm right behind you big guy," Oliver replied.

"OK, let's do it. Follow my lead," Slick said.

"You got it, boss," Oliver replied.

The two gargantuan and bloodthirsty sea monsters swam as rapidly as they could towards *The Knight Shark's* hull and viciously rammed it again with their heads. This time nobody fell overboard. Slick and Oliver swam up to the surface to scope things out.

"There it is! Fire the silver harpoons and guns!" Clayton commanded.

Augustus and Zeus fired two silver harpoons at Slick's upper body between his upper limbs. Both struck Slick in his chest cavity and they stuck in there. Clayton fired another silver harpoon at the Silver Serpent, while Rodney fired a rifle at Oliver. Clayton's silver harpoon struck Slick in the head and stayed stuck in Slick's skull. Rodney's rifle round hit Oliver in his head and caused him to stop moving. Slick noticed that and attended to Oliver.

"Get the other two silver harpoons!" Clayton exclaimed.
Zeus ran to the cabin and grabbed the last two silver harpoons.
"Here they are, Captain," Zeus said.

"Take one for yourself, and give me the other one," Clayton replied. Zeus handed Clayton one silver harpoon and kept the other one.

"OK Knight Sharks. There are three silver harpoons stuck in the Silver Serpent's body. It looks like he is getting weaker! Be prepared to be pulled once the Silver Serpent starts to swim away. Try to make these last two harpoons count when you fire them! Aim for his heart. Try your hardest to hit the Silver Serpent in the heart!" Augustus said.

"Get ready to fire that silver harpoon at the Silver Serpent's heart when he pops back up again, Zeus! Rodney, keep firing your rifle at the heads of the Silver Serpent and the octopus!" Clayton exclaimed.

"What should I do Captain?" Augustus asked.

"You and Ringo, load the guns and keep firing them at the two sea monsters," Clayton replied.

"Aye-aye Captain!" Augustus said.

"Aye-aye Captain!" Ringo replied.

"Are you okay, Oliver?" Slick asked.

"I don't know. I can barely move. They hit me in the head with a gunshot," Oliver replied.

"Hang in there, buddy. I'm gonna get you outta here," Slick said.

"Are you sure? Don't you want to finish those fishermen off once and for all?" Oliver replied.

"I do, but now is not the right time. I will have to slay them some other time. I need to get you outta here and to safety. This battle is over, but the war has just begun," Slick said.

Slick grabbed Oliver with his lower limbs and dragged him back to his cave. Slick still had three silver harpoons stuck in his body. There were two in his upper body, between his upper limbs, and one in his head. He painfully ripped those out with his upper limbs.

They arrived back at Slick's cave, so Slick could perform emergency surgery on Oliver and medicate him with some magical emerald seaweed. That emerald seaweed had special healing powers for all types of wounds, infections, and illnesses.

"Are we there yet?" Oliver mumbled.

"Yes, we just arrived. Let me fetch that emerald seaweed, so you can eat some, and we can put some on your wounds. First, I have to take that bullet out of your head," Slick replied.

"Are you gonna cut me open to take it out? Isn't that risky?" Oliver asked.

"Yes it is, but not as risky as it would be to leave it in there. If it stays in there, it's just a matter of time before you die. I have to do it," Slick replied.

"OK, if you have to do it, then just do it. Just get it over with," Oliver said.

"Eat some of this emerald seaweed to help with the pain, infection, and bleeding," Slick replied.

"OK," Oliver said groggily.

Slick handed Oliver some lush, emerald seaweed for him to devour. Oliver consumed the seaweed. He was drifting in and out of consciousness. Slick placed some other clumps of the spongy, emerald seaweed on Oliver's gunshot wounds.

"Has the seaweed kicked in yet?" Slick asked.

"Yeah, it is just starting to take effect," Oliver replied.

"OK, be strong. This will probably hurt," Slick said.

Slick, as delicately as possible, dug into Oliver's head with his claw. He cut Oliver's head open just enough to where he could see the lead slug.

"Son of a sea wench! That really hurts! Do you see the bullet?" Oliver said.

"There it is. I see it. Be strong, I'm going to dig it out," Slick replied.

"OK," Oliver said. Slick stuck his scythe like talon into Oliver's head and dug out the piece of led.

"There it is. It's done. The bullet is out of your head. It was just inches from your brain," Slick said.

"Thank the great Sea God and thank you, Slick. You saved my life," Oliver replied.

"No problem, buddy. What are friends for after all? Do you want to see the bullet? Slick said.

"Sure, why not?" Oliver replied. Slick showed Oliver the bullet.

"Wow, that thing was just inches from my brain. A few more inches, and I would've been fried calamari," Oliver said. Slick chuckled.

"That is true. You have to look at the bright side of things and figure that it could have been worse," Slick replied. Slick placed some emerald seaweed on Oliver's wound to patch it up.

"You are right. I'm glad I have you in my corner Slick. You are a true pal," Oliver said.

"Thanks Oliver. I'm glad I was able to help. I'm not gonna let those wretched humans slay one of my best friends. Not on my watch," Slick replied.

"This war against those bloody humans is getting out of control and extremely perilous. I don't know if I can continue going along with you on these killing sprees," Oliver said.

"I really appreciate all of your help. I understand if you don't want to help me battle the humans anymore, because of the danger element. I won't force you to do anything that you don't want to do," Slick replied.

"I don't know. I will think about it. Right now, I just need to heal up and get some rest," Oliver said.

"OK Oliver. You rest here as long as you need to. I'm gonna lay low here and get some rest as well. I need to devour some emerald seaweed also and put some on my wounds," Slick replied.

"Thanks buddy. I'm lucky to have the king of the ocean as my best friend," Oliver said as he dozed off on a comfortable bed of soothing kelp. Slick devoured some fresh and tasty, emerald seaweed and placed some on his wounds. Then he laid down on his gummy bed of colorful kelp for some much needed rest and recuperation.

Chapter Sixteen
Fresh Fillets

"Holy smokes! I can't believe that Silver Serpent just slaughtered Gregory and Polly like animals! That was insane!" Augustus exclaimed.

"Stay calm Augustus. Panicking won't help anybody," Clayton replied.

"Where did those hellish beasts go? They were lightning quick. We had to have done some damage to them!" Rodney said.

"What do you want to do Captain?" Zeus asked.

"I say that we drift towards Hammerhead Hedge to see what bites our baits. We will have our silver harpoons and guns locked and loaded, just in case we encounter that Silver Serpent and his octopus sidekick again," Clayton replied. It was late afternoon the next day on Friday, August 18, 1904. The blazing orange sun was sinking sluggishly into the deep-purplish, western horizon.

"I can't believe that Silver Serpent has slain two of our own crewmates. We have to slay that spawn of Satan!" Augustus exclaimed.

"That is what we are trying to do! We must keep our wits about us if we are to even have a chance of slaying that freak of nature," Clayton replied.

"How can you be so calm? Don't you realize what that barbaric beast has done to us and our entire town? It has terrorized us long enough, and it won't stop until there is a silver harpoon through its icy, black heart," Ringo said.

"I realize more than you will ever know. Now shut up and start making yourself useful," Clayton replied.

"Does anybody want a beer? I think we all could use one," Augustus said.

"Grab us all some beers and bring out the rum bottle," Clayton replied.

Augustus went to the cabin and fetched the beers along with the rum. The Knight Sharks were trolling and moving towards Hammerhead Hedge hoping to catch some yellowfin or bluefin tuna along the way. Clayton lit up a fine Cuban cigar. All of a sudden, one of the fishing rods received a massive tug.

"Grab that rod!" Clayton commanded.

Zeus grabbed the rod and yanked back as hard as he could to set the hook. The hook was set, and the ancient battle between man and beast, was on.

"Holy smokes! This feels like a real whopper!" Zeus exclaimed.

"Reel that son of a gun in Zeus!" Clayton exclaimed.

"I'm trying! This sucker feels really heavy!" Zeus replied. Zeus was battling that huge fish with all his might.

"What do you think it is?" Rodney asked.

"It feels like a huge tuna or a huge shark. I can't tell just yet," Zeus replied.

"Keep the rod up and keep the line tight," Clayton said.

"Aye-aye Captain," Zeus replied.

The sinister skies were darkening over the ominous Atlantic Ocean. It was about 7:00 in the evening when another rod received a ferocious yank on its line.

"Grab that rod!" Clayton ordered. Augustus grabbed the rod and jerked back violently to set the hook.

"I got it! This feels like a serious monster!" Augustus exclaimed.

"Get us some more shots of rum!" Zeus said.

"Set that hook Augustus!" Clayton exclaimed.

"Aye-aye Captain! I think the hook is set!" Augustus responded.

"Reel that beautiful brute in!" Clayton exclaimed.

"Get us those drinks Rodney!" Zeus exclaimed.

Now that Augustus and Zeus had the hooks set, the glorious contests commenced.

"Damn, this behemoth is wearing me out. I don't know how much longer I can go," Zeus said.

"Do you want me to take over for you?" Clayton asked.

"Sure. Take the rod," Zeus replied.

Zeus handed the fishing rod to the Captain.

"Wow! You weren't kidding. There is something monstrous and massive at the end of this line," Clayton said.

"What does it feel like?" Augustus replied.

"It feels like a gigantic shark," Clayton said. Just then the Knight Sharks spotted a large shark fin pop out from the ocean's glossy, black surface.

"There it is! I see it! It's a shark alright!" Zeus exclaimed.

"Yeah, I see it too! It looks like a giant lemon shark," Ringo said. The shark that they stared at was an 11-foot long lemon shark with a colossal body.

"Wow, that thing is humongous!" Augustus shouted.

Just as the lemon shark was getting closer to the boat, it suddenly swam down deeper into the ocean. Sharks were no dummies. They knew that when they were being pulled towards a boat by a hook in their mouth, that something wasn't right. That lemon shark knew it was fighting for its life, so he gave it one last soulful burst and dove back down into the deeper waters.

"There it goes again. Damn, this is a battle of epic proportions!" Clayton said.

"What do you think is on your line Augustus?" Rodney asked.

"It feels like a titanic tuna. It's got to be 250 pounds or more, at least," Augustus replied.

"Stay calm and reel that bad boy in," Ringo said.

Clayton was starting to tire also reeling in that enormous lemon shark.

"Stay strong, Captain. You can do it," Rodney said.

"Thanks Rodney. I'm trying. This shark is truly putting up a serious fight and doesn't want to be reeled in," Clayton replied. The bluefin tuna at the end of Augustus's line was tiring also, and Augustus was reeling it in at a steady pace.

"It's coming in. I can feel it getting closer," Augustus said.

Augustus was the first one to catch a glimpse of the herculean bluefin tuna just below the ocean's glassy, coal surface.

"There it is! That's a trophy tuna!" Clayton exclaimed.

Oh yeah! That baby is gorgeous!" Augustus replied.

Augustus reeled the tuna right next to the side of the boat.

"Ringo, grab the gaff, and gaff that son of a gun!" Clayton ordered. Ringo grabbed the gaff and leaned over the side of the boat. He gaffed the magnificent bluefin tuna. Ringo yanked the gaff's hooked barb through the tuna's gills and tried to pull it up onto the boat deck, but it was too heavy for him, alone.

"I need some help here. This whopper is too heavy for me to pull up on the boat by myself," Ringo said. Rodney lent Ringo a helping hand and together they landed the tuna up and onto the boat deck. That tuna was gargantuan and looked to be between 300 and 400 pounds.

"Wow, this is the catch of a lifetime! It's beautiful!" Augustus exclaimed.

The enormous bluefin tuna was a glistening, metallic silver with navy-blue on top.

"That's a great job landing that giant tuna Augustus!" Clayton exclaimed triumphantly.

"Thanks Skipper. It was tough, but I knew I could do it. And there's no way in hell I was gonna give up," Augustus replied.

"Alright. Somebody pull the hook out of that titanic tuna, and put it on ice," Clayton ordered.

"Aye-aye Captain," Rodney replied.

Rodney removed the hook from the tuna's mouth and then stabbed its brain with a sharp blade, so it would die quickly and stop flopping around. Then he gutted the giant tuna and threw the guts overboard. Next, he measured the giant bluefin. It was 6 feet long and robust. Finally, he placed the dead tuna on ice to keep it preserved. Meanwhile, Clayton was still battling the powerful lemon shark.

"How are you doing, Captain?" Zeus asked.

"I'm becoming exhausted. The shark at the end of my line is a true warrior," Clayton replied.

"Stay strong, Captain. Hang in there," Rodney said.

Clayton felt a release of tension on the line. He started to reel in faster.

"It's running out of gas. I'm gonna reel it in zealously and land this hulking creature," Clayton said. Clayton was reeling in the lemon shark at a steady pace. The lemon shark was getting very close to the boat.

"I see it! There it is!" Zeus exclaimed. The lemon shark was about twenty-five yards away from the boat.

"Get the gaff ready. This shark is coming in!" Clayton exclaimed.

Rodney grabbed the gaff and prepared himself to gaff the shark. Finally, the lemon shark was right next to the boat.

"Gaff that son of a gun Rodney!" Clayton commanded. Rodney stuck the sharp gaff through the gills of the massive lemon shark and cherry-red blood spilled out.

"Grab the other gaff as well. We're going to need to gaff this shark again," Augustus said.

Zeus grabbed the other gaff and stuck it through the belly of the shark. There were two gaffs stuck in the lemon shark.

"OK, let's pull that beast onboard," Clayton said. Four of the Knight Sharks grabbed the two gaffs and pulled the heavy shark on board their boat. It was an 11-foot long lemon shark.

Rodney and Zeus grabbed two machetes and chopped the impressive shark's head off immediately, so that it couldn't bite any of them. Rodney and Zeus threw the massive lemon shark on ice.

"What a catch! That is the biggest shark I've seen caught this year!" Zeus exclaimed.

"That shark is definitely something to brag about," Augustus said.

"We could either keep the meat or sell it. Or we could keep some and sell some. The same goes with the tuna. It's a win-win situation," Clayton replied.

"What should we do now?" Rodney asked.

"Let's head back to shore and end this trip with these last two monumental catches," Clayton said.

"Aye-aye Captain. That sounds good," Ringo replied.

The Knight Sharks packed up all their equipment and headed back to shore. They were all still grief-stricken about losing two beloved crewmates. There used to be seven of them, but now that they had lost two to the Silver Serpent, there were only five Knight Sharks that still drew breath.

Chapter Seventeen
Zelda

The next day it was Saturday, August 19, 1904. Slick woke up at 10:00 am and swam outside his cave. Oliver had regained some of his strength and swam back to his cave yesterday. Slick spotted a pod of lounging lobsters hanging around on the ocean floor. He deduced to go down there and devour some of them for breakfast. Then he decided to swim over to Oliver's cave near Squid Alley.

Slick arrived there in about fifteen minutes and sent off his hydro-sonar signal to notify Oliver of his arrival. Oliver swam out of his cave and greeted Slick.

"How's it going, buddy?" Oliver asked.

"I'm great. How are you doing buddy? Have you healed up?" Slick replied.

"I'm feeling better. My head still hurts some, but I'm regaining my strength, little by little. That emerald seaweed has been helping too. I just woke up. I'm famished," Oliver said.

"I'm glad to hear that bud. I just munched on some succulent lobster, but I could go for something else. Let's go grab something to fill our bellies then," Slick replied.

"Where did you find lobster? That sounds delicious. I haven't had lobster in a while," Oliver said.

"There was a pod hanging around the ocean floor just outside my cave when I woke up, so I made a quick meal of them. They were plump, juicy, and a perfect snack to start to the day," Slick replied.

"I could definitely go for some lobster right now, but I'm so hungry that just about anything will do," Oliver said.

"OK, we always find something to devour in this vast ocean. How has your head been feeling after we took that led slug out of it?" Slick replied.

"It still hurts some, and my vision is still kind of blurry, but I feel like it's getting better," Oliver said.

"Hang in there, buddy. You are a sea warrior. Don't ever forget that. You will be okay," Slick replied.

"Thanks for your encouragement, Slick. Your advice and support are always appreciated," Oliver said.

"No problem. Let's go grab some lunch. Where would you like to go?" Slick replied.

"Let's check out Squid Alley. There was a lot of action there the last time we went," Oliver said.

"That's a great idea. And it's close by too. Let's head over there killer," Slick replied.

The two sea monster buddies swam out towards Squid Alley. They arrived there shortly and spotted a shiver of sharks ferociously devouring something that looked like a human body. Slick and Oliver swam closer to investigate. The two sea monsters also viewed a boat on the surface in that area.

"Wow, those sharks are ravenously tearing into something," Slick said.

"What do you think it is?" Oliver replied.

"It looks like a human from here. Plus, there is a boat just above the surface. Maybe they are devouring an overboard victim," Slick said.

They got close enough to the sharks feeding frenzy and discovered that their meal was indeed a human. The bull sharks were devouring it limb by limb. Clouds of crimson blood filled the glittering, sapphire waters.

"It is a human. I can see the head and the limbs from here," Slick said.

"It's kind of blurry, but I see it too," Oliver replied.

"I'm gonna ask those sharks how they slayed that human," Slick said.

Slick swam up to the bull sharks and talked to the leader of the gang, Tommy.

"How's it going Tommy? I see that you and your buddies are feeding on a human. Did you and your gang slay that human yourselves?" Slick asked.

"What's going on Slick? My buddies and I were patrolling these waters and hunting for a meal when we noticed this human spearfishing. We decided to attack it and devour it. I believe that the human came from the boat that is hovering above us on the surface," Tommy replied.

"Oh, I see. Maybe we should hang around here long enough, so that more humans come to look for him," Slick replied.

"That's not a bad idea," Tommy said.

"In the meantime, Oliver and I are going to devour some of those king mackerel swimming over there by the kelp," Slick replied.

Slick and Oliver swam over to the mackerel and swiftly struck at them and grabbed them in their claws and tentacles. They each grabbed two and devoured them on the spot. Tommy swam back to his goon squad and finished devouring the remaining pieces of the spear fisherman. Slick and Oliver devoured some more king mackerel, and then they moved on to devour a fever of stingrays.

About half an hour went by, and then they saw three more humans drop into the ocean.

"There they go. I told you they would come looking for that spear fisherman," Slick said.

"You called it, buddy. Should we attack them now?" Oliver replied.

"Let's wait until they get a little bit closer," Slick said. Tommy and his shark goons were about seventy-five yards away feasting on some hefty haddock.

Slick sent a hydro-sonar signal to Tommy that alerted him to swim over. Tommy received the signal and swam over to Slick and Oliver with his shark goons.

"What's going on, Slick?" Tommy asked.

"Do you see that over there? Three more humans dropped into the water. I told you that they would come looking for their missing comrade," Slick replied.

"You were right. That looks like lunch to me. Let's go get them," Tommy said.

"OK Tommy. That sounds good. There are enough humans for all of us?" Slick replied.

"Yup. Plus, there is always strength in numbers," Tommy said.

"Let's go feast on some fresh, human flesh," Oliver replied.

"That sounds like a plan to me," Slick said.

The two sea monsters and the bull sharks swam over to the three humans. The humans noticed them and started to swim for their lives back towards their boat.

"They are turning back towards the boat! We have to get them now!" Slick exclaimed.

Slick, Oliver, and the sharks turned on their internal jets and accelerated towards the three humans. The sea monsters got within thirty yards of the humans and saw that they were armed with spear guns. The humans pointed their spear guns at the oncoming sea creatures and fired. The spear guns hit Slick, Oliver, and one of the bull sharks. Slick barely felt a thing. Oliver got hit in one of his tentacles and immediately ripped it out with another one of his tentacles. A bull shark named Mookie got hit right in the head and stopped swimming. He was dead. That pissed off Tommy, and he darted and snapped at the human that shot his comrade. Tommy chomped down fervently on the human's head and tore it off with his inexorable jaws. Slick grabbed another human with his upper limbs and stuck his claw through the human's heart. He sliced the human's torso open and snatched the heart with his forked tongue. Then Slick devoured it like an exquisite morsel. Oliver wrapped his lethal tentacles around the last human's head and squeezed it like a vice clamp until it burst like an overgrown, festering boil. All the humans were dead. The sea monsters devoured them piece by piece, while thick, blood clouds spread all around them that turned the blue water, red.

After a couple of minutes, all the humans were completely devoured, bones and all.

"AHH, that was exquisite. I'm sorry about your fallen comrade, Tommy," Slick said.

"Thanks Slick. Mookie was a good soldier. Sometimes soldiers die in this never-ending war against the haughty humans," Tommy replied.

"Well, our work is done here. Let's explore elsewhere, Oliver," Slick said.

"OK, lead the way, General," Oliver replied.

"It was a pleasure doing business with you. See you fellas later," Tommy said.

"Likewise, Tommy. See you later," Slick replied.

"Take care, Tommy," Oliver said.

Tommy and his gritty goons glided away towards the southwest part of the Atlantic. Slick and Oliver swam northeast towards Dolphin Point to scope out the scene. It was 4:00 in the afternoon and the sky turned lavender and gray with some heavy rain clouds moving in. It was very overcast and gloomy when it started to rain and thunder. The golden sun was still barely visible through all the heavy rainstorm clouds. The two sea creatures arrived at Dolphin Point and saw a pod of bottlenose dolphins playing and jumping out of the water. The dolphins were doing flips and tricks in the air despite the thunderstorm that was brewing.

"What do you want to do now Slick?" Oliver asked.

"Let's munch on some of that blue and orange seaweed over there. I hear it gives you special powers, like the emerald seaweed," Slick replied.

"Let's give it a try," Oliver said.

The two sea buddies swam over to a large hedge of the colored seaweed and started to snack on some of it.

"This stuff tastes pretty great. It kind of tastes like fresh sea berries," Slick said.

"Yes it does. The fact that this stuff is good for us also is a double bonus," Oliver replied.

Slick and Oliver devoured some good-sized chunks of the brightly colored seaweed and then noticed some swordfish swimming by.

"Look at those swordfish Oliver. They look really tasty," Slick said.

"Do you want to go devour some of them?" Oliver replied.

"Sure. Let's move on them," Slick said.

The dynamic duo swam towards the school of sleek swordfish. They got within about ten yards of the swordfish and ferociously plunged themselves towards them. Slick grabbed one of them in his jaws, while Oliver grabbed another one with his tenacious tentacles.

"I got it!" Oliver exclaimed.

"Good job buddy! I got one too!" Slick replied.

The other swordfish swam away frantically, but Slick and Oliver each had one to devour. They bit into the tender flesh and tore off solid chunks to chew and relished every second of it. Both sea monsters devoured the entire swordfish, sword-like bill and all.

"Wow, today has been an excellent day for hunting and feasting. We are devouring whatever we like, whenever we like," Slick said.

"Yeah, tell me about it. We are devouring humans and swordfish on the same day. That is a real treat," Oliver replied.

"You really like to devour humans now. I remember when you were not so fond of the sport or the taste," Slick said.

"I know. I just recently realized that they do taste pretty damn good. It's an acquired taste," Oliver replied.

"Are you still hungry, or do you want to head back to our caves?" Slick asked.

"Let's hang around here a little bit longer to see if any more fresh meals swim our way," Oliver replied.

"OK, that sounds good to me buddy," Slick said.

The sky was still overcast, but the rain and thunder were dying down. Slick and Oliver were hiding in some massive beds of kelp. The Atlantic's dynamic duo was trying to stay as hidden and as camouflaged as possible in case something swam their way. Just then, Slick spotted an enormous figure from the corner of his glowing, red eye that swam towards them.

"Holy smokes. Something gigantic is coming our way. Do you see that Oliver?" Slick asked.

"Yes, what is that? It's humongous," Oliver replied.

"It looks like a whale or something," Slick said.

"It looks like another one of you," Oliver replied.

"Do you think so? There hasn't been another Silver Serpent in these waters since my late lover, Sandy. May the almighty Sea God rest her soul," Slick said.

"I know. Sandy was really special and beautiful, inside and out. I miss her too buddy. Damn those blasted humans for slaying her," Oliver replied.

"It's getting closer, so we can take a better look," Slick said.

The large, looming creature swam right next to the towers of kelp and to the immense surprise of Slick and Oliver, it was another Silver Serpent.

"Holy smokes! It's another Silver Serpent! I never thought that I'd see the day!" Slick exclaimed.

"SHHH. Keep it down, buddy. It will hear you." Oliver replied.

"I don't care if it hears me. I'm gonna go say hello," Slick said.

Slick swam out from the towering hedges of green and yellow kelp and confronted the new Silver Serpent.

"Hello there. My name is Slick. What is your name, friend?" Slick said.

"Oh my God! You scared the crap out of me. Why did you just pop up on me like that?" The Serpent replied.

"I'm sorry. It's just that I haven't seen another Silver Serpent in these waters in two years and I got a little excited. Please excuse me," Slick said.

"Oh I see. I didn't see you in all of that kelp. My name is Zelda. What's your name?" Zelda replied.

"It's nice to meet you, Zelda. My name is Slick. Where are you from?" Slick said.

"It's nice to meet you too, Slick. I'm from Bonita Bay. It's a part of the Atlantic Ocean off the New England Coast. Where are you from?" Zelda replied.

"OK. I'm from these waters around here. My cave is located at Cod Channel. It's a spectacular spot located between Boat-Wreck Lane and Hammerhead Hedge," Slick said.

"Oh, I've heard of the notorious Boat-Wreck Lane. I've heard about all of those brutal battles between Silver Serpents and whale hunters in those waters," Zelda replied.

"You have heard of Boat-Wreck Lane all the way over there off the New England Coast? Wow! That's incredible!" Slick said.

"Yes of course. That place is very infamous because of the mighty battles that have taken place there," Zelda replied.

"Yes, that is true. There have definitely been some gruesome battles that have occurred there," Slick said.

Slick thought of his late lover, Sandy, who was slayed there, but he did not say anything regarding that sore and sorrowful subject.

"Wow! I would love to go there sometime," Zelda replied.

"I would love to take you there sometime," Slick said.

"That sounds wonderful and exciting," Zelda replied.

"Many sea creatures and humans have died there," Slick said.

"That's what I've heard," Zelda replied.

"Would you like to go there right now or some other time?" Slick asked.

"We can go whenever you like," Zelda replied.

"Let's go over there when the sun goes down, because it is more peaceful and serene then," Slick said.

"OK Slick. That sounds lovely," Zelda replied.

"Oliver, come on out of there," Slick said. Oliver swam out from the giant beds of green and yellow sea kelp.

"Hello," Oliver said.

"Hello," Zelda replied.

"Zelda, this is one of my best buds, Oliver. Oliver, this is my new friend, Zelda," Slick said.

"It's nice to meet you Oliver," Zelda said.

"It's a pleasure to make your acquaintance, Zelda," Oliver replied.

"Zelda is from Bonita Bay. It's located off the New England Coast," Slick said.

"Oh, that's neat. I hear the waters are really nice out that way," Oliver replied.

"Yes, it has its perks. The crab and lobster are in abundance there and are absolutely mouthwatering," Zelda said.

"You're so lucky. I could devour crab and lobster every day. What brings you to our neck of the ocean?" Oliver replied.

"I wanted to visit the famous Boat-Wreck Lane and see this part of the ocean," Zelda said.

"OK. We can take you to Boat-Wreck Lane. It's not too far of a swim from here," Oliver replied.

"Yes, that's what Slick was telling me. That sounds fabulous. I would be delighted and honored to be escorted to that historical landmark by such powerful and magnificent sea beasts, such as yourselves," Zelda said.

"We were going to wait until the sun went down," Slick announced.

"OK. The sun should be going down soon," Oliver replied.

"What do you want to do until then?" Slick asked.

"I'm kind of hungry. What is good to eat around these parts?" Zelda replied.

"You name it, we got it," Slick said.

"I feel like eating some amberjack," Zelda said.

"OK. We can find some of those at the coral reefs near Boat-Wreck Lane. Let's head over that way, so we'll get there by the time the sun goes down. We can kill two birds with one stone," Slick replied.

"That sounds wonderful. You two lead, and I'll follow," Zelda said.

The two Silver Serpents and the giant octopus swam towards Boat-Wreck Lane. Slick felt all tingly and warm inside to have made friends with another Silver Serpent. And a gorgeous one, at that. Slick felt an instantaneous and undeniable attraction towards Zelda. She was sleek, ferocious, and a brilliant, shimmering silver. The tips of her scales shone a vivid purple and pink, and she had ardent, ruby-red eyes, like Slick.

The three sea monsters took their time gracefully swimming over to the ominous Boat-Wreck Lane. They were taking in the sites while Slick and Oliver provided commentary on them.

"Wow, you guys sure do know a lot about this area," Zelda said.

"It's only natural since we've lived here all our lives. It's wise to have an abundant knowledge of your environment," Slick replied.

"Slick and I were both born in these waters about forty years ago. We grew up together here," Oliver said.

"I'm sure you both have seen a lot in your time here. I would love to hear some of your stories," Zelda replied.

"I would love to hear some of your stories and history as well. Do you have family back in Bonita Bay?" Slick said.

"I used to have a family, but they were either slayed by serpent hunters or they died of old age," Zelda replied.

"I'm sorry to hear that. The same thing happened to my loved ones also. That is why I despise humans and especially serpent and whale hunters," Slick said.

"I hate them too. I try to avoid them at all costs," Zelda replied.

"Now that we know each other, you are always safe with me. I won't let anything happen to you," Slick said.

"Thanks Slick. That is very sweet and reassuring of you to say," Zelda replied.

"No problem. We are almost at Boat-Wreck Lane," Slick said.

The rain and the thunderstorm were still fading, and the sun was barely visible again through the heavy, purplish-gray rain clouds.

"We're here. This is Boat-Wreck Lane. It's a graveyard for sunken boats and ships," Slick announced. At that time, it was eerily silent around Boat-Wreck Lane, and there were no boats around.

The only activity going on was a school of black marlin hunting for some amberjack. Zelda looked around in astonishment, and she noticed the multiple, wrecked and sunken ships and boats resting at the bottom of the ocean floor.

"So this is the infamous Boat-Wreck Lane. It's very beautiful here. It's quite charming with a lot of character," Zelda replied.

"It's nice and quiet, because there are no whale or serpent hunters here causing chaos right now," Oliver said.

"The coral reef here is absolutely gorgeous. I see some amberjack over there too," Zelda replied.

"Let's go sink our teeth into some," Slick said.

"OK," Zelda replied.

The two Silver Serpents swam towards the amberjack, and that spooked the black marlin. They swam away frantically. Oliver stayed back to keep a lookout for anything unfamiliar. Slick and Zelda crept as stealthily as possible towards the school of amberjack, so that they could attack them from the proper angle. They got within ten yards from the amberjack and then savagely struck at them with their mighty and powerful claws and jaws. Slick and Zelda both grabbed a jaw full of amberjack and some more with their claws as well.

They bit down on the juicy fish and devoured them instantly. Then they fed themselves the other amberjack that they had caught with their claws.

"This amberjack is amazing!" Zelda exclaimed.

"It sure is. Is it better than the amberjack from your waters?" Slick replied.

"It has a different taste. It is even more delectable than the amberjack from my waters," Zelda said.

"I'm glad you like it. Are you still hungry?" Slick replied.

"A little bit. I'm rather fatigued from my long journey and all that swimming, though," Zelda said.

"We can hang around here longer, or we can go somewhere else, if you like. It's up to you," Slick replied.

"Let's explore some place else," Zelda said.

"Where would you like to go? Your wish is my command," Slick asked.

"That is very kind of you. You're a real sweetheart. I don't know. I'm too tired to swim all the way back home," Zelda replied.

"We can go back to my cave to get some rest and relaxation," Slick said.

"We can do that," Zelda replied.

"OK, let's go. Oliver, get over here. We are going home," Slick announced.

"OK Slick. I'll see you later. It was a pleasure to meet you, Zelda. I hope to see you again soon," Oliver said.

"It was a pleasure meeting you as well, Oliver. Thank you so much for showing me the gorgeous waters that you and Slick reside in. I hope to see you again soon. Take care," Zelda replied. The three sea monsters swam toward their desired destinations. Oliver swam back to his cave near Squid Alley, while Slick and Zelda swam towards Slick's cave, near Cod Channel, together.

Chapter Eighteen
Newfound Love

Slick and Zelda arrived at Slick's cave at about 10:00 that evening.

"Welcome to my cave, Zelda. Make yourself at home," Slick said.

"Thank you Slick," Zelda replied. The two Silver Serpents entered Slick's enchanting and mystical cave.

"Wow. This is a charming place," Zelda said.

"Thanks Zelda. I live alone, but I try my best to maintain my cave and keep it looking sharp," Slick replied.

"You have done a stellar job," Zelda said.

"Thanks Zelda. You are very kind to say that," Slick replied.

"Don't mention it. It's the truth," Zelda said.

Slick's cave was very tidy despite some human and shark bones that decorated the floor. There were also some treasure chests filled with gold, silver, and precious gemstones that Slick looted from sunken pirate ships. It had different color seaweed and kelp all over the place to give it a brilliant and charismatic look.

"There isn't much here. Just some old bones, seaweed, and treasure," Slick said.

"I like it. Where do you sleep?" Zelda replied.

"Right over there in that bed of kelp. Would you like to lie down with me?" Slick said.

"Sure. That looks very comfortable. Let's go lie down together," Zelda replied.

"OK, great. Come with me," Slick said.

The two Silver Serpents swam to Slick's massive bed of cushy kelp and lied down together.

"This is really nice and comfortable," Zelda said.

"I'm really glad that I met you Zelda. I haven't seen another Silver Serpent in two years. I didn't think that any more of our kind existed. That thought would make me sad," Slick replied.

"I'm glad that I met you as well Slick. You are such a sweetheart," Zelda said.

Slick leaned over and kissed Zelda. His forked tongue went into her mouth and hers into his. Then he got into position to mate with her. He wrapped his long, powerful body against her sleek back and mounted her. They made passionate serpent love for about five glorious minutes.

After that was done, they cuddled up with one another and fell asleep in each other's limbs. The two Silver Serpents enjoyed a deep and pleasant slumber all through the night. That night Slick dreamed of his newfound love, Zelda, and thought that he had died and gone to heaven.

The next day it was Sunday, August 20, 1904. Slick awoke in his mammoth bed of spongy kelp next to his newfound lover, Zelda.

"Good morning, Zelda. How do you feel?" Slick said.

"Good morning, Slick. I feel fabulous. I really needed a good night's rest like that," Zelda replied.

"Would you like some breakfast? I can swim outside the cave and snag us some fish," Slick said.

"Sure. That sounds delicious," Zelda replied.

"OK, wait here. I'll be right back," Slick said.

"OK sweetheart," Zelda replied.

Slick swam outside his cave and spotted a school of plump black sea bass swimming around. He immediately torpedoed himself in their direction and snatched four of them in his claws. Then he grabbed two more of them in his steel-trap jaws. Slick slayed all six of the black sea bass in a heartbeat and brought them to the cozy confines of his clandestine cave.

"I snatched up some ripe black sea bass for us," Slick said.

"That's great, because I'm starving," Zelda replied.

Slick laid the six, fresh black sea bass on a huge, flat boulder that he used as a dining table.

"Breakfast is served. Enjoy," Slick said. Zelda grabbed one of the sea bass and licked it. Then she chomped down on it and chewed on it before she swallowed it.

"Yummy. This sea bass is excellent," Zelda replied. Slick grabbed a sea bass with his right upper limb and popped it into his salivating mouth. After he chewed it up and his taste buds were delightfully satisfied, he gulped it down his gullet.

The two Silver Serpents devoured all six of the black sea bass for a savory breakfast.

"That was really tasty. Thank you so much for everything Slick. You are truly a hospitable and courteous host," Zelda said.

"It's my pleasure, Zelda. I do anything for my loved ones," Slick replied.

"Do you really consider me as one of your loved ones?" Zelda asked.

"I would love for you to be. Would you like to be?" Slick replied.

"Yes, Slick. I'd be honored to be one of your loved ones," Zelda said.

"Great. You just made me the happiest sea creature in all the seven seas. Why don't you stay here with me forever?" Slick replied.

"OK. I will stay here with you. I don't have any family to return to in Bonita Bay anyway," Zelda said.

"Perfect. This way we can be together forever," Slick replied.

Slick kissed Zelda with his slithery, forked tongue and gently caressed her body with his body and limbs. They made love to each other again and again that day. Both Silver Serpents knew that they had found true love once again.

"I will always take care of you and never let anything bad happen to you or allow anything or anyone to hurt you for as long as I live. I love you Zelda," Slick said.

"Thank you my love. I love you too Slick," Zelda replied.

The two Silver Serpents fell asleep in Slick's bed again. They awoke at night.

"Are you hungry Zelda? Would you like to hunt for some dinner?" Slick asked.

"Yes, you read my mind. Let's go for a swim and see what we encounter," Zelda replied.

"Say no more. Let's see what the Atlantic has to offer tonight," Slick said.

The two Silver Serpents kissed and swam out of Slick's cave and toward Squid Alley. They arrived there and saw that there was an active and sumptuous supply of sea-life. There were sharks, stingrays, and squid that swam around the schools of smaller fish and lush sea vegetation.

"It looks like we have a full menu tonight. What would you like to devour first, my love?" Slick said.

"Those squid sure do look splendid. Let's devour some of those first," Zelda replied.

"OK, some calamari for appetizers it is," Slick said. Zelda giggled and smiled an inviting smile that displayed her rows of metallic, razor-sharp teeth.

The two giant sea monsters crept slowly towards a squad of color-changing squid. They swam close enough to attack them with their lethal sets of jaws and claws. Both serpents snagged a mouthful of plump, juicy squid. Then they decided to go after the frenzy of lemon sharks in that area. As the two Silver Serpents were swimming towards the lemon sharks, they spotted a boat hovering above on the surface.

"Look, it's a boat Slick," Zelda said.

"I see it. I'm gonna ravage it," Slick replied.

"Be careful Slick," Zelda said.

Slick shot through the water like a cannonball straight toward the boat and slammed into it headfirst with all his might. The violent blow created a good sized hole in the boat's hull and the boat started to sink.

"What the hell was that!" Leander exclaimed.

Leander was the Captain of the boat. The boat was named *The Pesky Pelican.*

"I don't know! Something just hit us really hard!" Pierre replied. Pierre was a passenger on the boat.

"I think we are sinking!" Dominic exclaimed. Dominic was another passenger on the boat.

"I bet it was that vile Silver Serpent! I've been hearing more and more stories lately about that malicious monster," Leander replied.

"What do we do? Our boat is sinking fast!" Pierre exclaimed.

"Get the harpoons and rifles ready!" Leander exclaimed.

Dominic went to the cabin and gathered the harpoons and the rifles.

"Load them up quickly!" Leander commanded

"What do we do about the sinking boat? We will be swimming in the ocean pretty soon!" Pierre replied.

"What can we do? We don't have another boat to climb into," Leander said.

"Holy shit! We're all gonna die!" Dominic replied.

"We might. If we do, we are gonna go out fighting with all our might!" Leander exclaimed.

"The harpoons and rifles are all loaded up and ready to fire Captain," Dominic said.

Slick swam back to Zelda.

"I hammered them really hard and made a hole in their boat. They are sinking fast and should be swimming in the ocean with us anytime now," Slick said.

"Great! You are so valiant my love. I don't like dealing with humans, but I sure do love to devour them," Zelda replied.

"We will dine on fresh human flesh tonight my love! Let's just wait for them to sink," Slick said.

"OK sweetheart," Zelda replied.

The Pesky Pelican was sinking rapidly and more than half of it was under water. The three passengers were still above the surface on the boat's bow, and they held two rifles and one harpoon. Dominic and Pierre each held a rifle, while Leander held a regular iron harpoon.

"Stay quiet. I don't see anything. Where is that damned beast?" Leander said.

"I don't know. Maybe it's waiting for us to sink," Pierre replied.

"You really think it is that smart?" Dominic asked.

"Yes. How else do you think its species has survived for so long? It's probably been around since the dinosaurs," Leander said.

"It's just a stupid beast. It can't premeditate murder," Pierre replied.

"How do you know it can't do that? It has a taste for human blood, and it knows how to kill," Leander said.

"Holy shit! We're gonna die! I'm not ready to die!" Pierre exclaimed.

"Don't think like that. Try and remain calm," Leander replied.

The Pesky Pelican was fully submerged in the cobalt-blue Atlantic Ocean. The three overboard victims were struggling to keep their heads above the surging sea's surface.

"There they are. Let's go slay them!" Slick said.

"I'm with you Slick!" Zelda replied.

The two Silver Serpents shot their silvery bodies towards the overboard victims like heat-seeking missiles.

"Holy shit Captain! I don't want to drown! I can't swim!" Pierre exclaimed.

"The more you panic, the more you are gonna drown yourself," Leander replied.

Dominic tried to swim away but Slick grabbed and pierced him with the sickle like claws of his left upper limb. Slick chomped down voraciously on Dominic's head and crushed it like a cantaloupe.

"Oh my God! I don't want to die!" Leander exclaimed. Zelda bit Leander in the chest area and ripped him open. Then she went for the kill and ripped his still-beating heart out of his chest and popped it into her mouth like a fine cut of bloody steak. She relished the taste of fresh blood from a human heart. She found it extremely invigorating.

"There's only one presumptuous human left. I'll finish him off," Slick said.

"OK Slick. I'll be right here devouring this crunchy and savory human," Zelda replied.

Slick darted at the panicking Pierre and sliced his guts out with one slash of his razor-edged claw. Slick devoured Pierre's guts while he was still alive. Pierre was screaming his lungs out in agonizing pain, but nobody was around to hear his last cries of terror. Nobody besides the Silver Serpents, that is. It just sounded like some gurgling sounds to them. Slick devoured Pierre's rubbery, tube-like guts and then snapped his head clean off his shoulders and chewed it up, triumphantly. Pieces of Pierre's brain and skull were mashed inside Slick's devastating jaws of death, until it was just a thick, bloody paste that slid down his gullet with ease.

The two Silver Serpents devoured the three human bodies in about three minutes flat. Every piece of bone, flesh, and organ were completely devoured by the rapacious and voracious sea monsters.

"That was delicious. I love the taste of fresh human flesh and blood," Zelda said.

"It sure was. I'm glad that you enjoyed it, my love," Slick replied.

"What do you want to do now?" Zelda asked.

"Let's go back to my cave and get a good night's rest," Slick replied.

"OK, that sounds great. Let's go, my love," Zelda said.

"After you, my love." Slick replied.

The Silver Serpents swam euphorically back to Slick's cave on full stomachs. Slick thought about his former lover, Sandy, and how he missed her. Then he thought about his newfound lover, Zelda, and how she set his heart ablaze. He knew that Sandy was looking down on him from the eternal sea kingdom in the sky and he wondered if she would be happy for Slick and his newfound love, or jealous.

Chapter Nineteen
Who's Going to Slay the Silver Serpent?

The next day it was Monday, August 21, 1904 in the harbor town of Cape Crusade. Clayton rode his horse and buggy over to the Sandbar to report the latest news on the Silver Serpent. Rodney, Ringo, Augustus, and Zeus were already there enjoying some ice-cold brews and crispy, golden, fried fish and fries.

"What's going on, fellas?" Clayton asked.

"How you doing, Captain?" The Knight Sharks replied.

Clayton sat down at the table with the remaining Knight Sharks. A waitress named Sally strutted over and took his order.

"What can I get you today, Clayton?" Sally asked.

"What's today's special?" Clayton replied.

"Today's special is all you can eat fried haddock," Sally said.

"I'll have some of that," Clayton replied.

"Can I get you anything to drink?" Sally said.

"I'll have an ice-cold Yellow Crab beer," Clayton said.

"OK, I'll come right back with your beer, and the fried fish will be out in a couple of minutes," Sally replied.

"Thanks sweetheart," Clayton said.

Sally came right back with his frosty, Yellow Crab beer. Two minutes later, she came back with his plate of fried haddock and fries.

"Has anyone seen Bruno around here today?" Clayton asked.

"Yeah. I saw him a couple of minutes ago. I think he walked into his office," Zeus replied.

"I need to tell him about our latest expedition and ask him if anybody has agreed to participate in the Silver Serpent bounty. I'll wait for him to come out," Clayton said.

The Knight Sharks enjoyed their fried fish and ice-cold beer. Bruno walked out of his office and toward the bar.

"There he is, Captain," Augustus said.

"How's it going Bruno?" Clayton asked. Bruno saw Clayton and the Knight Sharks and headed over to their table.

"What's going on, fellas? Did you guys have any luck on your Silver Serpent expedition?" Bruno replied.

"We had a very rough and traumatic experience. We lost two of our crewmates to that insidious Silver Serpent. Polly and Gregory, may they rest in peace," Clayton said.

"Are you serious? The Silver Serpent got them too? I'm really sorry to hear that fellas," Bruno replied.

"That Silver Serpent and his giant octopus sidekick dragged them away right in front of our eyes. They came back and we hit the Silver Serpent with three silver harpoons, and we hit that giant octopus with some rifle shots to its head. The harpoons slowed the Silver Serpent down some, but they didn't kill it. The rifle rounds stopped the octopus dead in its tracks, and then the Silver Serpent dragged him away from the scene. That was the last we saw of them," Clayton said.

"That is beyond abhorrent. That monster is incredibly difficult to slay," Bruno replied.

"That's putting it mildly. It's like a highly-sophisticated death-machine," Augustus said.

"I'm really sorry for your loss, guys. I know Polly and Gregory were like brothers to you guys. That Silver Serpent has to be stopped, somehow," Bruno replied.

"Has anybody showed interest in the $10,000 reward for the slaying of the Silver Serpent?" Clayton asked.

"Yes. A couple of whale hunting crews asked about it yesterday. They said they were willing to go after it for $10,000," Bruno replied.

"Are they hunters that we know, or are they some new faces?" Zeus asked.

"I recognized one of the Captains, because he and his crew are always here eating fish and drinking beer. They must be from here in Staten Island. I didn't recognize the Captain from the other crew. They said they were from Long Island. Those have been the only ones that have acquired about the bounty," Bruno replied.

"What exactly did they say?" Clayton inquired.

"They said that they were going to gather up their supplies and go after the Silver Serpent," Bruno replied.

"That's great news. I hope and pray that one of those crews can slay that monstrosity," Clayton said.

"Does that mean that you and your crew aren't going after the Silver Serpent anymore?" Bruno asked.

"That's right. I think that my crew and I have suffered enough calamities from that God-awful beast. We could all use that money, but not at the risk of losing our lives. What good is that money if we're not alive to spend it?" Clayton replied.

"I understand that. The Silver Serpent has slain too many people recently," Bruno said.

"I think we're going to stick to what we do best, which is fishing," Clayton replied.

"We caught a couple of other kinds of sea monsters on our latest journey," Rodney said.

"Is that right? What kind of sea monsters did you guys catch?" Bruno replied.

"We caught an 11-foot lemon shark and a 6-foot bluefin tuna," Zeus said.

"Holy Toledo! Those are some real sea monsters. What did you guys do with them?" Bruno replied.

"We kept half of the steaks and fillets for ourselves, and we have the other half for sale if you are interested," Clayton said.

"I sure am. I would love to serve up some fresh shark and tuna steaks here at the Sandbar, and I'm sure my customers would love it too. How much do you want for them?" Bruno replied.

"I'll sell you the rest of the shark and tuna fillets for $200. That is a hell of a bargain, considering the size and freshness of the fillets. Also considering, how hard it has been to catch lemon sharks and Atlantic bluefin lately," Clayton said.

"You are right. That is a damn good deal. I'll take it. How soon can you bring me the fillets?" Bruno replied.

"I can have them for you by today. The fillets are in my icebox at home. I just have to go pick them up and bring them back over here," Clayton said.

"OK, no hurry. Whenever you have a chance to deliver them is fine. I'll have the cash waiting for you here," Bruno replied.

"I'll go pick them up after I finish eating," Clayton said.

"That sounds excellent. Enjoy your meals gentlemen," Bruno replied.

"Thanks Bruno. We'll talk later," Clayton said.

"Thanks Bruno," The Knight Sharks replied.

The Knight Sharks devoured their all you can eat fried haddock and fries like hungry sharks and drank about six beers each. Clayton decided to go to his house to pick up the fillets. After all, his house was right down the street.

"I'll be right back fellas. I'm gonna go pick up the fillets. Ringo, ride with me so you can help me carry the shark and tuna steaks." Clayton said.

"Aye-aye Captain," Ringo replied.

"Alright. We'll be here drinking some beers and holding the fort down," Augustus said.

Clayton and Ringo walked out of the bar and into his horse drawn buggy. They rode down the street to his beach house and picked up the fresh fillets. Then they rode back to the Sandbar and delivered them.

"Here they are Bruno," Clayton said. Clayton and Ringo were carrying the tightly wrapped, large slabs of fresh, shark and tuna meat.

"Excellent. Here is your $200 in cash buddy. I'm gonna go grill some of these fillets right away and offer them on the menu. Would you gentlemen take the meat back to the kitchen?" Bruno said.

"That sounds incredible. Of course we will. I might just have to order some of those succulent steaks, myself," Clayton replied.

"Well, you definitely should since you and the Knight Sharks caught them yourselves," Bruno said.

"Augustus caught the blue-ribbon bluefin and I landed the laudable lemon shark," Clayton replied. Clayton and Ringo hand delivered the fresh meat to the Sandbar's kitchen, themselves. Clayton and Bruno completed the transaction by shaking hands.

"It was a pleasure doing business with you. Let me know if you have anything else to sell," Bruno said.

"It's always a pleasure doing business with you, Bruno. I'll keep you posted on anything we have to sell in the future," Clayton replied. At that moment a group of whale hunters walked through the bar's front doors.

"That's the fellas I was telling you about," Bruno said.

"Are you referring to the ones from here or the ones from Long Island?" Zeus replied.

"The fellas are from here I believe, because I have seen them eating and drinking here more than a couple of times," Bruno said.

"That's interesting. I've never seen them around before," Zeus replied.

The whale hunters took a seat at a table by a window. There were four of them.

"I'm gonna go say hello," Clayton said.

"I'll go with you," Augustus replied. The two Knight Sharks walked up to the whale hunter's table.

"How are you fellas doing? My name is Clayton, and this is my buddy, Augustus. We are members of a fishing crew called the Knight Sharks," Clayton said.

"I'm doing alright. It's nice to meet you fellas. My name is Ricky, and these are my comrades, Willy, Nicky, and last but not least, Al. We are a whale hunting crew called the Sea Snakes, and I'm the Captain. We're from Port Andrew, here in Staten Island," Ricky replied.

"Oh yes, Port Andrew. I've been there before. It's an excellent fishing village. It's nice to meet you gentlemen, as well," Augustus said.

"It's got its perks. What can we do for you guys?" Ricky asked.

"I heard that you and your crew are interested in the Silver Serpent Bounty. Is that true?" Clayton replied.

"Yes, that is true. My crew and I heard about that bounty and we could definitely use that prize money. Who couldn't, am I right?" Ricky said.

"Great. When are you fellas planning on going on that expedition?" Clayton replied.

"We decided to head out there tomorrow. We just need to gather some last-minute supplies," Ricky said.

"OK. I wish you fellas the best of luck, and I really hope that the Sea Snakes can slay that beast. It has slayed and devoured too many people from our own community. It has to be stopped," Clayton replied.

"We will try our best to slay it and drag its dead body back to shore as proof. Or at least its head," Willy said.

"Be extremely cautious. That Silver Serpent is an intelligent killing machine. It does not die easily. The only way to slay it is to penetrate its heart with a harpoon made of pure silver," Augustus replied.

"Is that so? Thanks for the advice. We will go to the Purple Octopus and buy some silver harpoons," Al said.

"We went after it also and it slayed two of our crew members. May they rest in peace. It also has a giant, octopus sidekick that is dangerous as well. You might try and slay that also, if it interferes, but the main objective is to slay the Silver Serpent. That is what will earn you and your crew the reward money," Clayton replied.

"OK. We got it. We appreciate the valuable tips," Ricky said.

"Enjoy your meals fellas. Good luck and God's speed," Clayton said.

"Thanks Clayton. It was nice to meet you fellas," Ricky replied. "It was nice to meet you guys also. Good luck, and I hope to cross paths again someday," Augustus said.

The Knight Sharks shook hands with the Sea Snakes and walked back to their own table. The Sea Snakes ordered some fried haddock and some rounds of Yellow Crab beers.

"What did they say Clayton?" Rodney asked.

"Those fellas are a crew of whale hunters called the Sea Snakes. They are from Port Andrew, here in Staten Island. They decided to go after the Silver Serpent tomorrow," Clayton replied.

"That's great news. I sure hope they are able to slay that noxious creature, once and for all," Zeus said.

"I hope so too. I think they can do it," Augustus replied. The Knight Sharks ordered another round of beers and continued to devour the all you can eat fresh, fried haddock and fries with tartar sauce and ketchup. Bruno walked back to the kitchen and checked on the shark and tuna steaks that were being grilled by his cooks.

Chapter Twenty
The Sea Snakes

The next day it was Tuesday, August 22, 1904. Ricky woke up at his house and got dressed. He climbed into his horse drawn buggy and rode over to Willy's house to wake him up. Willy answered the door, and Ricky walked inside his house.

"Are you ready to go, buddy?" Ricky asked.

"Yeah. Let me just put some clothes on and grab my stuff," Willy replied.

Willy put his clothes, grabbed his stuff, and the two headed out the door. They entered Ricky's horse drawn buggy and rode over to the Purple Octopus to buy the silver harpoons that they needed. After they bought four silver harpoons, they headed to the boat launch to meet with the other Sea Snakes. The Sea Snakes earned their name because they all owned a snake or two as pets.

It was about 10:00 am when the Sea Snakes met at the boat launch. The Sea Snakes loaded their supplies onto their boat called *The Sea Snake*, and they headed out into the inscrutable depths of the Atlantic Ocean. The day was bright and sunny with clear, blue skies. The first spot that they headed to was Hammerhead Hedge. Oliver and Bo were there lurking about and searching for some breakfast.

They spotted *The Sea Snake* and decided to swim to Slick's cave to alert him of the boat's presence. They arrived at Slick's cave and signaled for him to come out. Slick swam outside his cave and greeted his two best friends.

"How's it going, buddies?" Slick said.

"Say, buddy. I can't complain too much. We came to inform you that we spotted a boat snooping around Hammerhead Hedge," Bo replied.

"Is that so? I guess those humans just can't get enough of me. Either that or they never learn their lesson. Let's go check it out. Let me ask Zelda if she wants to come along," Slick said.

"OK Slick," Oliver replied.

Slick swam back inside his cave and gently nudged the serene Zelda with his head.. Zelda felt his touch and opened her sparkling, ruby-red eyes.

"Rise and shine, darling. How are you feeling this morning?" Slick said.

"Good morning, my love. I'm feeling fabulous this morning. How are you feeling?" Zelda replied.

"I'm just dandy. My buddies are outside my cave. They said they spotted another boat at Hammerhead Hedge. We are gonna go check it out. Would you like to come along?" Slick said.

"No, that's okay. I think I'm gonna hang out here and get some more beauty rest on your dreamy bed of kelp," Zelda replied.

"OK sweetheart. I'll be back later," Slick said.

"Be careful Slick. I couldn't take it if anything were to happen to you," Zelda replied.

"Don't worry, my queen. Nothing is going to happen to me. I'll always come back to your loving embrace. I'll see you soon," Slick said.

"OK. See you soon, my king," Zelda replied.

They passionately kissed each other goodbye with their long, red, forked tongues. Slick swam outside his cave to meet his best buds and they headed toward Hammerhead Hedge. They arrived there and saw that the boat was still there.

"What should we do, Slick?" Bo asked.

"Let's do what we do best. Let's demolish that boat and slay the passengers onboard," Slick replied.

"That sounds good to me, boss," Oliver said.

"If we all slam that boat at the same time, we can sink it. That's what we need to do," Slick replied.

"OK. I'm ready when you are," Bo said.

The three sea monsters rapidly sliced through the refreshing, cobalt-blue water toward *The Sea Snake* at their maximum speeds and viciously crashed into it with their gigantic bodies and devastating strength.

"Holy shit! What in the hell was that?" Ricky said. Then Al spotted the three giant sea creatures in the vicinity.

"It's the Silver Serpent and a giant whale shark!" Al exclaimed.

"There is a giant octopus with them also!" Nicky exclaimed.

"Get the silver harpoons and guns ready to fire at them!" Ricky yelled.

Willy and Nicky rushed to the cabin and collected four silver harpoons and four handguns.

"I got them, Captain," Willy said. Each Sea Snake grabbed a silver harpoon and a gun. The three sea monsters swam out of sight for the moment.

"When you see the Silver Serpent again, fire the silver harpoons at its heart and fire your guns at all of the sea monsters," Ricky ordered.

"Aye-aye Captain," The Sea Snakes replied. The Silver Serpent and his sidekicks were fifty yards under the choppy surface and were not visible to the Sea Snakes.

"That hit didn't do much damage. We didn't make a hole in the boat, and nobody fell overboard. Either that boat is very well built, or we are losing our touch," Slick said.

"Should we drill it again?" Bo asked.

"They're going to be ready for us this time," Oliver replied.

"That's why we have to swim up from directly underneath them and explode into the hull. That way they can't see us coming, and they won't have as good of a chance to hit us with harpoons and guns," Slick said.

"OK, let's do it," Bo replied.

The three sea monsters swam even deeper and positioned themselves directly underneath the Sea Snake. Then they rushed up with tremendous velocity and brutally banged the boat's hull with their heads. This time, they did create a hole in the boat's hull.

"They hit us again!" Ricky exclaimed.

"There they are!" Willy yelled.

The boat was starting to sink. The three sea monsters were now visible.

"Fire the guns at their heads! Wait for the Silver Serpent to emerge from the water, so we can fire the harpoons at its heart!" Ricky commanded.

"How do we know where his heart is?" Al replied.

"It's got to be somewhere between its upper limbs," Ricky said. Slick and Oliver were just underneath the surface to the left side of the boat, while Bo was a little bit deeper underneath the surface to the right side of the boat. The Sea Snakes fired gunshots at the three sea monsters and peppered them with hot lead. They didn't hurt Slick or Bo that much, but Oliver took some more rounds to his head and suddenly he stopped swimming, again. Slick saw that Oliver was motionless and bleeding heavily in the royal-blue water. Slick went over to check on Oliver.

"Oliver, are you okay?" Slick asked. Oliver did not reply. He was dead.

"Those sons of bitches slayed Oliver! I'm gonna annihilate them all and pick my teeth with their bones! Bo, get over here!" Slick exclaimed.

Slick grabbed Oliver with his upper limbs and pulled him deeper under the water, so that the humans couldn't shoot at him any longer. Bo heard Slick's distressed call and swam over to his side. Then they swam deeper into the water, so that they couldn't be seen by the Sea Snakes.

"What's going on, Slick?" Bo asked.

"They slayed Oliver! We have to slay them now!" Slick replied.

"I can't believe it. Is Oliver really dead?" Bo asked.

"Look at him! He isn't moving or responding! He is also bleeding profusely out of his head," Slick replied.

"Damn those insufferable humans! Take a deep breath and try and relax. They will be under the water with us in a matter of minutes. Let's just hang back here and be patient. We don't want to stick our heads and bodies too far above the surface and possibly catch some harpoons and bullets to the head or heart," Bo said.

"You are right. I'm just so infuriated that I want to go and pulverize them all now! I have to keep my composure," Slick replied.

"I know how you feel, but that's what we have to do," Bo said.

The Sea Snake was sinking fast, and the Sea Snakes were starting to panic.

"We are sinking fast you guys! What do we do?" Nicky asked.

"Try and remain calm, so that if we see those beasts again, we can throw the harpoons accurately at our targets," Ricky replied.

"Reload those handguns for good measure," Al said.

"I'm on it." Willy replied. Willy and Nicky reloaded their Browning handguns.

"We are going to be swimming in this ocean in no time at all! Then what are we gonna do?" Al said.

"Stay calm, Al. Keep it together man," Ricky replied.

Three quarters of the boat were now underwater. The Sea Snakes were barely remaining above the churning surface by standing on the boat's bow and still sticking out above the surface.

"I can't wait any longer. I'm gonna nail that boat one last time and send them all flying into the water," Slick said.

"Are you sure, Slick? They might see you coming and fire their harpoons and guns at you," Bo replied.

"I don't care if they see me! I'm enraged, and I'm doing it for Oliver!" Slick replied.

"Be careful buddy," Bo said.

Slick positioned himself directly underneath the sinking boat and shredded through the water rapidly toward the already damaged hull, to destroy it.

"I see it! It's headed straight toward us! Get ready to fire those silver harpoons at its heart!" Ricky exclaimed.

Ricky and Al got in a ready position to fire the silver harpoons at the rapidly approaching Silver Serpent.

"There he is! Fire the harpoons!" Ricky yelled. Ricky and Al saw the colossal, silvery creature approaching quickly toward them when they fired the silver harpoons at the area between Slick's upper limbs. The harpoons pierced the ocean's surface and flew towards the upper part of the dashing Silver Serpent. One of the harpoons hit him just below the head, while the other one pierced through his left eyeball and into his skull, and stopped just short of his brain. Waves of sharp pain shot and disbursed through Slick's head and upper body just as he rammed the boat's battered hull. Slick's body had such vehement velocity and force that he completely demolished the hull and sent the Sea Snakes flying into the Atlantic Ocean.

The harpoons in Slick's head and upper body caused him immense pain and rattled him. He also became light headed. He grabbed the silver harpoons with his two upper limbs and pulled them out of his upper body and skull. His left, ruby-red eyeball stayed stuck to the sharp harpoon barb. Bo swam up to Slick.

"Are you okay, Slick? What happened?" Bo asked.

"I think I'm okay. They hit me with two harpoons. One in my eye and the other just below my head. I'm kind of dizzy right now. My left eyeball is gone," Slick replied.

"Those humans are swimming in the ocean as we speak. Do you want to go finish them off?" Bo asked.

"Yes. Let's go finish those miserable bastards right now. Let's do it for Oliver," Slick replied.

The Sea Snakes were trying to find various floating objects from the boat, but most of it was sinking. Nicky and Willy were still holding onto the last two silver harpoons, while Ricky and Al were still gripping their handguns.

"Where did those hellish beasts go?" Ricky asked.

"I don't know. They could be anywhere," Willy replied.

"They are probably lurking below us and watching us," Nicky said.

"Thank you for saying that," Willy replied sarcastically.

"Be prepared at all times. If those demons come to get us, then try your best to fight them away. Willy and Nicky, you stick those silver harpoons right through that devil's heart! Don't ever stop fighting!" Ricky exclaimed.

"Aye-aye Captain," The Sea Snakes replied.

Slick and Bo were swimming towards the floating Sea Snakes in the tumultuous, blue water.

"Are you ready to finish them, Bo?" Slick asked.

"I sure am, boss. Let's slay those sons of bitches for Oliver!" Bo replied.

"I'll go after them. You just watch my back," Slick said.

"You got it, comrade," Bo replied.

The two sea monsters were approaching the four floating Sea Snakes when Ricky spotted them.

"There they are! They are coming right at us!" Ricky exclaimed.

"I see them too! God help us!" Al said.

"Get those harpoons ready!" Ricky exclaimed.

"Aye-aye Captain!" Willy replied. The Silver Serpent plunged himself toward Willy, just as Willy threw the silver harpoon at him. It struck Slick in the neck as he clamped down on Willy's head with his fatal jaws. Slick bit Willy's head clean off his shoulders and pulverized it with a loud, juicy crunch. Then he swallowed it and ripped the silver harpoon out of his neck.

Nicky threw his silver harpoon at the Silver Serpent, and it bounced off the steely spikes on his back. Slick went after Nicky and slashed him into bloody pieces with his claws. Ricky fired his handgun at Slick's head and upper body, but his armory scales prevented them from going too deep. Al fired some shots at Slick's head also, when all of a sudden, Bo popped out from the sparkling, sapphire surface with his jaws wide open and swallowed him whole.

"Way to go Bo!" Slick exclaimed. Bo gulped and swallowed.

"You know I don't like humans, but I had to get some revenge for our fallen comrade, Oliver. Are you gonna devour the last human, or should I?" Bo replied.

"I'll finish this one myself," Slick said.

Slick grabbed Ricky with the honed claws of his upper limbs and dangled him in front of his last, ardent, blood-red eye. His sword-like, salivating teeth, were dripping with human blood and pieces of flesh, guts, and organs. Ricky screamed bloody murder and struggled to wriggle free, but his body was already impaled on Slick's claws. Then Slick sliced Ricky in half vertically from groin to the top of his head. After that, he feasted on the two halves of Ricky's corpse. Just like that, the Sea Snakes ceased to exist.

"That's all of them. That's for Oliver you worthless humans!" Slick exclaimed.

"I'm glad we got rid of them. They deserved that for what they did to Oliver," Bo replied.

"You are damn right they deserved that. How did the human that you swallowed whole, taste? I thought you didn't like to devour humans," Slick said.

"I had to do it for Oliver. They slayed one of our best friends in all the seven seas. I couldn't really taste much since I swallowed him whole. I can still feel him squirming around in my belly. I'm sure he'll run out of breath and life, soon," Bo replied.

"He'll panic and scream and die a horrible and punishing death. Then your stomach acid will turn him into a pasty waste, and you will digest him. That was very impressive. You can be my new human-hunting partner," Slick said.

"We'll see. Next time I'll chew the human up before swallowing, so I can get a better taste of the flavor and actually use my teeth for a change," Bo replied.

"OK killer. You just devour whatever you want. You are one of the biggest creatures in the ocean, after all. Don't ever forget that, and use your size to your advantage. With you on my side, no one will be able to harm us," Slick said.

"I always got your back Slick. Don't ever forget that," Bo replied.

"Thanks buddy. I always got your back too," Slick said.

"What happened to your eye Slick?" Bo asked.

"Those blasted humans shot a harpoon through my eye. I only have one eye left now, but thank the great Sea God that it didn't reach my brain. That would have been much worse," Slick replied.

"Well at least we slaughtered them all. Let's go home," Bo replied.

"Yeah, let's go brother," Slick said.

The white-tip sharks detected the blood and started to devour Oliver's dead carcass.

"Do you see that, Slick?" Bo asked.

"See what?" Slick said.

"The white-tip sharks are devouring Oliver's corpse," Bo replied.

"What can we do for him now? He is gone. It is only natural for the ocean creatures to feed on other creatures, dead or alive. That is the cycle of life. That is what keeps us all moving and living. Oliver's physical presence will be gone, but he will live forever inside of our hearts and minds," Slick said.

"Perhaps you are right. I guess that is the cycle of life. One creature devours another creature to survive. I am going to miss him," Bo replied.

"So am I. Oliver was one of the best friends a serpent could ask for. He was like a brother. I loved him," Slick said.

"I loved him, too," Bo replied.

"Let's go home, partner," Slick said.

"OK comrade. Let's go," Bo replied. The two sea monsters were melancholy and grief stricken as they swam back to their caves. Slick and Bo were terribly sad that they lost a dear friend, but they were able to find some sort of closure knowing that they slayed and devoured the humans that brought about the demise of their beloved brother, Oliver the Octopus.

Chapter Twenty-One
Emerald Seaweed and Jellyfish

The next day it was Wednesday, August 23, 1904. Slick awoke next to his newfound love, Zelda.

"Good morning, my darling. How are you feeling this morning?" Slick said.

"I'm feeling phenomenal this morning. How are you feeling, my love?" Zelda replied.

"I'm really heartbroken because of what happened yesterday. The humans slayed Oliver right in front of my eyes. And they shot a harpoon through my left eye. Now I only have my right eye left," Slick said.

"Oh my God Slick! Are you ok? What happened yesterday?" Zelda replied.

"One of my best friends, Oliver, was slain by some hunters and their guns. They shot him in the head, and he had already been shot there before. I think this time the bullet reached his brain. He is gone forever," Slick said. Slick looked like he was about to cry. It was truly amazing how a lethal killing machine, such as Slick, could feel such love for his friends.

"Oh my God! I can't believe it. I'm so sorry about your loss Slick. I could tell that you two were very close," Zelda replied.

"We were extremely close. Oliver was one of the few ocean creatures that I considered to be a true brother of mine," Slick said.

"That's terrible. I'm so grateful to the great Sea God that you are still alive. Was Bo hurt?" Zelda replied.

"Bo wasn't hurt. He just took some gunshots to his backside, but since he is so huge, he barely felt a thing. They struck me with three harpoons. One went through my left eyeball and stuck in my skull, until I ripped it out, along with my eyeball. The other two pierced my neck and upper body. Those harpoons slowed me down some and rattled my cage for a while, but I ripped them out and kept on fighting until all those repugnant humans were slaughtered.

I slayed and devoured three of them. Bo swallowed one of them whole," Slick said.

"Wow, I'm glad you guys got them back for slaying Oliver and hurting you," Zelda replied.

"Yes, we had to obliterate them for what they did. I was gonna slaughter them anyways, but once they slayed Oliver, something inside of me awakened and it demanded blood and vengeance," Slick said.

Slick had some wounds around his head and upper body. He had incredible and mystical blood. His wounds could heal and scar up in just a couple of days. These wounds were still somewhat fresh and not completely healed yet.

"Let me put some emerald seaweed on those wounds, so they can heal up even faster," Zelda suggested.

"OK Zelda. The emerald seaweed is in some jars on the table," Slick replied. Zelda fetched the brilliantly glowing, emerald seaweed and returned to Slick.

"Here you go, my love," Zelda said.

She applied the emerald seaweed to Slick's wounds and Slick devoured some as well. The emerald seaweed started to work its magic immediately.

"Thanks darling. I really appreciate your caring for me," Slick replied.

"No problem, my love. You know I love and care for you with all my heart and soul. It's my job and I'm happy to do it," Zelda said.

"Thank you, my love. I feel the same way about you. I love you with all my heart and soul, too," Slick replied.

"What would you like to do today?" Zelda asked.

"I don't know. Let's just hang around the cave and feast on whatever is around here. I don't feel like going anywhere too far today and expending too much energy. I need to rest and heal up," Slick replied.

"OK Slick. Let's do whatever you want to do. You just rest up and recover, so those wounds can heal," Zelda said.

"OK, thanks for understanding," Slick replied.

"Of course I understand," Zelda said.

"I'm so glad and blessed that I found you Zelda. I thank the great Sea God every day," Slick said.

"I'm so happy and blessed that I found you as well Slick. I also thank the great Sea God for placing you in my life," Zelda replied.

"Let's swim outside and see what we can catch and devour. I'm getting kind of hungry," Slick said.

"That sounds good to me," Zelda replied.

The Silver Serpent lovers swam outside the cave and spotted a school of yellowfin tuna swimming around in that area.

"Look at those plump tuna over there. Let's go devour some of them," Slick said.

"That sounds like a tasty treat to me. Those tuna look delicious," Zelda replied.

The two Silver Serpents slowly crept up on the tuna and when they got close enough, they struck like vipers with their dragon-like heads and impaled the tuna with their fulsome fangs. They each snatched one in their jaws and chomped down hard, giving the tuna quick deaths. Then they chewed on the bloody and nutritious chunks of tuna flesh and devoured them. The other tuna sped away frantically to avoid the Silver Serpent's mighty and ferocious jaws of death.

"Let's go after the rest of them. We can catch them," Slick said.

"OK, let's go," Zelda replied.

The two serpents sped swiftly after the school of yellowfin and caught up to them. Then they savagely snapped and shredded their way to a hearty helping of prized yellowfin tuna. Together they slayed and devoured eight yellowfin. Only two yellowfin escaped with their lives.

"That's more like it," Slick said.

"Yes. This is quite a delectable and bountiful meal. Enjoy, my darling," Zelda replied.

"You enjoy it as well, my love," Slick said.

The Silver Serpents devoured the succulent pieces of yellowfin. They seemed to be thoroughly enjoying and savoring the fresh meal that the great Atlantic Ocean provided. The loving Silver Serpents finished devouring the eight, good-sized yellowfins, and then they burped and rubbed their scaly bellies.

"That hit the spot," Slick said.

"It sure did. Are you still hungry Slick?" Zelda replied.

"I'm good for right now. If I catch some other tasty creature swim in our territory, I'm going to gladly devour it anyway though," Slick said.

"I could go for some seals for dessert. Are there any seals in this area?" Zelda replied.

"Seal Island is about thirty miles away if you want to go. I'm still in too much pain to swim that far today. I'm gonna stay here," Slick said.

"No. That sounds too far to swim without you. I'm gonna stay here with you," Zelda replied.

"There are copious amounts of jellyfish just about five minutes from here. Those taste pretty good for dessert," Slick said.

"I can handle that. Where do we have to go?" Zelda replied.

"Just swim to that sunken, red pirate ship up ahead and make a right. That is where the jellyfish like to congregate," Slick said.

"OK, would you like to come with me, or would you rather that I bring some back for you?" Zelda replied.

"Bring some back for me, please. I'm just gonna stay right here for today," Slick said.

"OK, I'll be right back," Zelda replied.

Zelda kissed Slick goodbye and swam towards the jellyfish. She arrived at the sunken, red pirate ship and made a right. Then she swam further and spotted the vibrant jellyfish. There were hundreds of bright, neon yellow, orange, and green jellyfish in that area. Zelda licked her chompers and dove into the giant pod of lengthy and colorful jellyfish.

Jellyfish were easy for Silver Serpents to catch because they moved around lethargically compared to a Silver Serpent. Zelda snapped her jaws down on several jellyfish and consumed them in a couple of mighty bites. The toxin in the jellyfish's tentacles tasted like ice-cream to a Silver Serpent. She grabbed some more with her claws and shoveled them into her mouth. Then she snatched eight in her claws and swam back to Slick's cave and delivered them to him. The flashy jellyfish were huge with long ice-cream tentacles.

"Here you go, my king. That was an exquisite dessert. It hit the spot," Zelda said.

"Thank you, my queen. I truly appreciate that," Slick replied.

Slick chewed on the savory jellyfish and crushed all the sweet fluids out of them, and then he slid them down his gullet.

"That really did hit the spot. I think I'm gonna take a nap. I really need my rest," Slick said.

"OK, I'll take one with you," Zelda replied.

They lied down on Slick's cushy bed of vividly colored kelp. They fell into a deep slumber in which they dreamed about hunting together and making love. A couple of hours passed by when Slick heard Bo's signal from outside his cave. It awoke Slick but not Zelda.

Slick sluggishly crept outside his imposing cave and greeted Bo.

"What's going on, Bo?" Slick said.

"Not much, buddy. I'm still shocked about Oliver's death. I miss him already," Bo replied.

"I know what you mean. Oliver was a gallant sea creature and a true friend. He is gone but never forgotten," Slick said.

"He has gone to the great sea in the sky. He will be looking down on us and always be with us in spirit," Bo replied.

"What's going on in your part of the old Atlantic?" Slick asked.

"I was at Hammerhead Hedge. The sharks there have been complaining about a lot of boats in their area. Some of their comrades have been getting caught lately by shark fishermen," Bo replied.

"Is that so? I bet we could help them out with that problem," Slick said.

"Do you want to go check it out?" Bo replied.

"Sure. Not today though, because today I'm just going to rest and recuperate. I'll go with you tomorrow if you want to go," Slick said.

"That sounds like a plan Slick. We'll go check it out tomorrow. You get some rest and heal up," Bo replied.

"Did you tell the sharks about Oliver's death?" Slick asked.

"Yeah, I told them that he was slain yesterday by some hunters. Then I told them that we paid the humans back by slaying and devouring every last one of them. They were glad to hear that we terminated those miserable humans but sad to hear about Oliver's death," Bo replied.

"The sharks are good allies for us. They can help us battle the hunters and fishermen. And also provide proper back up when the situations get sticky. We need them on our side. That's why tomorrow we will go and see if we can help fix their problem. That way, they will owe us a favor," Slick said.

"That's very clever and strategic thinking Slick. We could definitely use them on our side in this war against the humans," Bo replied.

"Did you eat already today, Bo?" Slick asked.

"Yeah, I had some krill this morning," Bo replied.

"Have you swallowed any humans whole today?" Slick asked.

"No. Not today. I only devour those bony suckers when I have to," Bo replied.

"What do you think about the way they taste?" Slick asked.

"They taste alright. I guess it's an acquired taste," Bo replied.

"An acquired taste huh? Have you acquired that taste yet?" Slick asked.

"I don't know. They don't taste all that bad. The one I devoured, I swallowed whole, so I couldn't really taste too much. If I must devour some humans to protect my life or your life, I'll do it," Bo said.

"That's very reassuring to hear, Bo. I admire your position and perspective," Slick replied.

"Us sea monsters gotta stick together right? We are the kings and the protectors of this ocean. We cannot let humans come in and take over," Bo said.

"You are exactly right bud. We are the kings of this ocean and we must protect it and ourselves. These humans want to slay us, so they can dissect and study us for their research. Or so they can slaughter us and brag about it. We can't let that happen," Slick replied.

"When you're right, you're right, Slick. How's your precious Zelda doing?" Bo asked.

"She is doing splendiferous. I love her with all my heart and soul. I still miss Sandy, but she has gone to the eternal sea kingdom in the sky. She will always hold a special place in my heart. I need to move on with my life and find somebody that is going to make me happy. Life is too short not to be happy. I finally found that special somebody that sets my heart on fire and makes me happy," Slick replied.

"Congratulations! That is great to hear my friend. I'm happy for you and Zelda, buddy. I wish I could find a female whale shark that would love me and be my companion. They are so hard to find these days because of all the whale hunters in this area. I think that most of them are scared to migrate to this part of the ocean, because they fear that they might be slayed. I don't know where to look for a lover," Bo said.

"Don't worry brother. You will find her someday. I will help you find her if I need to. Keep your head up brother," Slick replied.

"Thanks for that encouragement Slick. You are a true friend and brother," Bo said.

"What are friends for?" Slick replied.

"I'm gonna swim home, because I'm getting tired. I'll see you later brother. Get some rest and take care," Bo said.

"OK Bo. Thanks for coming to my cave and giving me the latest information. We will visit the sharks tomorrow," Slick replied.

"Alright brother, I'll see you tomorrow," Bo said.

"I'll see you tomorrow Bo. Be careful on your way home. The whale hunters could be anywhere this time of the year. Stay low so they can't see you," Slick replied.

"You got it, boss," Bo said.

Bo swam back to his home near Hammerhead Hedge. On his way home, Bo spotted another whale species. It was an enormous north Atlantic right whale. Bo swam up to it to greet it.

"Hello there. I'm Bo. What's your name?" Bo said.

"Hello Bo. My name is Sloopy. I came here for the endless swarms of krill in this area," Sloopy replied.

"It's a pleasure to meet you, Sloopy. I like your name, by the way. It's so unique and cool sounding. There are tons of krill in this area. Help yourself. Just beware of the whale hunters. They like to hunt these waters as well. Try and stay low and out of sight. That's just some friendly advice to help you survive," Bo said.

"I appreciate that. I most definitely will do that. Thanks Bo. I like your name too, by the way. It's very rugged and masculine. I hope to see you in the future. Take care Bo," Sloopy replied.

"No problem. I hope to see you in the future too. I'm usually around these waters. Take care Sloopy," Bo said. Sloopy glided toward the plethora of krill with jaws wide open, while Bo cruised toward the cozy confines of his cave.

Chapter Twenty-Two
News on the Sea Snakes

The next day rolled around it was Thursday, August 24, 1904. It was a quiet and breezy day in Cape Crusade. Molly woke up to the sound of seagulls squawking and waves crashing. Her house was located right on the beach. She went outside and collected her newspaper. On the front page, it read; "The Silver Serpent is still out there!"

She picked it up and headed back inside her beach house. Molly brewed herself a pot of coffee and sat down to read the newspaper. The article about the Silver Serpent was very captivating and bone chilling. She couldn't stop reading it. It talked about all the recent slayings of whale hunters, fishermen, and party goers. Molly started to cry as the article brought back painful memories of her deceased boyfriend, Marco. She gathered her emotions and continued reading. The article also mentioned the bounty on the Silver Serpent and how that had motivated some courageous whale hunters and sea captains to venture out to the dreaded depths of the Atlantic to attempt to slay the menacing monster.

Molly decided to ride over to the Sandbar to get the latest news on the Silver Serpent. She hopped in her horse drawn buggy and rode over to the renowned watering hole and eatery. Molly parked her buggy and walked inside. It was about 2:00 in the afternoon.

She took a seat at the bar and ordered a Stingray beer. The Knight Sharks were also in the bar drinking and eating as usual. Bruno brought Molly's beer to her and asked her if she wanted anything to eat. Molly ordered some grilled lemon shark steaks.

"Isn't that the lady that was asking about her boyfriend the other day?" Augustus asked.

"Yeah, that's her alright. Why don't you go talk to her and ask her how she's doing?" Clayton replied.

"I guess I can do that. I'll be right back," Augustus said.

Augustus walked up to Molly and asked her how she was doing.

"Do I know you?" Molly replied.

"Yes. We met the other day, when you asked us if we'd seen your boyfriend and the Bloodhounds. My name is Augustus," Augustus said.

"Oh yes. Now I remember. You are the guys that went out searching for them, right?" Molly replied.

"That's right. It's nice to see you again," Augustus said.

"It's nice to see you too. How are you and your crew doing?" Molly replied. There was a definite and instantaneous attraction between the two.

"My crew and I are doing okay. We could be better. We lost two of our crew members, Polly and Gregory, to the Silver Serpent. May they rest in peace," Augustus said.

"I'm terribly sorry to hear that. That demonic beast has claimed too many lives. It really must be stopped," Molly replied.

"I know. I feel the same way," Augustus said.

"Has anybody else journeyed out there to try and put an end to that monster?" Molly replied.

"Yes, a group of whale hunters called the Sea Snakes went out a couple of days ago and have not returned. My crew and I believe that their trip might have taken a turn for the worst," Augustus said.

"They were probably killed by the Silver Serpent also, right?" Molly replied.

"I'm afraid so. We were trying to decide whether we should go search for them or not. It's just so damn dangerous out there. We fear for our lives," Augustus said.

"I don't blame you. That Silver Serpent has killed so many people lately and none have been able to kill it. I wouldn't want to go out there anymore either," Molly replied.

"Yes, that is true. They say that a silver harpoon through its heart can kill it, but it's so hard to hit it in the heart, because it's so fast and elusive," Augustus said.

"I would stay on land where it is safe. That monster definitely calls the shots out there in those deep, dark waters," Molly replied.

"It definitely defends its territory with deadly force and an iron claw. It has backup now too. We saw a giant octopus with it the last time, and some people say that they've seen it with a humongous whale shark as well. That makes it even harder to slay," Augustus said.

"Is that so? It sounds like he and his buddies are joining forces and hunting the hunters," Molly replied.

"Yeah, I guess you could say that. Would you like to come join us at our table Molly?" Augustus said.

"Sure. That sounds fine," Molly replied.

Molly and Augustus walked to the Knight Shark's table.

"You knuckleheads remember Molly, right?" Augustus said.

"Of course we do. How could we forget the lovely, Molly?" Zeus replied.

"I remember her. How are you doing Molly?" Rodney said.

"Hello, Molly," Clayton said.

"Hello, gentlemen. I'm still very grief stricken and heartbroken about Marco's death. How are you guys doing?" Molly replied.

"I can imagine. I'm sorry to hear that, honey. Keep your head up and stay strong. It will get better with time. Have a seat and join us," Clayton said.

"Thank you. I don't know if I'll ever stop grieving for my lost love. I hope and pray that it does get better with time," Molly replied.

"It will, Molly." Augustus said.

Molly sat down next to Augustus.

"Can I get you another beer Molly?" Augustus asked.

"Sure, I'll have another one. Thank you," Molly replied.

"You got it. Any of you sea slugs want another round?" Augustus asked.

"Damn straight sunny boy!" The Knight Sharks rejoiced.

"A simple yes would have sufficed, wise guys," Augustus replied. Augustus signaled for the waitress, Sally, to attend to him.

"What can I get you?" Sally asked.

"We'll take five Yellow Crab beers and one Stingray beer, please," Augustus replied.

"Can I get you guys anything else?" Sally asked.

"That's it for now. Thank you Sally," Augustus replied.

Sally returned quickly with five ice-cold Yellow Crab beers for the Knight Sharks and one frosty Stingray beer for Molly.

"That'll be $1.20," Sally said. Beers were only twenty cents each at the Sandbar in 1904.

"Just put that on my tab," Augustus replied.

"OK, will do," Sally said.

"Cheers to old friends and to new friends!" Augustus toasted.

"Cheers to that!" The Knight Sharks replied.

"Cheers!" Molly said.

They all took some healthy gulps from their ice-cold beers. Just then, Bruno came running to their table.

"The Sea Snakes are all dead!" Bruno exclaimed.

"What? Where did you hear that?" Clayton replied.

"A friend of mine who is a shrimp boat captain told me earlier that he was out shrimping yesterday, and he came across pieces of the Sea Snakes boat. He said there were some floating pieces of that boat and he recognized it as the Sea Snake's boat, because the pieces were purple and green, and one of them had a sea snake painted on it. Purple and green were the Sea Snakes colors and the Sea Snake was their symbol," Bruno said.

"Was there any sign of the Sea Snakes?" Zeus asked.

"No. The only evidence that was there were some pieces of the boat and a couple of life preservers. The rest of the stuff and the boat had already sunk to the bottom of the ocean," Bruno said.

"Holy smokes. Those poor fellas. The Silver Serpent has struck again," Clayton replied.

"When and where did your buddy see all of that?" Rodney asked.

"He witnessed that yesterday around Hammerhead Hedge," Bruno replied.

"What are we gonna do now? Nobody else has shown interest in the Silver Serpent Bounty," Augustus said.

"Let's just give it some time. I'm sure that somebody else will be motivated to slay the Silver Serpent for that $10,000 bounty. Let's be patient. In the meantime, we will lay low and fish other areas away from the Silver Serpent's territories," Clayton replied.

"It sounds like that sinister serpent ran us out of our own fishing territories," Zeus said

"He is not running us out. We will just fish in other areas until somebody can put a silver harpoon through the heart of that cold-blooded creature. They are his territories also. We have to remember that," Clayton replied.

"I think that's a great idea Captain. I'm with you all the way," Ringo said.

"What do you think about that Augustus?" Clayton asked.

"I think that all of you fellas have valid points. I will always do what's best for the Knight Sharks," Augustus replied.

"Good answer Augustus. I admire your attitude and loyalty," Clayton said.

"I think you guys should wait for another crew to slay that malignant monster. It has already claimed the lives of two of your crewmates and numerous other victims including my boyfriend and the Bloodhounds, and now the Sea Snakes. That foul creature is nearly impossible to destroy. Someone must pierce its heart with a silver harpoon, but that is beyond difficult to accomplish because of its quickness, strength, and elusiveness. I have already lost too many loved ones to that dreadful devil. I don't want to lose you guys also," Molly replied.

"That is very nice of you to say. I don't want to die either. I want to live to be a happy, old fisherman and surrounded by my loved ones," Augustus said.

"Do you really think that another crew is going to go after the Silver Serpent, once the latest news on the Sea Snakes gets out? Crew after crew is falling victim to the Silver Serpent's wrath," Rodney stated.

"I think so. That $10,000 bounty will inspire and motivate them. Trust me," Clayton replied.

"OK Captain. I trust you. We need to plan another fishing trip soon though, because money is getting kind of tight around here," Zeus said.

"That sounds like a stellar idea, Zeus. I'm ready to go whenever you guys are," Clayton replied.

"Let's plan one for tomorrow," Rodney said.

"That sounds grand to me. I definitely could use the extra coin," Augustus replied.

"What kind of fish do you guys catch?" Molly asked.

"We catch sharks and tuna. We catch other fish as well from time to time, but sharks and tuna are our bread and butter. They provide good sources of money and food. We catch them and sell the bulk of it and keep some for ourselves to enjoy at our dinner tables," Clayton replied.

"That sounds thrilling. I love to eat shark and tuna. They taste so delicious," Molly said.

"If you have eaten shark or tuna in Cape Crusade, then there is a good chance that it was caught on our boat. We provide Cape Crusade and the rest of Staten Island a great deal of the shark and tuna it serves here locally," Augustus replied.

"Wow. That is good to know. I ate some exquisite lemon shark here earlier when I had just arrived at the bar. Maybe it was the Knight Sharks that caught that shark," Molly said.

"Yes, as a matter of fact it was. We caught an eleven-foot, 600 lb. lemon shark. We kept half of it for ourselves, and sold the other half to The Sandbar. I'm one hundred percent sure that that was what you were eating earlier," Clayton replied.

"That is incredible. That shark tasted so fresh and delicious," Molly said.

"We also caught a 350 lb. bluefin tuna. We kept some of that and sold the rest to Bruno and the Sandbar. That is our livelihood, and that is what puts money in our pockets and food on our tables. It keeps our heads above water, financially, so to speak," Augustus replied.

"I am very impressed. Next time I'll try some of that bluefin tuna as well," Molly said.

The Knight Sharks ordered another round of beers and some shots of Jamaican rum. They did the same for Molly. The alcohol was starting to take effect on the heavy drinking locals. They were starting to loosen up a bit after being so devastated by their loved one's deaths in the past few weeks. They were laughing and singing and having a jolly good time.

The spark between Molly and Augustus was starting to grow into a flame as they smiled, laughed, and flirted with each other all night. They playfully giggled and touched each other while they exchanged lustful, googly eyes. Then Augustus mustered up the courage and planted a deep and passionate French kiss on Molly's luscious lips. Molly was pleasantly surprised and she kissed back. The Knight Sharks all just watched in amazement and admiration for their lucky comrade, Augustus. Molly was most definitely a great catch.

There was an awkward silence as the Knight Sharks remained quiet and tried not to laugh.

"How about that Jamaican rum, it'll get you every time," Clayton said.

"You said it. That Jamaican rum is pure fire water. The true nectar of the gods," Zeus replied.

"I think it sneaks up on people and sometimes they can't handle it. Me, I handle it just fine," Rodney said. Augustus and Molly stopped kissing for the moment.

Augustus looked at his crewmates and smiled.

"Are you coming up for air, buddy?" Ringo asked. The Knight Sharks all burst out laughing.

"Let me get you fellas another round of beers, so you'll stop busting my balls," Augustus said. Augustus beckoned Sally. Sally came over to take his order.

"What will it be?" Sally asked.

"Get us all another round of beers please," Augustus replied.

"OK, coming right up," Sally said. She returned promptly with their beers.

"Put that on my tab," Augustus said.

"Thanks Augustus," The Knight Sharks said.

"Thanks Augustus," Molly said.

"Cheers to good health, good fishing, and good times!" Augustus cheered.

They all raised their beer bottles and toasted them in the air together.

"I haven't felt this good in a long time. It has been fun hanging out with you and the Knight Sharks," Molly said.

"I'm glad that you're enjoying yourself. Life is short. We must live every day to the fullest and make the most of what we have. Would you like to come back to my place for a nightcap?" Augustus replied.

"Sure. That sounds lovely," Molly said.

"That's just grand. Let me pay my tab, and we'll get out of here," Augustus replied.

"OK Augustus," Molly said.

"We are gonna get out of here fellas. What time are we gonna meet tomorrow at the docks?" Augustus said.

"You're leaving already? I think I know why. We are gonna meet at 2:00 pm tomorrow at the boat launch. We're all probably gonna be a little sluggish, so go ahead and sleep in," Clayton replied.

"OK Captain. I'll see you sea urchins tomorrow," Augustus said.

"See you tomorrow, buddy. Have fun," The Knight Sharks replied.

"Goodbye. It was a delightful hanging out with you gentlemen," Molly said.

"The pleasure was all ours. You're always welcome at our table. See you around Molly," Clayton replied.

"Goodbye, Molly. Take care," The Knight Sharks said.

Molly and Augustus walked out of the Sandbar and into his horse drawn buggy.

"Let's go in my buggy. We can leave yours here overnight. It will be safe here. Tomorrow I'll bring you back, so you can pick it up. You shouldn't be riding alone tonight anyway," Augustus said.

"OK. That is probably the wisest decision," Molly replied.

"My house is just about seven minutes from here," Augustus said. It was about 11:00 in the cool and starry evening. The perfectly round moon was full, and the stars were twinkling amid an obsidian sky with smoky gray clouds. There was a slight and crisp breeze with the scent of sea salt and grilled fish in the air. Augustus led Molly's gray and white persheron horse into the Sandbar's stables and locked the gate with his key.

The new friends hopped into Augustus' rugged buggy and rode out toward his beach house. He had a medium sized, two-bedroom house right on the Atlantic's enchanted surf. They arrived at Augustus' beach house and went inside. As soon as they got inside, they started kissing and fondling each other. Augustus led Molly into his master bedroom and took her clothes off. Molly helped Augustus take his clothes off as well, and they hopped into his bed, naked.

Molly had a jaw-dropping body with silky-smooth, buttermilk skin and lustrous curves. Her peridot-green eyes glinted like exotic gemstones that complimented her gleaming, jet-black hair that flowed over her shoulders like the night's sky. They laid on top of each other and kissed and caressed each other. Then Augustus placed his head between Molly's creamy thighs to give her oral sex. She was so slick and juicy down there, and tasted as delicious as homemade peach cobbler. She grabbed Augustus's head and pushed it firmly into her southern region as she moaned seductively with pleasure. He licked and kissed her beautifully shaped vagina until she was percolating with euphoric orgasms. Molly returned the favor and gave Augustus phenomenal oral sex. Augustus was fully aroused at that point, and he climbed on top of Molly and penetrated her tight, slippery clam in the missionary position. She let out some toe-curling moans and really started to get into the passionate deed. They made erotic and epic love to each other for a solid fifteen minutes, before August spilled his seed onto her glistening belly. Then they kissed deeply one last time, before they fell asleep blissfully in each other's arms.

Chapter Twenty-Three
The Fishing Trip

The next morning it was Friday, August 25, 1904 in the fishing village of Cape Crusade. Augustus woke up to a beautifully naked Molly right next to him. He became aroused again, and he woke Molly up with a kiss. They began to fondle each other's bodies. Molly climbed on top of Augustus and straddled him. Augustus entered inside Molly's sweet, southern region and she moaned out in ecstasy. They made love to each other for a good while when Molly climaxed on top of Augustus. He felt her heavenly vagina as it contracted and climaxed on his manhood. That triggered Augustus to explode effervescently inside of her. They both let out an enjoyable sigh of relief and then wrapped their arms around each other and kissed.

"Would you like some breakfast? I have some bacon, eggs, and toast with some coffee and orange juice," Augustus said.

"That sounds wonderful," Molly replied. The new lovebirds put on their clothes and headed into the kitchen. Augustus placed the bacon and eggs in the frying pan and brewed a pot of coffee. After breakfast and coffee were ready to be served, Augustus prepared their plates and coffee and set them on his cedar-wood dining table.

"Breakfast is served, my lady," Augustus said.

"Thanks Augustus. You are quite the host and gentleman," Molly replied. The slightly hung-over pair ate their breakfast with toast and drank their coffee and orange juice.

"How do you like it?" Augustus asked.

"It's delicious. You're an excellent cook, Augustus," Molly replied. "

"Thank you. I really appreciate it," Augustus said.

Augustus and Molly felt a real, fiery connection toward each other. They had an insatiable lust for each other and their personalities meshed well together as well. Augustus was thirty years old and Molly was twenty-six years old.

"You're more than welcome Molly. Thank you for spending time with me and being such a delight," Augustus replied.

"No problem. I hope we can do it again soon," Molly said.

"That sounds like a great plan to me," Augustus replied.

"What time do you have to go fishing today?" Molly asked.

"I have to meet my crew at the boat launch at 2:00 this afternoon. I'll drop you off at the Sandbar before I go, so you can pick up your horse and buggy," Augustus replied.

"OK, that will work just fine. Good luck on your fishing trip. I hope you catch lots of big ones. Be careful though. It's still perilous out there in those waters," Molly said.

"Thank you, and I will. We should be relatively safe since we are gonna stay clear of the Silver Serpent's main territories," Augustus replied.

"That is very wise indeed," Molly said.

"Well, we better get going. It's already 1:00 pm. Let me just grab a couple important belongings," Augustus replied.

"OK. I'll wait for you right here," Molly said.

Augustus gathered his belongings and headed out the door with his sexy, newfound lover, Molly. They hopped into his horse drawn buggy and rode over to the Sandbar.

"Goodbye, Augustus. Thanks again for everything. I haven't been with anyone since Marco passed away. I truly relished it," Molly said.

"You don't have to thank me. It was my pleasure. Thank you for being such spectacular company. I cherished every moment of it, as well. If you ever need to find me, you know where I live or just come by the Sandbar, I'm there often," Augustus replied.

"OK, sounds good. See you later. Take care, Augustus," Molly said.

"I'll see you later, Molly. Take care," Augustus replied.

They kissed each other and Molly got out of Augustus's buggy and walked to her buggy. Augustus unlocked the stable's gate and led Molly's persheron horse back to her buggy and harnessed him for her. They exchanged phone numbers and agreed to call each other. Molly climbed in her buggy and headed toward her beach house. Augustus rode over to the boat launch to meet with his crew for departure. He arrived there at 2:00 sharp and saw the rest of the Knight Sharks already there. They were loading supplies onto their boat.

"Look it's Augustus," Zeus said.

"Come and help us load the boat Augustus!" Clayton ordered. "Aye-aye Captain. Keep your shirt on," Augustus replied.

Augusts joined his crewmates and helped them load the supplies onboard their prized and sacred vessel.

"Do we have any more silver harpoons, just in case we see that Silver Serpent? Augustus asked.

"Yes, we still have five silver harpoons, just in case we do encounter that Silver Serpent," Zeus replied.

"Good. I feel a little bit safer now," Augustus said.

"Don't worry so much Augustus. We are gonna fish the Northeast Banks and the Rocky Shores. Those areas are very far away from the Silver Serpent's territories," Clayton replied.

"I pray that you are right. It seems to me that the entire Atlantic Ocean is the Silver Serpent's territory," Augustus said.

"We will be alright. That monster won't even detect us. Besides, we can't let that beast keep us from doing the job that puts food on our tables and money in our pockets," Clayton replied.

"I guess you're right. I just don't want to die. There's too many things that I haven't done yet, and I think I'm in love," Augustus said.

"Holy shit! Listen to lover boy over here. Who are you in love with?" Zeus replied.

"I'm in love with that lady from last night, Molly," Augustus said.

"Are you serious? You just met her. You barely even know her, buddy," Rodney replied.

"I know, but I feel this undeniable connection with her that I've never felt with any other woman before in my life. It's definitely the real deal this time. I'm in love," Augustus said.

"Listen to this lovesick dog. She must have really done something special to you last night, or she must have a golden clam between her legs," Zeus said. The Knight Sharks burst out in raucous laughter.

"I guess you could say that," Augustus replied.

"I knew you were gonna get lucky. You two were all over each other all night at the Sandbar," Clayton said.

"Last night was a blast. We planned on seeing each other again soon," Augustus replied.

"OK, enough of that mushy stuff. We have some other types of fish to catch!" Clayton said.

The Knight Sharks finished loading their guns, liquor, food, and water onboard their boat and headed out toward the Northeast Banks. The Northeast Banks were located about 100 miles northeast of the boat launch. It would take them between two to three hours to get out there. That was a good distance from Boat-Wreck Lane and Hammerhead Hedge, so the Knight Sharks felt somewhat safe.

On their way over there, they cracked some beers open and made sure that they were steering themselves in the right direction. The Knight Sharks arrived at the Northeast Banks just after 4:00 pm. The Northeast Banks were known for their outstanding fishing. All kinds of sea creatures congregated there during this time of year because of the cornucopia of aquatic life.

The commercial fishermen all loved to fish these waters during the summer months because of the various species, sizes, and amounts of fish that they caught here.

"Drop the anchor Zeus!" Clayton ordered.

"Aye-aye Captain!" Zeus replied.

"Prepare to drop the lines," Clayton said.

Rodney and Augustus baited the hooks at the end of the lines with large chunks of fish and squid. Then they dropped six lines into the water.

"The lines are in the water Captain," Rodney said.

"Good job Rodney. Grab me a beer," Clayton replied.

"Does anybody else want one?" Rodney asked.

"Sure," Augustus said.

"Yes sir," Zeus replied.

"Grab me one," Ringo said

Rodney went to the icebox and grabbed five ice-cold Stingray beers. Rodney returned with the icy beers and distributed them to his crewmates. The Knight Sharks popped open their beer cans and took some seats by the fishing rods.

"This is nice. Now, all we have to do is catch some fish," Clayton said.

"You said it Captain. I have a good feeling about today. It's perfect out here right now," Ringo replied.

"It's a gorgeous day today. It's not too hot or too windy. It's just right with a slight breeze and calm, sparkling, blue waters," Zeus said.

The beers were going down smooth and the Knight Sharks were starting to catch a buzz. Clayton pulled out some Cuban cigars.

"Does anybody want a cigar?" Clayton asked.

"Sure, I'll take one. Are those Cuban?" Augustus replied.

"You bet they are. I only smoke the best," Clayton said.

"I'm okay for now," Zeus said.

"I'm good. Thanks," Rodney replied.

"I'll take one of those stogies," Ringo said.

Clayton handed fresh, Cuban cigars to Augustus and Ringo, and they sparked them up.

"These taste really fresh. Where did you get them?" Augustus asked.

"I bought them from that Cuban guy on Sunny-Side Street. He gets them directly from Cuba," Clayton replied.

"That's pretty cool man. I like these. Does he give you a good deal?" Augustus asked.

"Yeah, he charges me $5.00 for twenty cigars, or twenty-five cents a cigar. That's not bad in my book, considering he gets them straight from Cuba, and they are always fresh," Clayton replied.

"That's a damn good deal, especially since he gets them straight from Cuba. That is pretty rare," Augustus said.

The Knight Sharks were enjoying their beers and the ideal weather, with their lines in the calm, glistening, azure water. All of a sudden, one of the rods bent violently. Clayton rushed to grab the rod with the cigar still in his mouth, and he pulled back hard to set the hook. The hook was set, and the fight was on.

"It's on! It feels like something massive!" Clayton exclaimed.

"What do you think it is Captain?" Zeus asked.

"It feels like a giant tuna!" Clayton replied.

"What kind of tuna do you think it is?" Rodney asked.

"Whether it's bluefin or yellowfin doesn't really matter to me. Both of those are prizes in my book!" Clayton replied.

Clayton's fishing rod was bending forcefully in the shape of a sickle moon.

"Reel that big boy in!" Augustus exclaimed.

"I'm trying, I'm trying," Clayton said. The fish was about halfway reeled in when it jumped out of the water. It was a magnificent yellowfin tuna.

"There it is! Did you see that? That was amazing!" Zeus exclaimed.

"Yeah, I saw it! It looks like a giant yellowfin!" Clayton replied.

Clayton battled the tuna and puffed on his cigar. The rest of the Knight Sharks guzzled their beers and glued their eyeballs to Clayton's epic battle with the monster yellowfin. They looked as excited as kids at a candy store.

"How's it going Captain? Is it tiring out yet?" Rodney asked.

"Yeah, it feels like it's tiring out. I'm reeling it in as fast as I can, Clayton replied.

"Don't put too much pressure on the line, or it'll bust," Zeus said.

"I know that genius. I'm the Captain for crying out loud," Clayton replied.

"I'm just trying to give you sound advice," Zeus said.

"Thanks so much for your expert advising," Clayton replied.

"I see it! It's coming in!" Augustus exclaimed.

The yellowfin tuna was being reeled in at a steady pace at that point. It was clearly visible because it was about five yards below the gleaming, cyan surface.

"It's almost here," Rodney said.

"Somebody, get the gaff ready!" Clayton ordered.

Zeus rushed into the cabin, grabbed the gaff, and rushed back to the side of the boat. Clayton reeled the tuna all the way to the side of the boat.

"There it is! Gaff that whopper!" Clayton exclaimed.

"I'm on it!" Zeus replied.

Zeus stuck the long gaff right through the gills of the gigantic yellowfin tuna. He hooked onto it and tried to pull it up onto the boat. It was too heavy for him to do it himself, so Rodney and Augustus helped him with the other gaffs. Together they landed the enormous tuna onto the boat's deck.

"We did it!" Augustus shouted.

"Damn straight! Great job Captain!" Ringo exclaimed.

"I couldn't have done it better myself. Congratulations Captain," Rodney said.

"Thanks fellas. I couldn't have done it without you. Hold the fish down, so I can pull the hook out," Clayton replied.

"Would you rather us hold it down or chop its head off?" Augustus asked.

"Try to hold it down first," Clayton replied.

The Knight Sharks did as they were told and tried to pin the tuna to the boat deck with their hands. The monster sized tuna still had a good deal of fight left in it and flopped around wildly. It was too big and too slippery for the Knight Sharks to hold down.

"OK. Grab the machete and stab its brain," Clayton ordered.

"Aye-aye Captain," Rodney replied.

Rodney rushed inside the cabin and returned with a razor-sharp machete.

"Finish it off," Clayton ordered. Rodney raised the shiny machete in the air and brought it down in a hard, stabbing motion that pierced the tuna's brain. The giant yellowfin flopped one last time and died.

"It's dead Captain," Rodney said proudly.

"There you go Rodney! Now somebody grab us all some beers, so we can celebrate this glorious catch!" Clayton said.

Augustus headed to the icebox and grabbed some icy Stingray beers.

"Cheers to the Knight Sharks and another impressive catch!" Augustus said. The Knight Sharks cracked their beer cans open and raised them in the air victoriously. They all took hearty guzzles from their beers.

"To a great catch and to the Knight Sharks!" Zeus exclaimed.

"To the Knight Sharks!" The Knight Sharks cheered.

"Let's weigh this beast and put it on ice. Somebody, help me carry it to the scale," Clayton ordered.

"Aye-aye Captain," Zeus replied.

"You got it Captain," Augustus said.

Augustus and Zeus helped Clayton carry the gargantuan yellowfin tuna to the scale. They positioned it on the scale's hook to be weighed. It weighed 450 pounds. It was a new yellowfin record that beat the old record of 420 pounds. The Knight Sharks measured the humongous yellowfin, and it was 7-feet in length.

"It's a new record! We are gonna collect a fortune for this monster," Clayton said.

"We sure are. We should keep some for ourselves, so we can enjoy it also," Ringo replied.

"We can do that. Or we can just sell the entire fish to Bruno and then eat it there at the Sandbar when it's offered on the menu. It's a win-win situation. OK, let's put this beast on ice," Clayton said.

Rodney and Ringo helped Clayton carry the marvelous, trophy catch to the icebox to keep it fresh. They opened the huge icebox and tossed it in there.

"That is a grand prize right there if I've ever seen one," Augustus said.

"OK, let's get back to fishing. Put some bait on that line and throw it back out there," Clayton ordered.

Zeus placed an entire bonito on the hook and tossed it into the shimmering Atlantic.

"I think this remarkable accomplishment calls for a shot of whiskey!" Rodney exclaimed. Rodney went into the cabin and returned with a bottle of New York whiskey.

He poured them all some shots in shot glasses.

"Cheers to another successful fishing trip and cheers to the Knight Sharks! A toast to those here with us right now and to those that aren't here with us right now," Zeus said.

"Polly and Gregory will always be with us in our hearts and minds. I hope and pray that they are fishing and drinking like kings in heaven right now," Clayton replied.

"Cheers to the Knight Sharks!" The Knight Sharks exclaimed.

The Knight Sharks continued drinking and fishing the Northeast Banks, and they were getting good and drunk as usual. At that point, all of them were pounding beers and puffing on Cuban cigars.

"Why was the ghost an alcoholic?" Zeus asked

"I don't know. Why?" Ringo replied.

"Because he likes boo's," Zeus said. The Knight Sharks laughed.

"What happens when ghosts drink booze?" Rodney asked.

"I don't know. What happens?" Augustus replied.

"They get sheet-faced," Rodney said. They all laughed again.

"Good one. I got one for you all. How do you know when you've really pissed off the bartender?" Clayton replied.

"I don't know. How do you know?" Zeus said.

"She leaves her rag in the Bloody Mary," Clayton replied. The Knight Sharks cracked up.

It was getting late and the bright, orange sun was setting amid the electric, bluish-purple skyline. The Knight Sharks had caught two more medium sized yellowfin tuna and two good sized lemon sharks. Their 1st icebox was filled to the brim with yellowfin tuna and lemon sharks. They had two iceboxes.

The sky was getting darker and the sinking sun was barely visible anymore amid the sable horizon.

"Should we head to the Rocky Shores, or should we continue fishing here? It is getting late, and we are all pretty drunk," Clayton said.

"I say we stay here," Augustus said.

"I say we head to the Rocky Shores," Zeus replied.

"I'm pretty drunk already. I'll do whatever the Knight Sharks want to do," Ringo said

"What do you say Rodney?" Clayton replied.

"I say we go home. I'm getting very tired," Rodney said.

"Everybody wants to do something different. The decision falls on me," Clayton replied.

"So what do you want to do Captain?" Augustus said.

"I say we fish here for thirty more minutes, and we go home. It's been a long day, and it's too far to venture all the way to the Rocky Shores right now," Clayton replied.

"I can live with that," Augustus said.

"I can too," Zeus said.

"That sounds about right. Great decision Captain," Rodney replied.

"Sounds good to me," Ringo said.

"Grab us all some more beers and some shots of rum," Clayton ordered.

Zeus went to the cabin and retrieved the beers and a bottle of rum. He poured the Knight Sharks all some shots and handed them their beers. Clayton and Augustus were still puffing away on their cigars. The Knight Sharks drank their shots of rum and cracked open their beer cans. They sipped on them and enjoyed the

Atlantic's crisp and cool night's breeze. All of a sudden, one of the rods bent drastically.

"Grab that rod!" Clayton commanded.

Augustus grabbed the rod and yanked back mightily to set the hook.

"It's on! I hooked it!" Augustus exclaimed.

"Good job. Take it nice and slow. What do you think is on your line?" Clayton replied.

"It feels like a proper sized shark at the end of this line. I don't know for sure yet though," Augustus said.

The line was being pulled aggressively, and the fishing rod bent dramatically.

"Keep playing with it. Let it tire itself out," Zeus advised.

"Holy smokes! This animal is putting up a serious fight!" Augustus said. The sky and the ocean were now completely dark and quiet. As Augustus was reeling in the large sea creature, Rodney spotted some lights from another boat.

"Look at that. It looks like a boat is coming toward us," Rodney said.

"I'll be damned. That boat is heading our way," Clayton replied.

"Don't worry about that right now Augustus. Concentrate and focus on landing that sea animal," Zeus advised.

"I will. I don't care about another boat heading our way. I just care about landing this fish or shark or whatever it is," Augustus replied.

"I wonder what they are doing out here this late," Clayton said.

"They are probably just fishing like we are," Rodney replied.

"First, let's land this fish, and then we can pay attention to that boat," Zeus said.

"I'm trying, I'm trying. I think this beast is tiring out. It's not battling as hard as it was earlier," Augustus replied.

"Good. Keep on reeling it in. It's getting closer," Clayton said.

The boat's lights were also getting closer. Finally, the shark was right next to the boat.

"Get the gaff ready!" Augustus exclaimed. Rodney grabbed the gaff from the deck. He rushed back to Augustus and looked for the shark.

"There it is. Gaff it already!" Clayton commanded.

Rodney stuck the gaff's hooked barb into the shark's head and yanked to set it.

"I got it. Somebody, help me pull it up," Rodney said. Clayton and Ringo helped Rodney pull the ferocious shark onboard the boat's deck.

"We did it!" Augustus exclaimed.

"Wow! What a magnificent catch. That is a beautiful Atlantic short-fin mako shark. It was a whopper. It was 10-feet long with a fierce, pointy head and rows of jagged, razor-sharp teeth. It's sleek, powerful body was a pristine silver color topped with a glorious, indigo-blue and deep shade of purple.

"Cut the head off immediately! We don't want that shark biting any of our asses," Clayton said.

Zeus went to the cabin and retrieved the machete. He returned with the machete and hacked at its head until it severed from the body.

"Let's weigh this herculean beast. Help me take it to the scale," Augustus said.

Ringo and Rodney helped Augustus drag the colossal shark to the scale. They hooked it up on the scale and weighed it. It weighed 300 pounds without the head.

"Let's put this monster in the icebox," Clayton said. The Knight Sharks placed the huge mako shark in the 2nd icebox.

"What a way to end the day!" Augustus rejoiced.

"Yes, this has been another successful and productive fishing trip," Zeus replied.

"Those lights are getting closer. Let's reel our lines in and go see what that boat wants," Clayton said.

The Knight Sharks reeled in the other five fishing lines and pulled the anchor up and in. Then they loaded up their guns just in case that oncoming boat tried something treacherous. Finally, they pulled up right next to the other boat.

"Hello there? Who is there?" Clayton said.

"Hello there. Who are you guys?" The man on the boat replied.

"I'm Clayton, and these are my crewmates. We are a fishing crew called the Knight Sharks," Clayton said.

"My name is Winston, and these are my crewmates. I'm the Captain, and we are a whale hunting crew called the Swordfish," Winston replied.

"Any luck today?" Clayton asked.

"Not today, but now we are going on a serpent hunting expedition," Winston replied.

"Are you guys going after the Silver Serpent?" Augustus asked.

"That's right. We heard about the bounty on its head, so we decided to go after it," Winston replied.

"That's great. I wish you and your crew the best of luck. It's about time somebody slayed that monster. I recommend you go to Boat-Wreck Lane and Hammerhead Hedge. That's where you'll most likely find the Silver Serpent, since those are its main hunting territories," Clayton said.

"Thank you for the advice. We'll most definitely check out those areas," Winston replied.

"We went after it, but we weren't successful. Some other people have tried also and been unsuccessful. May God be with you and may your results be different than the others," Clayton said.

"Thanks again. Did you guys have any success fishing today?" Winston replied.

"Yes, we caught three yellowfin tuna and three sharks. It was a successful and bountiful trip today," Clayton said. "Congratulations. That is a real score. Well we better head toward Boat-Wreck Lane to find that Silver Serpent. See you fellas later," Winston replied.

"OK Winston. It was nice to meet you and your crew. God's speed and good luck," Clayton said.

"Likewise. Thanks again, and take care," Winston replied.

Winston and the Swordfish headed out toward Boat-Wreck Lane to the west. Clayton and the Knight Sharks headed southwest and back toward the boat launch. They arrived there and unloaded all of their supplies and their catches. The Knight Sharks placed one icebox in Clayton's buggy and the other icebox in Augustus's buggy.

"Today has been a great day. I'll see you fellas tomorrow at the Sandbar for lunch, so we can sell and eat our catches there," Clayton said.

"Aye-aye Captain," Augustus said.

"OK Captain," Zeus replied.

"It's a deal," Rodney said.

"Sounds good to me Captain," Ringo replied.

"Get home safely and I'll see you guys tomorrow," Clayton replied. The Knight Sharks climbed into their horse drawn buggies and rode home happy as larks on that lucky and fruitful night of deep-sea fishing in the perilous, yet bountiful, Atlantic Ocean.

Chapter Twenty-Four
The Swordfish

The Swordfish arrived at Boat-Wreck Lane at about 2:00 am on Saturday, August 26, 1904. Their vessel was appropriately named, *The Swordfish*. The Swordfish earned their name because they all owned a collection of various battle swords at their houses. It was pitch black besides the boat's lights. A miasma of eerie fog was enveloping the ocean's glassy surface.

"Alright, we're here. Drop the anchors," Winston said.

"Aye-aye Captain," Derek replied. Derek was a member of the Swordfish.

There were a total of five Swordfish crewmates. Their names were Winston, Derek, Wally, Monty, and Colby.

"Keep your eyes peeled for the Silver Serpent and any other monstrous sea creatures such as whales, sharks, and octopuses. I heard that those creatures are the Silver Serpent's allies," Winston said.

"Damn, it sounds like he's got the Atlantic's heavy hitters with him," Monty replied.

The Swordfish popped open a bottle of rum and some beer cans. They sat vigilantly and drank their beers and rum, while they waited and hoped to see something extraordinary.

"Did anybody bring any cigars?" Wally asked.

"Yeah, I brought some," Colby replied.

"Good. I'll want one later," Wally said.

"I didn't bring any cigars, but I did bring a couple of joints," Derek said.

"That's great. I'll want one of those later too," Colby said.

"I'm gonna light this beauty up right now," Derek replied.

Derek sparked up the marijuana cigarette. He took a couple of drags on it and inhaled. Then he passed it to Colby. Colby took some hits and passed it to Monty.

"Do you want to hit this, Captain?" Monty asked.

"No. Not right now. I want to stay as sharp as I can in case we see that monster," Winston replied.

"You can smoke weed and still stay sharp. It's all in the power of the mind," Derek said.

"It helps to relax and ease the mind," Monty replied.

"I'm good for now. Maybe I'll try some later," Winston said.

"I'll take a rip off of that," Wally said.

Monty passed the joint to Wally.

"Here you go Wally," Monty replied. Wally puffed, inhaled, and blew the smoke out slowly.

"Man, this is some good smoke. It tastes like blueberries and pine trees," Wally said.

"When have you tasted pine trees?" Monty asked. The Knight Sharks chortled.

"I meant it tastes like blueberries and smells piney, wise guy," Wally replied.

"You're damn right. This herb is homegrown. I grow it myself in my backyard with lots of love. Lots of sun and water are good also," Derek replied. The Swordfish chuckled. The Swordfish were starting to catch a good buzz off the weed and alcohol. Winston was the only one that didn't partake in the weed smoking session.

"Pass me one of those cigars Colby. Where are they from?" Winston said.

"OK, let me grab some. They are in my bag in the cabin. They are from the Dominican Republic," Colby replied.

"How did you get cigars from the Dominican Republic? Are they any good?" Winston asked.

"My cousin gave me a big box full of them for my birthday last month. I don't know how he got them. I just know that they are from the Dominican Republic, because that is what my cousin told me, and that's what's printed on their box and labels. Yeah, they are pretty damn good," Colby replied.

"That makes sense. Let's try them out," Winston said.

Colby handed Winston a Dominican Republic cigar. Winston sparked it up with his lighter. Derek took the last couple of hits from the roach and tossed it into the ocean.

"What did you guys think? Was that some good cannabis or what? Derek said.

"Yeah, I gotta hand it to you Derek. That was some top-grade smoke right there," Colby replied.

All the Swordfish, except for Winston, were stoned but still sharp and vigilant. The thought of encountering the Silver Serpent was sobering and frightening enough to keep them that way.

"This cigar isn't half bad. I didn't know the Dominicans knew how to roll good cigars," Winston said. The Swordfish were relaxed but still very aware of their surroundings. They knew that they were in the infamous Boat-Wreck Lane and that all kinds of sea life could pop up at anytime, anywhere.

"Grab me another beer Wally, since you are the closest one to the icebox," Monty said.

"Man, you are lazy as a three-toed sloth," Wally replied.

"C'mon man. Be a pal would ya? I can move faster than a sloth, by the way," Monty said.

"Yeah, keep your pants on. Anybody else want one?" Wally replied.

"I think we are all ready for one," Derek said.

Wally went to the icebox and retrieved five Yellow Crab beers. He distributed them to the Swordfish.

"Did you see that?" Colby said.

"See what?" Winston replied. A huge tail just came out of the water.

"What kind of tail?" Monty asked.

"It looked like a whale shark," Colby replied.

"Do we really want to hunt whale sharks right now? Shouldn't we wait for the Silver Serpent?" Derek said.

"I think Derek is right. Let's wait for the Silver Serpent," Winston replied.

The whale shark that they spotted was Bo. Bo saw the boat and deduced to warn Slick about it. Bo swam to Slick's cave. Bo signaled for Slick to come out. Slick heard that familiar signal and exited his impervious cave.

"What's going on Bo?" Slick said.

"Did I come at a bad time?" Bo replied.

"I was asleep with Zelda. What's on your mind buddy?" Slick said.

"I was feasting on swarms of krill at Boat-Wreck Lane when I spotted another boat there. It looked to be a good-sized boat, so I assumed that they might be whale or serpent hunters," Bo replied.

"I'm still very tired right now. We'll go check it out later, during the day, to see if it is still there," Slick said.

"OK Slick. That sounds good. Get some rest, and I'll see you later during the light of day," Bo replied.

"OK Bo. I'll see you later buddy," Slick said.

Bo swam back to his cave to get some rest, and Slick reentered his cave to do the same.

"What was that all about?" Zelda said.

"It was Bo. He said he saw another boat at Boat-Wreck Lane," Slick replied.

"What did you say to him?" Zelda said.

"I told him that we'll check it out later, during the day," Slick replied.

"OK. Get some rest baby. Goodnight. I love you," Zelda said.

"Thanks my love. You do the same. Sleep with the angels. Goodnight. I love you too," Slick replied.

The Silver Serpent lovers kissed with their long, slithery, forked tongues and fell back asleep nuzzled against each other's scaly, sturdy bodies. The Swordfish were still drinking steadily and puffing on cigars.

"Wow, it's almost time for the sun to come up. It looks like we pulled another all nighter," Colby said.

"Yeah, it must be about 5:30 am right now," Monty replied.

"Grab me another beer. I'm just starting to wake up," Wally said.

"Get us all another one," Winston said.

"Who is gonna get them?" Colby replied.

"You are Colby," Winston said.

"I am?" Colby replied.

"Yes, you are and that's an order!" Winston said as he laughed. "OK, OK. Take it easy. You don't have to yell at me," Colby replied.

"I'm just fucking with you. But, I'm still the Captain, so you must do as I say," Winston said as he chuckled.

Colby went to the icebox and fetched five more icy Yellow Crab beers. He passed them out to his crewmates and took a seat by the cabin.

"I'm gonna go in the lower cabin to get some rest. Wake me up if you guys see the Silver Serpent, or if you guys need help with anything," Monty said.

"OK Monty. Get some rest man," Wally replied.

Monty went into the cabin and laid down on one of the beds in the lower cabin.

"Do we have anymore rum?" Derek asked.

"Yeah, I think there is some left in the cabin. Let me go check," Wally replied. Wally walked into the cabin and retrieved the last unopened bottle of rum left.

"I knew there was some left," Derek said.

"I'll take a shot of that," Winston said.

"I'll take one also," Colby said.

Wally poured Derek, Winston, Colby, and himself some shots of rum. They took the shots and cracked open some more beer cans.

"What kind of food did we bring with us on this trip?" Colby asked.

"We brought some cold cuts, hot dogs, potato chips, and vegetables with lime and salt," Wally replied.

"That sounds pretty good. I think I'm gonna make myself a sandwich," Colby said.

"Make one for me too," Derek said.

"I'll make you one for a quarter," Colby replied.

"That's a deal," Derek said.

"OK, I'll be right back," Colby said.

Colby walked into the cabin to the kitchen section.

"Damn, this beer tastes great. I love drinking cold beer in the middle of the ocean. It's an invigorating feeling," Winston said.

"You said it Captain. Drinking out in the ocean gives you peace of mind and lets you really put life in perspective. It's us versus the elements. Nature has a mysterious way of letting us know who we really are," Wally replied.

"That's pretty deep Wally. Did you think of that just now?" Derek said.

"No, I have always felt that way about the ocean. It is like my sacred sanctuary," Wally replied.

"I love the ocean also. We must keep our guard up all the time, because we came here to do a job. That job is to slay the Silver Serpent. We can become heroes and earn a boatload of money doing it!" Winston exclaimed.

"I'm with you all the way Captain. We can accomplish this monumental feat. I believe in our crew," Derek replied.

"Good, Derek. Keep your eyes and ears open at all times," Winston said.

"Aye-aye Captain," Derek replied.

Colby returned with the pastrami sandwiches that he made.

"Breakfast is served. Where is my quarter Derek?" Colby said.

"Here you go buddy," Derek said. Derek flipped a shiny new quarter to Colby. Colby made sandwiches for everyone except for Monty, because he was sound asleep in the cabin.

"Thanks Colby. You are a jolly good fellow," Winston said.

"Thanks Colby. A tasty sandwich always hits the spot," Wally said.

"No problem. You fellas owe me one though," Colby replied.

The Swordfish enjoyed eating their fresh sandwiches and chips, and washed them down with ice-cold beer. The sun arose in the east. It was a vibrant, reddish-orange fireball that shone and gleamed above the pellucid, cerulean sea. It was about 7:00 am and Monty still slept like a baby in the cabin. The other Swordfish drank and surveyed the waters like osprey for any activity. They were being very vigilant despite their intoxicated states.

A flock of seagulls dove down at a large school of bluefish. As they were diving down and feasting, a shark popped up from the foggy, cornflower-blue surface and devoured two seagulls in one bite.

"Did you see that? A shark just came up and devoured some of those seagulls. It looked like a great white," Derek said.

"No, I didn't see anything," Winston replied.

"Damn, you missed it. That was amazing. It was enormous. Maybe it'll do it again," Derek said.

The seagulls dove down like heat-seeking missiles at the large school of bluefish. The great white shark jumped out of the water and clamped its jaws shut on three more seagulls.

"There it goes again. I saw it this time," Winston said.

"I saw it too. That was an absolute hulk of great white shark. I haven't seen many of those in these waters lately," Colby said.

"Yup, that was definitely a great white. It must be impetuously ravenous," Wally replied.

The seagulls scattered away in a frenzy for their lives, so the rapacious great white claimed the feast of bluefish for itself.

"How big do you think it was?" Derek asked.

"It looks like it was at least 12-feet long. It's most likely a fully-matured, alpha male," Wally replied.

"If it comes this way, we should throw a harpoon through it," Colby said.

"I don't think that is wise. We only have four silver harpoons and four regular harpoons. We should save those for the Silver Serpent and the whales," Winston replied.

"A great white shark's steaks sell for a pretty penny these days. Are you sure you don't want to nail that impressive specimen for ourselves?" Colby said.

"I'm positive. Let's just wait for the Silver Serpent," Winston replied.

The Swordfish drank some more beer and sparked up some more Dominican cigars. It was about 10:00 in the morning. The great white shark lurked around Boat-Wreck Lane and hunted for some more quick and easy prey. The golden sun was peeking out from the puffy, white clouds and the fog was rising and evaporating into the crisp sea air. At Slick's cave, Slick woke up next to his beloved Zelda.

"Good morning, Zelda. How are you feeling?" Slick said.

"Good morning, Slick. I'm feeling strong and well rested this morning. How are you feeling?" Zelda replied.

"I'm feeling better today. My left eye is gone, but it doesn't hurt as much. I gotta go meet Bo later, so we can go check on that boat he saw in the middle of the night," Slick said.

"I feel so bad for you my love. You still look sexy with only one eye. Do you have to go? I know you can handle yourself quite well around those whale and serpent hunters, but I still worry when you have to battle with them. They are so malevolent and have such fierce weapons," Zelda replied.

"Don't worry about me, my love. I'll be just fine. Those hunters cannot slay me. They have tried many times and failed. I'm always the one doing all the slaying," Slick said.

"I know that you are a proud and courageous Silver Serpent. I also know that those hunters can win sometimes. Look at our loved ones that they have taken from us in the past," Zelda replied.

"I appreciate your concern, my love, because I know it comes from a place of love. The bloody war against the humans has gone on for centuries. How can we stop it? They invade our territories with intentions of destroying us. It falls on us to destroy them. That's just the cruel nature of this savage and cutthroat, creature planet," Slick said.

"I understand where you are coming from. What if we just stay away from them when they travel to our territories? I just worry about you. I've lost all my loved ones already, and I don't want to lose you too," Zelda replied.

"They will just keep on coming and coming until something happens. They are out for blood and it's my blood they are after," Slick said.

"If we stay away long enough, maybe they will think that we have moved elsewhere, and they will stop coming after us," Zelda replied.

"They would still come in these territories to hunt all of the other sea life. These waters are a primal feeding ground for a plethora of sea life. That is why it is so attractive to all types of predators including myself. Besides, I won't let them run me out of my own territory," Slick said.

"We can travel elsewhere to conquer and claim a new territory that is ripe with sea life. One where there is just as much sea life but less whale and serpent hunters," Zelda replied.

"Wherever there is blessed sea life, there are presumptuous and noxious humans. They thrive on it just like we do," Slick said.

"I'm sure we can find somewhere far away from here where there is an abundant supply of food and no signs of humans," Zelda replied.

"I don't know. You are quite an imaginative Silver Serpent," Slick said.

"We have to be creative to survive sometimes," Zelda said.

"I don't want to leave this territory, because it has been my home my entire life, and I love to devour humans and pick my teeth with their bones. I've been doing it all my life. I also don't want to disappoint you, because I love you. I don't want to lose you, and I want you to always be happy, comfortable, and safe. Don't you think that we can stay here and slay any humans that threaten to slay us?" Slick said.

"I think that we can be happy wherever we go, as long as we are together. I don't know if I can be happy here with the constant battles against humans," Zelda replied.

"You've put me in a tight spot here, my love. I promised Bo that I would go check out that boat with him today," Slick said.

"You can go check it out, but you don't have to attack it. If you stay low and far away, they probably won't see you," Zelda replied.

"OK, I will try my best to remain out of sight," Slick said. "Please promise me you won't attack them, and you'll stay far away," Zelda replied.

"I promise you, my darling. It's a shame though, because I really had the taste for human flesh and blood on my tongue today," Slick said.

"I know you do, my king, but just stay composed and think of us being together," Zelda replied.

"OK. Will do, my queen," Slick said.

"Thanks my love. I love you," Zelda replied.

"I love you too," Slick said.

The two, majestic Silver Serpents kissed each other.

"Would you like anything to devour before you leave? I can go catch some fish for us outside the cave," Zelda replied.

"That's okay baby. I'll grab something on the way to Bo's residence. I better be on my way. Bo is probably waiting for me," Slick said.

"OK Slick. Remember what I said and be careful. I'll see you later. I love you," Zelda replied.

"No problem. I'll see you later Zelda. I love you too," Slick said.

Slick swam outside his cave and headed towards Bo's residential waters. On the way he saw some silvery tarpons, so he chased after them and devoured them. He arrived at Bo's cave and signaled for him to come outside. Bo heard the signal and swam outside to greet his friend.

"How's it going killer?" Bo said.

"It's going just fine. I feel healed and rejuvenated. How's it going for you my brother?" Slick replied.

"I'm spades. Let's go to Boat-Wreck Lane to check if that boat is still there." Bo said.

"OK, let's go," Slick replied.

The two sea monsters swam out toward the infamous and deadly Boat-Wreck Lane. They arrived there at about noon that day and saw that the boat was still there. Slick and Bo stayed far away and below the surface for now, so that they couldn't be seen. They just peeked their eyes above the surface to check for the boat. *The Swordfish* floated on while its crew drank and monitored the wondrous waters.

"That boat is still there Slick," Bo said.

"Yes, I see it," Slick replied.

"What should we do about it?" Bo said.

"I don't know. I promised Zelda that I wouldn't attack them," Slick replied.

"Why did you do that?" Bo said.

"I did that, because I love her," Slick replied.

"Are you saying that we are just gonna let them roam this territory in peace without any repercussions? Bo said.

"I don't want to do that, but yes that's what I'm saying. I'm a Silver Serpent of my word," Slick replied.

"This is a totally new Slick. You have changed overnight my brother," Bo said.

"I have changed. I'm in love with Zelda now, and I realize that those whale hunters might slay me if I keep attacking them. They have slayed a loved one of mine and Zelda's loved ones in the past. They almost brought about my demise the last couple of times. They took one of my eyes already," Slick replied.

"This is an absolute shocker coming from the King of the Ocean," Bo said.

"I'm still the King of the Ocean. I'm just more elusive and calculative now," Slick replied.

"If you want to run these humans out of our territories, I'm with you. If you don't, I'm with you also. I'll follow your lead, because you are the king," Bo said.

"I'm glad to hear that Bo. Thanks for understanding. You have always been a true and loyal friend," Slick replied.

"What do you want to do now?" Bo said.

"Let's go to Squid Alley and grab some lunch," Slick replied.

"That sounds good. Let's go buddy," Bo said.

"Let's boogie, big Bo," Slick replied.

The two sea creatures swam out toward Squid Alley. It was the first time in a long time that they didn't attack a boat at Boat-Wreck Lane. The ocean floor at Boat-Wreck Lane was becoming littered with destroyed and sunken boats and ships. Back on the Swordfish's boat, the Swordfish, drank heavily, smoked cigars, and devoutly surveyed the waters.

"We haven't seen anything all day besides that great white shark. Where in the bloody hell is that Silver Serpent?" Derek said.

"I don't know comrade. Just be patient," Winston replied.

Monty arose from his slumber and rejoined the Swordfish.

"What did I miss?" Monty said.

"Not much. Just a herculean great white shark devouring some seagulls and bluefish," Wally replied.

"Is that so? How big was it?" Monty asked.

"It was about twelve-feet," Colby replied.

"Yup, that was the biggest one I've seen in awhile," Derek said.

"Have you seen any signs of the Silver Serpent?" Monty asked.

"Nope. We haven't seen any trace of that menacing monster," Winston replied.

"That's not good. How long are we gonna wait out here for it?" Monty said.

"I don't know yet. We'll play it by ear," Winston replied.

Monty grabbed a beer from the icebox.

"Does anybody else want a beer?" Monty asked.

"Yeah," The Swordfish replied. Monty grabbed some icy Yellow Crabs for himself and his crew. Winston and Colby puffed on the cigars from the Dominican Republic.

"Do you still have one of those joints left Derek?" Wally asked.

"Yeah, I got one more in the cabin. Do you want me to get it?" Derek replied.

"Yeah, let's spark that baby up," Wally said.

"OK, I'll be right back," Derek replied.

Derek went into the cabin and retrieved his last joint from a travel bag he had brought with him and returned to his crewmates.

"Let me spark it up," Winston said.

"Look who wants to smoke now. The mighty and fearless Captain of the Swordfish, himself," Colby replied.

"I want to try it. I saw all of you smoke one and nobody did anything that messed up. Plus, I like the way it smells," Winston said.

"Here you go, Captain. Knock yourself out," Derek replied.

Derek handed the joint and a lighter to Winston. Winston put down his cigar momentarily and lit up the joint.

"This does taste piney," Winston said.

"Here we go again with the piney taste," Derek replied. The Knight Sharks chuckled.

"Look at our fearless leader getting stoned. This is a day to remember," Colby said. Winston took a couple of drags and coughed. Then he passed it to Derek. Derek took a couple of pulls and passed it to Monty. The Swordfish all took turns puffing and passing the joint. They were feeling pretty good when they spotted something big on the horizon. It was a huge humpback whale.

"Do you see that?" Monty asked.

"See what?" Winston replied.

"That massive figure about 100 yards north of us," Monty said.

"I see it. It looks like a whale," Colby replied.

"Should we harpoon it?" Derek asked.

"I thought we wanted to save our harpoons for the Silver Serpent?" Winston replied.

"We can save the silver harpoons for the Silver Serpent, but what if we don't see the Silver Serpent? We would have come all this way for nothing," Derek said.

"I don't feel that way. This trip has been a blast," Colby replied.

"It's been a jolly good time, but I don't want to go home empty handed," Derek said.

"I'll leave it up to you fellas. We can go after the whale or we can wait for the Silver Serpent to show itself," Winston replied.

"We can slay that whale with the regular harpoons and save the silver harpoons for the Silver Serpent," Wally said.

"That makes sense," Monty replied.

"If we slay the whale and the Silver Serpent, how will we pull both of them back to shore?" Winston said.

"I hadn't thought of that. Is that even possible?" Colby replied.

"I say we harpoon that whale," Derek said.

"OK, let's do it. Pull up the anchor, so we can go after it," Winston replied. Monty and Colby pulled the anchor up.

Wally cranked up the motor and Winston grabbed the helm. The whale didn't notice them headed toward it, so it stayed there. The Swordfish were getting very close to the whale.

"Prepare the whale irons!" Winston commanded.

Derek and Wally went to the cabin and retrieved the regular harpoons.

"Here they are, Captain. They are ready to fire," Derek said.

"We're getting close. When we reach within firing range, you two fire the whale irons at its back," Winston commanded.

"Aye-aye Captain," Wally said.

"Aye-aye Captain," Derek replied.

The Swordfish positioned themselves within ten yards from the enormous whale.

"It's a humpback whale. Look at the size of it. Those provide a lot of bones, blubber, and oil we can sell," Monty said.

"OK, steady. Aim the whale irons. Now, let him have it!" Winston commanded. Winston was at the helm. Derek and Wally were in proper position at the bow, and they fired the harpoons at the whale's back. Both whale irons found their mark and pierced the humpback whale's blubbery back and stuck. The humpback thrashed in pain and rocked *The Swordfish*. The line coils uncoiled out of the buckets as the Swordfish were now involved in what whale hunters call "The Nantucket Sleigh-Ride." That was when the fastened whale towed the boat in an escape effort. Derek and Wally tied the lines around two small posts called loggerheads to slow it down as it ran out. The lines were being pulled so vigorously and caused so much friction that hot smoke arose from the loggerheads.

"We got it Captain!" Wally exclaimed.

The indigo sky darkened with charcoal-gray clouds.

"OK, Wally. Take it easy now. Keep an eye on the ropes," Winston replied.

"Jesus, Mary, and Joseph! That is a mammoth humpback whale!" Derek exclaimed. The whale towed *The Swordfish* at twenty mph as it ruggedly bounced along the waves. The tempestuous sea sprayed and soaked the Swordfish. The massive, blackish-gray whale dragged the Swordfish for about thirty minutes until it finally tired out. The Swordfish pulled up right next to the exhausted whale and shot it in the head multiple times with rifles until it turned fin out on its side, and died.

Chapter Twenty-Five
The Humpback Whale

It was about 7:00 that Saturday evening. The luminous, crimson sun had set amid a hazy, lavender sky in the west. The Swordfish steered their boat right next to the humongous, dead humpback whale. It was about 46 feet long and weighed about thirty metric tons.

"OK, let's drag this Goliath back to shore," Winston said.

"I thought we were going to hang out here longer and wait for the Silver Serpent," Wally replied.

"I've decided that we should head back to shore, because if we stay out here too long with this giant whale tied to our boat, the sharks will come and feast on it," Winston said.

"That's true," Monty replied.

"OK, let's go," Colby said.

"I thought we came out here to slay the Silver Serpent," Derek replied.

"We did, but we have been out here for seventeen hours and not a single sign of it. We will have to check out some other areas next time, like Hammerhead Hedge and Squid Alley. I've heard that the Silver Serpent has been spotted there as well. The task at hand is to take this walloping whale back to shore," Winston said.

"That makes sense. I'm okay with that. Besides we can always come back for the Silver Serpent some other time," Wally replied.

"We're gonna make a pretty penny with this humpback whale. We need to get it back to shore and sell it," Colby said. The Swordfish attached a line through a hole in the whale's tail that they made with a cutting spade. Then they cranked up the engine and towed the whale southwest, toward the boat docks.

The sun went down, and the ghostly darkness of the night stretched across the sky.

"Keep the harpoons and guns ready to fire in case we see the Silver Serpent," Winston ordered.

"Aye-aye Captain. The silver harpoons are ready to fire, and the guns are loaded," Monty replied.

"Good. Now get me another beer," Winston said.

"Aye-aye Captain," Monty replied. Monty grabbed five yellow crabs and distributed them to the thirsty Swordfish.

The Swordfish drank their beers and took turns at the helm. Winston sparked up another cigar.

"Let's do a shot of rum to celebrate the slaying of this magnificent beast," Derek said.

"OK, pour us some shots," Wally replied.

Derek grabbed the rum bottle and shot glasses from the cabin and returned with them. Then he poured himself and the Swordfish some shots of rum.

"Cheers to another successful trip and to the Swordfish!" Colby said.

"Cheers to that and to this glorious humpback whale!" Winston said.

"Cheers!" The Swordfish said.

"We didn't get to slay the Silver Serpent, but it has been a blast, and at least we're returning to shore with an impressive humpback whale," Monty replied.

"Yeah, we didn't even see the Silver Serpent for that matter, but it has been a grand, jolly-good trip. We slayed a monstrous sized and very valuable whale. Besides, we can always come back for that sly Silver Serpent," Derek said.

"Cheers to that!" The Swordfish exclaimed.

The Swordfish drank their rum shots and opened some more beer cans for the trip back to shore. They moved slower than usual, because they pulled an animal that weighed thirty tons. However, they traveled at a steady pace.

It was about 10:00 pm when they finally arrived at the boat docks. The Swordfish docked their boat and unloaded their belongings. Then they cut valuable strips of blubber from the whale. The Swordfish chopped and dissected the entire humpback whale and separated the blubber, bones, and flesh. They left nothing except its guts to throw back in the ocean.

"OK, let's put these bones in some bags and the blubber and meat on ice. Tomorrow we will take the blubber to our warehouse, so we can boil it down to extract the oil. Then we'll notify our contacts about our merchandise," Winston said.

"Aye-aye Captain. That sounds wise to me. What time are we gonna meet at the warehouse?" Monty replied.

"Let's meet there at noon. It's been a long day. Let's all go home and get some rest," Winston said.

"Aye-aye Captain. I'll see you tomorrow at the warehouse," Colby replied.

"See you tomorrow Captain," the rest of the Swordfish said. They loaded the bags of bones, and iceboxes filled with meat and blubber onto their carriages and rode home. The Swordfish arrived at their houses and jumped in their beds. They fell asleep as soon as their heads hit their pillows and got a good night's slumber.

The next day it was Sunday, August 27, 1904. The Swordfish woke up and rode over to their warehouse on Blue Marlin St. Their warehouse was located about five miles south of the Sandbar in Cape Crusade.

They unloaded the iceboxes that were full of fresh whale blubber and meat from their buggies and placed them in the warehouse.

"Get the flame going under the cauldron," Winston said. After the scorching flames were blazing under the cauldron, the Swordfish boiled strip after strip of blubber, until every last ounce of precious oil was rendered. They poured the oil in large casks and set them aside to cool. Now that the casks of oil were cooling, they would be ready to sell soon. The bones could be sold separately or an abundance of them at once. And the meat could be sold the same way. It just depended on what the customer wanted. After drinking and playing cards for a while, the oil had finally cooled and was ready for the market.

"OK, we have all of the casks sealed up and cool, the meat is tightly wrapped, and the bones are in the bags. Let's go out to our contacts and put the word out on the street that we have humpback whale bones, meat, and oil to sell," Winston said.

"Aye-aye Captain. Let's do some wheeling and dealing," Monty replied.

"Aye-aye Captain," The Swordfish said.

They left the meat, bones, and oil locked up in the warehouse as they hit the streets to advertise their merchandise. Winston visited the house of a fellow business man named Ripley. Ripley was a major wholesale buyer of whale bones, meat, and oil. After he bought the whale products from the Swordfish, he sold them to different businesses and earned his profit.

Ripley answered the front door.

"If it isn't my favorite whale hunter. How's it going Winston?" Ripley said.

"It's going just great. How are you doing, old friend?" Winston replied.

"I'm well. I've been looking for some whale products if you've got any," Ripley said.

"Today is your lucky day. My crew and I slayed a magnificent humpback whale yesterday. We have its bones, meat, and oil ready to sell from our warehouse," Winston replied.

"That's splendid news. Humpback whale products are getting harder and harder to come by these days. I'll take the trifecta of bones, meat, and oil," Ripley said.

"OK, let's head to the warehouse, so we can make that transaction," Winston replied.

"That's a grand idea. I'll follow you over there," Ripley said.

Winston and Ripley headed over to the Swordfish warehouse. Monty and Colby rode together and headed over to another major wholesale buyer named Sippy. They parked their buggy and knocked on Sippy's front door.

"Look who it is. How are you guys doing?" Sippy said.

"Hello there, Sippy. I'm good and you?" Monty replied.

"What's going on, Sippy? I'm spades. How about you?" Colby said.

"I'm doing well, chaps. Same old stuff, different day. Come on in," Sippy replied.

"Thanks buddy," Monty said.

"OK, we have a peach of a proposal for you today, Sippy," Colby said.

The three men walked into Sippy's house.

"What kind of proposal?" Sippy replied.

"We have some fresh humpback whale bones, meat, and oil to sell," Colby said.

"A humpback whale huh? That is some grade-A stuff right there," Sippy replied.

"Yes sir. We have tons of it in our warehouse," Monty said.

"Yeah, I could definitely use some of that precious stuff. A lot of my contacts have been asking me for that kind of merchandise lately, and I've been completely out of everything. When can I purchase it?" Sippy replied.

"We can go right now. The merchandise is freshly wrapped, sealed, and ready to go," Colby said.

"What are we waiting for? Let's go," Sippy replied.

"OK, let's head on over there," Monty said.

The three Cape Crusaders climbed into the horse drawn buggies and rode over to the Swordfish warehouse. Derek rode in Wally's buggy as they headed towards the house of another legit businessman and entrepreneur named Dagger.

Dagger was the proprietor of a lumber company called Dagger's Lumber. Wally parked his buggy, and the two Swordfish climbed out. They knocked on Dagger's door.

"Who is it?" Dagger asked.

"It's the Swordfish," Wally replied.

Dagger was very cautious of who he let into his house, because he had lots of money and valuable collectibles inside. Dagger opened the door.

"What do you say, fellas?" Dagger said.

"How you doing, Dagger? It's good to see you," Derek replied.

"Come on in," Dagger said.

"Thanks," Wally replied.

The three business men walked into Dagger's house.

"What can I do for you gentlemen today?" Dagger asked.

"We have some whale products for sale if you're interested. Fresh bones, meat, and oil," Wally said.

"That sounds excellent. What kind of whale is it if you don't mind me asking?" Dagger replied.

"It's not a problem. The merchandise we are selling comes from a humpback whale," Wally said.

"A humpback whale you say? That is a true treasure," Dagger replied.

"Are you interested?" Derek said.

"Sure I am. How soon can I purchase some of this merchandise from you gentlemen?" Dagger replied.

"You can purchase these products right now if you would like to. The merchandise is ready to go from our warehouse," Wally said.

"OK. Let me put on some proper clothes, and we'll take a ride over there," Dagger replied.

"That sounds great Dagger. We'll be waiting for you at the warehouse," Derek said.

"OK. I'll see you fellas there in a New York minute," Dagger replied.

"OK, we'll see you there," Wally said.

Derek and Wally walked out of Dagger's house and climbed into Wally's horse drawn buggy. Then they rode back to the warehouse. Dagger got dressed and headed out towards the warehouse as well. As Derek and Wally arrived at the warehouse, they saw that their crewmates were already there with some customers. Everyone climbed out of their buggies and entered the warehouse.

Dagger arrived shortly after everyone else and entered the warehouse.

"Thank you all for coming. Let us know what we can get for you," Winston said. The Swordfish had a total of 100 casks of whale oil, 150 wrapped meat packages, and 120 bags of bones. Each cask of oil sold for $8, each meat package for $7, and each bag of bones for $6. When all was said and done, the crew should have made a total of $2,570. Each crew member would claim an equal cut of the profit. After it was divided among the five Swordfish, each one would walk away with $514.

"I'll take fifty casks of whale oil, forty meat packages, and twenty-five bags of bones," Dagger said.

"You got it Dagger. That'll come out to $830," Winston replied.

"No problem," Dagger said. Dagger handed Winston $830 in cash.

"It's always a pleasure doing business with you Dagger. You are a loyal and preferred customer to our organization. My crewmates will help you load your merchandise onto your buggy," Winston said.

"It's always a pleasure doing business with the Swordfish as well. Keep me posted on any new merchandise in the future. I'm always interested," Dagger replied.

Derek and Wally loaded up the casks of oil, bags of bones and meat packages onto Dagger's horse drawn buggy.

"Who's next?" Colby said.

"I'll take twenty-five jugs of oil, fifty meat packages, and fifty bags of bones," Sippy said.

"You got it, Sippy. That comes out to $850," Winston replied.

"Here you go, Captain," Sippy said. Sippy handed Winston $850 in cash.

"It's a pleasure doing business with you Sippy. You have always been a loyal customer. My crewmates will help you load the merchandise onto your buggy," Winston replied.

Colby and Monty helped Sippy load the purchased whale products onto his buggy.

"That's another satisfied customer. Who's next?" Winston said.

"I'm the only one left," Ripley replied.

"OK Ripley, what can we do for you?" Winston said.

"I'll take the last twenty-five jugs of oil, sixty meat packages, and forty-five bags of bones," Ripley replied.

"You got it Ripley. That comes out to $890," Winston said. Ripley handed $890 in cash to Winston.

The Swordfish sold all of their whale merchandise and earned a total of $2,570. Colby and Monty helped Ripley load the merchandise onto his buggy. The three customers paid, and their buggies were all loaded up with the whale products. They shook hands with the Swordfish and rode away. The Swordfish counted all the money and divided that by five, so that every member would get his equal cut.

"That was a job well done, Swordfish. Here is everybody's fair share of the profits," Winston said. Winston distributed $514 to his fellow Swordfish and kept $514 for himself.

"That's not a bad day's pay," Colby said.

"You got that right, Captain!" Monty replied. The Swordfish popped open a bottle of whiskey and took some shots to celebrate their successful operation. Then they rode over to the Sandbar to splurge and spend some of their hard-earned money.

Chapter Twenty-Six
The Brawl

The Swordfish arrived at the Sandbar that Sunday night at about 8:00. The Sandbar had a sizable crowd that evening. The Knight Sharks were there drinking heavily and womanizing. Some other whale hunting and fishing crews were there partying as well.

There were lots of attractive women there including Heather, Tiffany, and Molly. The Swordfish walked into the Sandbar and found a table to sit at. Sally came over to take their orders.

"What can I get you guys?" Sally asked.

"Get us all some Stingray beers and some shots of your finest New York whiskey," Winston replied.

"OK. Can I get you fellas anything to eat?" Sally asked.

"What do you have on special for tonight?" Monty replied.

"Tonight's special is all you can eat fried striped sea bass," Sally said.

"OK, I'll have that," Monty replied.

"I'll have the same," Colby said.

"I'll have fish soup and some crab legs," Derek said.

"I'll have the sea bass," Wally said.

"I'll have the sea bass also," Winston said. Sally wrote down the orders.

"OK, I'll be right back with your drinks, and the food should be out shortly," Sally replied.

"Thanks Sally," The Swordfish said.

Sally came right back with their beers and shots of whiskey.

"Cheers to the Swordfish and another successful operation!" Winston said.

"Cheers!" The Swordfish replied. Meanwhile, the Knight Sharks were drinking and partying at another table across the room. Molly was sitting next to Augustus and kissing him from time to time. In the middle of the establishment there was another whale hunting crew called the Sea Wolves eating and drinking at their table. The

Sea Wolves earned their name, because they liked to howl at the full moon when they were out at sea.

Heather and Tiffany spotted the Knight Sharks and walked over to their table to say hello.

"Hi, Clayton. How are you doing?" Heather said.

"Hi, Heather. What a pleasant surprise. I'm doing alright. How are you doing?" Clayton replied.

"It's a pleasant surprise indeed. I'm doing well, thank you," Heather said.

"Hi, Clayton. Where is Polly?" Tiffany said.

"Hello, Tiffany. I'm afraid I have some bad news regarding Polly," Clayton replied.

"What do you mean? What happened?" Tiffany said.

"Polly has passed away. He and Gregory were slayed by the Silver Serpent a little over a week ago," Clayton replied.

"What? Oh my God! That is terrible!" Tiffany said. She burst into tears.

"I'm sorry my dear. We are still mourning ourselves," Clayton replied.

"It was a horrible tragedy. They are gone but never forgotten. They will always be with us in spirit," Ringo said.

"Have a seat. Let us buy you ladies some drinks," Zeus said.

"OK, thank you. I can't believe that Polly is dead. That is truly heartbreaking," Heather replied.

The two ladies sat down at the Knight Shark's table.

"It is crushing. They are in a better place now. What can I get you lovely ladies to drink?" Clayton said.

"I'll take a Long Island iced tea," Heather replied.

"I'll have a Yellow Crab beer," Tiffany said. She was still sobbing.

"OK. Are you ladies hungry?" Clayton replied.

"No, that's okay. We had some dinner at Tiffany's house. Thank you for the offer though," Heather said. Clayton beckoned the waiter, Jack.

"Yes sir, what can I get you?" Jack said.

"Get my two lady friends a Long Island iced tea and a Yellow Crab beer," Clayton replied.

"OK, that's coming right up," Jack said.

"Thanks," Clayton replied.

Jack fetched the drinks.

"Here you go ladies," Jack said.

"Thank you," Heather replied.

"Thank you," Tiffany said.

"Just put that on my tab," Clayton said.

"OK, will do," Jack replied. Rodney raised his beer.

"Here's a toast to our fallen Knight Sharks, Polly and Gregory," Rodney said. The table raised their drinks.

"To Polly and Gregory," the table replied.

Tiffany was still crying over the tragic news.

"It's okay Tiffany. They are in a better place now. They will always live in our hearts and minds," Zeus said.

"I know. It's just so terribly sad. How old were they?" Tiffany replied.

"Gregory was thirty-seven and Polly was thirty-eight," Zeus said.

"That is still relatively young. They could have lived many more years," Tiffany replied.

"You're absolutely right. That damned Silver Serpent has claimed the lives of too many loved ones from our town. It has to be stopped. It's just so immensely difficult to stop such a lethal and malevolent force." Zeus said.

"I hope and pray that someone can bring about that Silver Serpent's demise," Tiffany replied.

"We all do. My name is Zeus. It's nice to meet you," Zeus said.

"I think we met last time, but we were all pretty drunk," Tiffany replied.

"Yeah, that night was kind of a blur," Zeus said.

"It's nice to meet you again, if we might have met last time," Tiffany replied. Zeus laughed.

"OK, that's fair enough," Zeus said.

"That is such horrific news about Polly. He was a great guy. I've heard about that Silver Serpent and how it has been killing lots of members of this community. Isn't there anyone that can slay it?" Tiffany replied.

"A lot of people have tried to slay it, including us, but no one has been successful. It's a devastatingly powerful and cunning beast. We have hit it with all types of firearms and harpoons, including silver harpoons, which are the only weapons that can slay it. The silver harpoon must pierce its heart to slay it," Zeus said.

"I see. So you guys haven't been able to pierce its heart with a silver harpoon yet?" Tiffany replied.

"No. We have been extremely close but no cigar. We have hit it in the head and upper body, but none through its heart," Zeus said.

"Wow. That is amazing. That Silver Serpent sounds like a tough foe to defeat," Tiffany replied.

"That is putting it mildly," Zeus said. Tiffany was still sobbing softly.

"That creature is the devil. It has been slaying and devouring everyone," Augustus said.

"Apparently it hasn't been slaying everyone. The Swordfish are drinking over there. How did they go after it and come back alive? Rodney, go and bring one of them over to our table, so we can talk to them about their latest Silver Serpent expedition," Clayton replied.

"Aye-aye Captain," Rodney said.

Rodney walked over to the Swordfish's table and spoke to their Captain, Winston.

"What can I do for you?" Winston said.

"I was wondering if one of you fellas could come to our table and discuss what you saw on your latest Silver Serpent expedition," Rodney replied.

"Sure. Who do you want to talk to?" Winston said.

"Anyone will do," Rodney replied.

"Monty, go over there and tell them what we saw on our latest expedition," Winston said.

"Aye-aye Captain," Monty replied.

Monty and Rodney walked over to the Knight Shark's table and sat down.

"Who is this, Rodney?" Clayton asked.

"This is Monty. He is going to tell us about his crew's latest Silver Serpent expedition," Rodney replied.

"How's it going? That's no problem. What do you guys want to know?" Monty said.

"How did you fellas come back alive? Did you see the Silver Serpent?" Zeus replied.

"No. We did not see the Silver Serpent or any of his sidekicks. The only sea creature that we saw was a giant great white shark and an enormous humpback whale. We slayed the humpback whale and sold its bones, meat, and oil," Monty said.

"Are you serious? What areas did you explore?" Augustus replied.

"We only went to Boat-Wreck Lane, because that is where we heard the Silver Serpent had been spotted most frequently. We also heard that it had been spotted at Hammerhead Hedge, and Squid Alley, but we did not get to check those areas. We figured since Boat-Wreck Lane was one of the Silver Serpent's main territories, he would discover that we were there and come after us," Monty said.

"That is very odd that the Silver Serpent did not attack your boat considering that is one of its main territories," Clayton replied.

"Maybe it was asleep or in one of its other territories. Or maybe it didn't feel like devouring humans that day. Who knows?" Monty said.

"Only God knows. It definitely has a taste for human blood and is extremely territorial. I think it would have attacked your vessel if it knew it was there," Clayton replied.

"Maybe it has turned over a new leaf and isn't violent towards humans anymore," Monty said.

"I seriously doubt that," Zeus replied.

"Maybe Monty is right. Maybe the Silver Serpent did spot their boat but didn't attack them because of all the wounds he has suffered lately from hunters like us. Maybe it has finally grown weary of waging war against humans," Augustus said.

"I don't know. That sounds kind of fishy," Ringo replied.

"Like I said; the only beasts that we saw were a ferocious great white shark and a massive humpback whale. We slayed the whale and sold its bones, meat, and oil," Monty said.

"I believe you. I'm just shocked that the Silver Serpent didn't attack your boat," Clayton replied.

"Is there anything else that you guys want to know?" Monty asked.

"No, I guess not. Thank you for your time and information," Clayton said.

"OK. I'll see you fellas later," Monty replied. As Monty was walking back to the Swordfish table, he accidentally bumped into one of the Sea Wolves, named Xavier.

"Excuse me," Monty said.

"Why don't you watch where you're going?" Xavier replied smugly.

"It was an accident. Take it easy," Monty said.

"Don't tell me to take it easy. Who the hell are you?" Xavier replied.

"Have another drink buddy," Monty said.

"I ain't your damn buddy," Xavier replied.

Xavier pushed Monty. Monty retaliated and landed a forceful punch, square on Xavier's nose. Blood burst out from his nose like deep-red, cherry syrup. Xavier swung back at Monty and they were in a full-blown, bare-knuckle, bar fight.

"Look, it's Monty! He's in a fight!" Colby exclaimed.

Winston and the Swordfish jumped up from the table and rushed to Monty's aid. Bruno saw the fight and rushed over there to stop it.

"Take that shit outside! Don't disrespect my bar!" Bruno yelled.

Monty and Xavier landed violent blow after blow on each other's faces. Another member of the Sea Wolves, named Ollie, jumped in the fight and punched and kicked Monty. Winston saw that and attacked Ollie. The other Sea Wolves stood up from their table and jumped in the brawl. The Swordfish jumped in as well. The two crews were engaged in a full-blown brawl.

"I said take that shit outside!" Bruno exclaimed.

The brawlers were too concerned with pummeling each other to pay any attention to Bruno's orders. The Knight Sharks obviously saw the raucous rumble, but decided it was not their fight. Xavier grabbed a beer bottle and cracked it over Monty's head. The bottle cut Monty just above his right eye and he started to bleed. Monty grabbed a chair and broke it over Xavier's back with a loud crack. Ollie and Winston squared off and attacked each other like ferocious jungle cats. Winston hit Ollie so hard that he knocked him down. Derek kicked Ollie in the head while he was down. Another member of the Sea Wolves, named Lobo, pulled out his pocketknife and attacked Wally with it. Lobo slashed Wally's chest and sliced a deep gash that oozed blood. Wally pulled out his pocketknife also and shanked Lobo right in the gut. Lobo started to bleed from that cut. There were a total of five Sea Wolves and five Swordfish involved in the barroom brawl, so the odds couldn't have been more even. The bloody and intoxicated gladiators viciously attacked each other and grunted like wild animals. They knocked over tables and chairs in the chaotic process. Customers stood up from their chairs and scampered as they tried to avoid being hit or trampled. Bruno ran frantically over to the Knight Sharks table.

"You guys gotta help me get these maniacs outside before they destroy my bar!" Bruno exclaimed.

"It's too late. They are already fighting. Just let it finish," Clayton replied.

"Oh my God! Those guys are animals!" Molly yelled.

"Tell me about it. Someone is going to get seriously hurt," Tiffany said.

"I think it's exciting," Heather replied.

Inside the tangled knot of sinister Sea Wolves and scrappy Swordfish, they tried their hardest to inflict severe pain on one another. Another member of the Sea Wolves, named Jet, jumped at Colby and punched him right in the mouth. The punch busted Colby's lip and knocked out one of his teeth. The stunned Colby kicked Jet square in the family jewels and temporarily paralyzed him. Then he landed a left hook and right upper-cut that sent Jet crashing to the floor with a loud thump.

Wally and Lobo were hurt and bleeding, but they were still waving their knives at each other. The people in the bar cleared out from that area and some were even leaving. Others stayed there and continued to drink their beverages and observe the brutal and bloody melee from a distance.

"People are starting to leave! This fighting is bad for business! What can we do?" Bruno said.

"Don't you have a pistol in your office?" Clayton replied.

"Yes, I do. I didn't want to use it unless I really had to," Bruno said.

"Just point it at the rowdy bastards and tell them to take it outside," Clayton replied.

"I guess I can do that. I'll be right back," Bruno said.

Bruno rushed to his office and grabbed his black and brown, Browning handgun. He returned with it and pointed it at the brawlers.

"Take that shit outside or I'm gonna start shooting!" Bruno exclaimed. The Sea Wolves and Swordfish stopped fighting for the moment.

"OK, take it easy Bruno. Let's finish this outside," Winston said.

The Sea Wolves and Swordfish caught their breath and headed outside to finish the barbaric battle.

"I told you that would work," Clayton said.

"I didn't want to pull my pistol in my own place of business, but I guess I had to. Those jackals were destroying my bar and causing my customers to leave," Bruno replied.

"Let's go outside and finish watching those maniacs beat the tar out of each other," Zeus said.

"OK, let's go," Heather replied.

The Knight Sharks walked outside with their girlfriends to watch the brawl. Bruno walked outside also and still held his gun. Some of the other customers walked outside to observe the ruckus as well. The Swordfish and the Sea Wolves were going at each other's throats once again. Lobo lunged at Wally with his blade, but Wally dodged his attack and counter attacked by slashing Lobo's throat. Lobo fell to the ground and desperately grasped his critically cut throat. He gurgled on his own warm blood and had the panicked look of imminent death in his eyes.

"They killed Lobo! I'm gonna kill all of you!" Xavier exclaimed.

Xavier pulled out his sharp, pointy stiletto and lunged at Monty.

"Look out Monty!" Derek exclaimed. Monty spotted Xavier from the corner of his eye and dodged his attack. Then Monty regained his balance and tackled Xavier as they both grabbed for the stiletto. Another member of the Sea Wolves, named Cisco, pulled out his brass knuckles and fitted them around his knuckles. Cisco punched Derek square on the jaw with the brass knuckles. Derek felt as though his jaw might have cracked, but he kept on punching Cisco with all his might.

The Sea Wolves and Swordfish were trying hard to rip each other's heads off. The blood continued to gush out of Lobo's throat, and he stopped moving, completely. He was dead. Both crews still battled courageously and vehemently. Monty head butted Xavier and disarmed him. Then they tried to punch each other's lights out. Monty got on top of Xavier and choked him with all his might. He choked him so forcefully that Xavier's face turned red and blue.

"OK, that's enough! Get off of him!" Jet exclaimed.

Monty stopped choking Xavier just before his oxygen ran out completely.

"Do you bastards give up yet?" Winston said.

"Yes, we give up," Xavier said out of breath.

"OK, get the hell outta here before we kill you!" Derek exclaimed.

"You killed Lobo! You sons of bitches are gonna be locked up in cages like animals forever!" Ollie yelled.

"I only did it to save my life! He pulled a blade on me first and cut me first! He kept coming at me with his blade trying to kill me! I didn't want, to but I had to do it! It was self defense for crying out loud!" Wally exclaimed.

"You didn't have to kill him!" Cisco exclaimed.

"He was gonna kill me! I didn't have a choice! It's called self-defense!" Wally replied.

"We are gonna go to the cops!" Xavier said.

"Go ahead and tell the cops! You started this whole calamity in the first place. We will tell the cops that it was self-defense," Monty replied.

"Let's get outta here guys," Jet said.

"Put Lobo's body in the buggy, so we can give him a proper burial. Tomorrow we will drop off Lobo's body at the funeral parlor, and then we'll go to the police department and tell them that these psychos murdered Lobo," Ollie replied.

"Go ahead. Do what you gotta do," Colby said. The Sea Wolves placed Lobo's dead and bloody corpse in one of their buggies and rode away.

The Swordfish walked back inside the bar with Bruno. The Knight Sharks walked back inside the bar with their girlfriends. "You guys better get outta here. If the cops do come by tomorrow, I'll tell them that those maniacs started the fight and that they were the first ones to pull their knives," Bruno said.

"My crew and I will tell the police the same thing if they talk to us about that incident. We saw everything. You guys better get outta here though just in case the Sea Wolves come back with guns," Clayton said.

"You guys are probably right. Thanks a million," Winston replied.

"We better get our stories straight just in case the cops do come to our houses tomorrow," Monty said.

"If the cops do come by our houses tomorrow, we will just tell them the truth. The truth is that the Sea Wolves initiated the fight and pulled a blade first. One of them tried to murder Wally with it. Wally pulled his knife in self-defense and killed that guy Lobo, because he feared for his own life. That's our story and that's the truth," Winston replied.

"OK, that sounds about right," Colby said.

"I got it, fellas. Let's get outta here," Wally replied.

It was about 1:00 in the morning as the Swordfish exited the Sandbar and climbed into their buggies. Then they rode to their houses and showered and washed all the blood off their bruised and battered bodies.

Chapter Twenty-Seven
Cape Crusade P.D.

The next day it was Monday, August 28, 1904 in Cape Crusade. The Sea Wolves dropped Lobo's body off at Morty's Funeral Home and prepared the arrangements. Then they gathered for breakfast at a diner called Bingo's. They ate breakfast with coffee and then rode over to the Cape Crusade Police Department in two buggies. It was about 11:00 am.

The Sea Wolves arrived at the station, parked their buggies, and walked into the police station. They were greeted by Sergeant Darwin.

"How can I help you fellas?" Sergeant Darwin said.

"Some crew called the Swordfish murdered our friend Lobo last night at the Sandbar. They slashed his throat in cold blood," Xavier said.

"They slashed his throat you say? Why did they do that?" Sergeant Darwin replied.

"We were in a brawl at the Sandbar, and one of them pulled out a knife and slashed Lobo's throat with it," Xavier said.

"So he pulled out a knife first? Did any of you fellas have knives on you?" Darwin replied.

"Yes, we always carry blades on us, but nobody pulled them out until one of them did first," Ollie said.

"How many people were involved in this brawl?" Sergeant Darwin replied.

"There were five of us and five of them. Now there are four of us, because they killed Lobo," Jet said.

"Is that all that happened? Is there anything else that I need to know? What started the fight?" Sergeant Darwin replied.

"One of their guys bumped into our Captain, Xavier. After that they started talking shit to each other, and all hell broke loose," Cisco said.

"What did you guys do with your friend's body?" Darwin replied.

"We took him to Morty's Funeral Home and prepared his funeral arrangements," Xavier said.

"You should have left the body there untouched and notified us immediately. It's illegal to tamper with evidence like that. Our investigators are gonna need to examine the body. I'm gonna head over to the Sandbar to get some more answers. First, I'm gonna tell the Chief about this incident," Sergeant Darwin replied.

"We're sorry about that. It's just that last night we were all intoxicated and banged up. We also feared that the Swordfish might have tried to get rid of Lobo's body and cover it up. May we give you our names, addresses, and phone numbers and go home for now, or do you want us to wait here at the station?" Xavier asked.

"The Swordfish would have been in trouble if they did that. Go ahead and give me your personal information, and I will get in contact with you after I question the other party involved in this incident and any other witnesses from the Sandbar," Sergeant Darwin said.

"OK. Thank you for your help Sergeant Darwin," Xavier replied.

The Sea Wolves wrote down their personal contact information on a piece of paper and left the police station. Sergeant Darwin walked into Chief Marble's office and notified him of this most recent incident.

"How's it going Chief? I have a recent and serious incident to report," Sergeant Darwin said.

"It's going just fine Sergeant Darwin. What do you have for me?" Chief Marble replied.

"Some fellas just came in here and reported a homicide. They claim that some sea crew called the Swordfish slashed their friend's throat last night at the Sandbar and killed him," Sergeant Darwin said.

"Did they say why they killed him?" Chief Marble replied.

"They claim that the two crews were involved in a barroom brawl, and one of the combatants pulled out a blade and slashed their friend's throat," Darwin said.

"Did you get the names of the people involved?" Chief Marble replied.

"Yes sir. I had them write down their names, addresses, and phone numbers, so I could contact them after I investigate the murder scene at the Sandbar," Sergeant Darwin said.

"Good job, Sergeant Darwin. Let's head over to the Sandbar right now and get some answers," Chief Marble replied.

"Yes sir, Chief," Sergeant Darwin said.

Chief Marble and Sergeant Darwin walked out of the police station and into their patrol vehicle. Then they rode over to the Sandbar. It was about 12:30 on that overcast and melancholy Tuesday afternoon. They parked their vehicle and entered the Sandbar.

Bruno was there with some customers having lunch.

"Good afternoon officers. How can I help you?" Bruno said.

"Good afternoon. We were informed that there was a murder that took place here last night. What can you tell us about that?" Chief Marble replied.

"I can tell you exactly what happened here last night. I saw everything with my own eyes," Bruno said.

"We appreciate that. What's your name?" Sergeant Darwin replied.

"My name is Bruno Sanders. I am the owner of this establishment," Bruno said.

"OK Bruno. My name is Chief Brad Marble, and this is Sergeant Jericho Darwin. Please enlighten us on the events that took place here last night?" Chief Marble replied.

A crew of whale hunters called the Sea Wolves started a brawl with another crew of whale hunters called the Swordfish. It was getting ugly when one of the Sea Wolves, named Lobo, pulled out a knife and attacked one of the Swordfish, named Wally, with it. Wally pulled out his knife and killed Lobo in self-defense. It was not a premeditated malicious murder. It was a self-defense survival reflex," Bruno said.

"Do you know the names of the Sea Wolves?" Sergeant Darwin replied.

"Yeah, I know their first names but not their last names. They have been coming here for a while now. Their Captain is a man named Xavier. The man that died was a man named Lobo. The others are named Ollie, Cisco, and Jet," Bruno said.

"I recognize those names from the paper they used to write their names down. Are you telling me that those fellas started the brawl and that Lobo was the first one to pull a knife and tried to use deadly force with it?" Sergeant Darwin replied.

"That is exactly what I'm telling you. I'm sure they told you that the Swordfish were the ones to start the brawl and pull out knives first, but that is a lie. It was the other way around. The Sea Wolves initiated the brawl and pulled out their knives first," Bruno said.

"Do you know the names of the Swordfish?" Chief Marble asked.

"Yes. They are some of my most loyal customers and stand up guys. Their names are Winston, Wally, Monty, Derek, and Colby," Bruno replied.

"Do you have their addresses?" Sergeant Darwin asked.

"No, I don't have that information. I've never needed it. They are usually at the docks or out at sea," Bruno replied.

"We're going to have to talk to those guys as well. Were there any other witnesses?" Chief Marble said.

"Their girlfriends also witnessed these unfortunate events. I think their names are Molly, Tiffany, and Heather. Molly lives just a couple of blocks from here in Cape Crusade, and the other two live in Long Island," Bruno said.

"OK, was there anybody else that witnessed that calamity?" Sergeant Darwin replied.

"Oh yes. A fishing crew called the Knight Sharks also witnessed these events. Their names are Augustus, Clayton, Ringo, Rodney, and Zeus. You can usually find them at the docks, too. Some of my other customers witnessed that bloody mayhem also, but I don't have all of their names," Bruno said.

"OK, the Knight Sharks. Where did all of this take place?" Sergeant Darwin asked.

"The brawl started inside the bar and finished outside the bar. Lobo pulled his knife inside the bar and Wally pulled his in self-defense. They slashed each other a couple of times inside the bar. I cleaned up the blood already. The two crews took the fight outside, and that was when Lobo attacked Wally with the knife again.

Wally dodged the attack, and slashed Lobo's throat and killed him," Bruno replied.

"Are you sure you're telling us the truth, because if you're not, that is a crime in itself?" Chief Marble replied.

"I swear on all that's holy that I'm telling you the absolute truth. I have no reason to lie or to protect anybody. I just want justice to be served," Bruno said.

"OK, thank you for your cooperation Bruno. We're going to have to check out a few more places, including the docks," Sergeant Darwin replied.

"They're at the boat docks often, because they're whale hunters. If they aren't launching or docking, they are hunting out at sea," Bruno said.

"Thanks a lot for your time and information. We will be in contact with you if we need any more information," Chief Marble replied.

"No problem officers. Like I said, I just want justice to be served. The Swordfish were innocent in this whole fiasco. Yes, they were involved in the brawl, but it was all in self defense. The Sea Wolves initiated the altercation, and they were the first ones to pull weapons and try to do some critical and lethal damage. One of the Sea Wolves even used brass knuckles," Bruno said.

"OK, we're headed to the boat docks to try and get in contact with the Swordfish. Thanks again for your cooperation and take care," Sergeant Darwin said.

"Have a good one," Chief Marble said.

"Thanks officers. Likewise," Bruno replied.

Chief Marble and Sergeant Darwin exited the Sandbar and climbed into their patrol car. They rode over to the boat docks. It was about 1:30 in the afternoon. Thick, gray clouds loomed in and covered the somber sky like infinite patches of smoke.

The police officers arrived at the boat docks and saw that there were some whale hunters and fishing crews loading and unloading their boats. The Swordfish and the Knight Sharks were there preparing to venture out into the ocean. The police officers approached the Knight Sharks and introduced themselves.

"Good afternoon gentlemen. My name is Chief Brad Marble, and this is Sergeant Jericho Darwin. We would like to ask you guys some questions," Chief Marble said.

"OK, that's no problem," Clayton replied.

"Do you guys know of a whale hunting crew called the Swordfish?" Sergeant Darwin asked.

"Sure we do. They are right over there," Clayton replied.

"Is this about that brawl at the Sandbar last night?" Augustus asked.

"Yes it is. How do you guys know about that?" Chief Marble replied.

"We were there to witness it," Zeus said.

"Is your crew called the Knight Sharks? What did you guys witness last night?" Sergeant Darwin asked.

"Yes it is. The Sea Wolves initiated the altercation, and they were the first ones to pull their weapons out. Two of them pulled out blades and another used brass knuckles," Rodney said.

"That's exactly what Bruno said. I trust that you fellas are telling the truth and aren't just protecting the Swordfish," Chief Marble replied.

"That's the God's honest truth. We have no reason to lie, and we barely met the Swordfish the other day. They just acted in self-defense," Clayton said.

"OK. That matches Bruno's story. Thank you gentlemen. We're gonna go talk to the Swordfish. What are your names?" Sergeant Darwin replied.

"No problem officers. We're glad to be of help. I'm the Captain of the Knight Sharks, Clayton. And this is Augustus, Ringo, Rodney, and Zeus," Clayton said.

"OK, thanks again gentlemen. Good luck with your whale hunting," Chief Marble replied.

The officers walked over to the Swordfish and introduced themselves. The Swordfish were doing some maintenance on their boat.

"Good afternoon, gentlemen. My name is Chief Marble, and this is Sergeant Darwin. We are with the Cape Crusade Police Department," Chief Marble said.

"Good afternoon, officers. What can we do for you?" Winston replied.

"Were you guys involved in a brawl at the Sandbar last night?" Sergeant Darwin asked.

"Unfortunately, yes. Some maniacs called the Sea Wolves started a scuffle with us and pulled out blades and brass knuckles," Winston replied.

"That is what we heard. We also heard that a man named Lobo was killed," Chief Marble said.

"Yes, that's the guy that pulled out his blade on me and tried to kill me," Wally replied.

"What did you do when he did that?" Sergeant Darwin asked.

"I pulled out my pocketknife and slashed his throat," Wally replied.

"So you acted in self-defense, because you feared for your life. That is not a crime," Chief Marble said.

"I didn't want to kill him, but I had no choice. If I didn't kill him, he would have killed me or one of my crewmates," Wally replied.

"What started this whole tussle?" Sergeant Darwin asked.

"I was walking back to my table, and one of their goons, named Xavier, bumped into me and pushed me. He started to swing at me, so I punched him," Monty replied.

"How did it turn into a full-blown brawl?" Sergeant Darwin asked.

"After Xavier and I started squabbling, our crews took notice and decided to jump in as well. Whale hunting crews always protect their own at all costs," Monty replied.

"Your story matches all of the other witnesses' stories. We just need to take care of a couple of other things," Chief Marble said.

"We are also going to inform the Sea Wolves that they shouldn't go around starting barroom brawls, and they shouldn't pull out deadly weapons on people. They are lucky we don't throw the book at them for disorderly conduct, assault, and tampering with evidence," Sergeant Darwin replied.

"Thank you for your understanding, officers. If there is anything else we can help you with, don't hesitate to ask," Winston replied.

"Thanks for your time, and be careful on the water. I've been hearing horrific stories about the Silver Serpent," Sergeant Darwin said.

"Thanks officers. We will. The sad part is that those stories are true," Zeus replied.

Chief Marble and Captain Darwin left the boat docks and headed back to the station to pick up the piece of paper with the Sea Wolves' contact information. They also looked up Molly Thompson's address while they were there. Then they climbed back into their patrol vehicle and rode to Molly's house. Molly's story was identical to Bruno's, the Knight Sharks, and the Swordfish. That was enough for them to realize that it was true and that the Swordfish acted in self defense.

After they thanked Molly for her cooperation, they headed to Xavier's house. Xavier lived in a house on the bay side of Cape Crusade. Chief Marble and Sergeant Darwin parked their patrol unit and knocked on Xavier's door. Xavier answered.

"Hello, Officers. Glad to see you again. What did you find out?" Xavier said.

"We found out that you and your crew were the ones that started the brawl and were the first ones to pull out weapons. That makes the Swordfish's actions justifiable, because they were in self-defense," Chief Marble replied.

"What the hell are you talking about? A friend of mine was murdered last night, and you want to say that we are responsible? What kind of justice is that?" Xavier said.

"We are sorry that your friend lost his life, but we have based our decision on identical information from multiple eye witnesses that were at the scene. All of them said that you and your crew started the ruckus and that Lobo was the first one that pulled out a deadly weapon and used it. You are lucky that we don't charge you and your crew with disorderly conduct, assault, and tampering with evidence," Sergeant Darwin replied.

"What witnesses have you talked to?" Xavier asked.

"We talked to multiple witnesses at the scene of the brawl from beginning to end," Chief Marble replied.

"Do you have any names?" Xavier said.

"Yes we do, but that doesn't matter now, and it's not your job to ask the questions," Sergeant Darwin replied.

"I think it does matter. What if I want to take this matter to court?" Xavier said.

"Do whatever you want to do. We have made our lawful decision to not file any charges based on matching information from multiple sources that witnessed the event," Chief Marble replied.

"That is some bullshit! I'm gonna take this matter to court!" Xavier said.

"Do what you have to do. Nobody will be charged in this situation, unless you want us to charge you and your crew with all of the previously mentioned charges. You're lucky we haven't done that yet, but you're pressing your luck," Sergeant Darwin replied.

"I heard from multiple sources that you were the one that started the brawl in the first place," Chief Marble said.

"That is bullshit! Everything that you heard was a lie! You haven't heard the last of me!" Xavier exclaimed.

"That's it! I've heard enough out of you. I was willing to give you a break, since your friend died and since it was a drunken barroom brawl, but you couldn't keep your mouth shut. I'm taking you in and charging you with disorderly conduct, assault, and tampering with evidence. Cuff him Sergeant Darwin," Chief Marble said.

"Yes sir, Chief. Put your hands behind your back Xavier," Sergeant Darwin said. Sergeant Darwin cuffed Xavier and told him that he was under arrest.

"This is bullshit! You can't get away with this! I was just making sure that Lobo received a proper burial and wasn't buried or thrown in the ocean by the Swordfish! You'll be hearing from my lawyer you lousy pigs!" Xavier exclaimed

"Bark all you want. It doesn't do you a bit of good now. Let's take him to the station and book him, Sergeant. Then we'll head over to the funeral parlor to observe Lobo's body," Chief Marble said.

"Yes sir, Chief," Sergeant Darwin replied. Xavier was still running his mouth and shouting obscenities at the officers. The officers escorted Xavier to their patrol vehicle and roughly placed him inside. Then they headed back to the station and booked him.

Chapter Twenty-Eight
Slick and Zelda Relocate

The next day rolled around and it was Tuesday, August 29, 1904. Slick woke up next to his beloved Zelda.

"Good morning, my love. How are you doing?" Slick said.

"Good morning, my sexy serpent. I'm feeling lucky and blessed to have found love again, with you. How are you doing?" Zelda replied.

"I feel the same way, darling. I'm kind of hungry though," Slick said.

"You're always hungry, Slick. That's good because I'm always hungry too. What should we devour for breakfast? Zelda said.

"Let's go outside and see what there is," Slick replied.

"OK, let's go," Zelda said.

The two Silver Serpents swam outside of Slick's cave to view the sea life that was around to put in their bellies. It was about 10:00 am and the ardent, yellow sun was gleaming through the dazzling, indigo water. There were some barracudas and some whiptail stingrays swimming around a plush coral reef just outside of Slick's cave.

"Look at those ripe barracudas. Let me snatch some for us," Slick said.

"OK. Do you need any help?" Zelda replied.

"Why don't you snag some of those stingrays, while I slay the barracudas?" Slick said.

"I can do that," Zelda replied.

"Let's get'em," Slick said.

The two Silver Serpents darted after their prey like the precise predators that they were. Slick snatched some fresh barracuda in his jaws and claws. They tried to wriggle free, but Slick clamped his lethal jaws shut and crushed them into jelly. He skewered the other ones with his claws. He devoured three of them and saved the other three for Zelda. Zelda snapped her jaws down on one large whiptail ray and slashed another one's head in half with her claws. They both died on the spot. She devoured one of them and saved the other one for Slick.

The two Silver Serpents met and exchanged the prey that they had slain for one another. They devoured their meals and kissed each other.

"When would you like to relocate to our new home, my love?" Zelda asked.

"We can do it today if you like?" Slick replied.

"That sounds ideal. Is there anything from your cave that you would like to take with you?" Zelda said.

"Yes, definitely. I'll take my treasure chests and my jars of emerald sea weed. They are much too valuable to leave behind for some other creature to steal, " Slick replied.

"OK. We can leave whenever you would like to," Zelda said.

"I'm gonna miss this place," Slick replied.

"I know my love, but we will be even happier and safer in our new home. Just wait and see. We must keep our everlasting faith in the almighty Sea God. If we do that, he will reward us with guidance, love, strength, protection, and wisdom," Zelda said.

"We most definitely will my love. We should stop by Bo's place on our way, so I can give him the news," Slick replied.

"That is a grand idea my love. I know how close you two are," Zelda said.

"Let's head out now then. Where would you like to go after we visit Bo?" Slick replied.

"I was thinking we should head northwest towards Oyster Island. There is a plethora of prey there and hardly any whale or serpent hunters," Zelda said.

"I've heard about Oyster Island. I heard there are tons of oysters there. Won't the oyster fishermen see us and inform the hunters about us?" Slick replied.

"I don't think so. We will try our best to remain out of their sight as much as possible," Zelda said.

"OK. I guess we can do that," Slick replied.

"Let's be on our way then. Gather your treasure chests and jars of emerald seaweed," Zelda said.

"OK. Let me collect them. Would you help me carry them?" Slick replied.

"Of course, my love," Zelda replied. The two Silver Serpents swam inside the cave and collected two treasure chests and four jars of emerald seaweed.

"Are you ready to go?" Zelda asked.

"Yes. First, let's pay Bo a visit, so we can inform him about our plans to relocate. In case he ever needs to contact me," Slick replied.

"OK Slick. Let's get going," Zelda said.

The two Silver Serpents headed out towards Bo's place near Hammerhead Hedge. It took them about fifteen minutes to arrive there. The Silver Serpents were exceptionally fast swimmers. Slick signaled and alerted Bo of his arrival.

Bo was devouring swarms of copepods when he heard his friend's familiar sonar signal. He followed the signal and found the two, mighty and majestic Silver Serpents.

"What's going on, my dear serpent friends?" Bo asked.

"How you doing, Bo? I came by today to let you know that Zelda and I are relocating to Oyster Island," Slick replied.

"So you weren't joking about relocating? How far is Oyster Island from here?" Bo said.

"It's about five hours northwest of here. I'm not sure about the exact mileage," Zelda replied.

"That is quite a swim from here. I sure am gonna miss both of you," Bo said.

"You should come with us," Slick replied.

"I don't know. This territory has been my home all of my life," Bo said.

"I know how you feel. Take some time and think it over. If you need to contact me, you know where to find me. I'm gonna miss you too Bo. You have been my best friend my entire life and you will always be my best friend. You hold a special place in my heart, my brother," Slick replied.

"You're my best friend too, Slick, and my brother. We have been through it all together. I'll think it over. Regardless of my decision, you will see me in the future. Even if I don't decide to relocate out there, I will still go visit you two from time to time," Bo said.

"That sounds splendid Bo. I'll see you later then," Slick replied.

"See you later my brother. Take care of Zelda, and take care of yourself. Try and stay away from the hunters and their harpoons," Bo said.

"I'll try. Take care of yourself as well my brother," Slick replied.

"See you later, Bo. Take care," Zelda said.

"See you later, Zelda. Take care of my brother for me," Bo replied. After all the goodbyes were said, Slick and Zelda headed northwest towards Oyster Island. They knew it would be a long journey, but they were content and relaxed in each other's company.

The first place they came across was Sailfish Point. A territory that was abundant in Sailfish and other sea life. It was located about one hour northwest of Hammerhead Hedge. The Silver Serpents stopped there for a quick bite to eat. They each caught and devoured a sailfish for some fresh fuel in their tanks. After that, they continued northwest on their journey toward Oyster Island.

Silver Serpents were excellent travelers and could slash and dash through the water like finely tuned machines. They also had extraordinary endurance that enabled them to cover vast distances. Slick and Zelda were shredding through the pristine, refreshing Atlantic water like gargantuan, silver torpedoes. They swam for another two hours and stopped for another quick breather at an area known as Albatross Landing.

That place earned its name because of a boozer pirate, named Yellow Beard. He swore he saw an albatross flying around his ship at nighttime. His crewmates never saw it, so they didn't believe him. They thought he was losing his mind from drinking too much rum and from being out at sea for too long. It was never seen in the daytime. Finally, one night, Yellow Beard shot the creepy albatross down with his shotgun. He retrieved the dead, floating bird with a net and showed it to his crew. Then he cooked it and served it up to them for dinner. After that, his crew finally believed him, but his ship became cursed, and it sank. All the pirates either drowned or were devoured by sharks. That spot was marked with Yellow Beard's sunken ship. All of the sunken pirate's treasure had been looted by humans many years ago.

"Wow! I remember my father told me stories about Yellow Beard's ship when I was a young Silver Serpent. It's incredible to see it with my own eye," Slick said.

"I heard about it also," Zelda replied.

"This looks like a nice spot to take a breather. Let's check out that sunken ship," Slick said.

"OK," Zelda replied.

The two sheeny Silver Serpents took their time gliding around the sunken ship and took in its enticing aura and charm. The sunken pirate ship had been stripped of all its treasures, trinkets, and artifacts. The only items that remained were some old rum bottles made of yellow glass. They were left there in homage of Yellow Beard and his crew.

"This used to be a mighty pirate ship, and now it's just a sunken ruin. Time manages to send everyone and everything to our inevitable fates," Slick said.

"That is so true, my love. Time defeats all creations eventually. No man nor creature leaves this savage planet alive," Zelda replied.

"Old Yellow Beard's sunken pirate ship is quite a sight though. A real, sunken, pirate ship. Just to see it up close and know the true story behind it makes it an extra special treat," Slick said.

"I'm glad you are enjoying it my love. I love to see you happy," Zelda replied.

"I am happy. I'm happy to be starting a new life with the love of my life, you, Zelda," Slick said.

"I feel the same way. I'm glad that our destinies have brought us together. Now we can be together forever," Zelda replied.

"That's right. I'm glad that you feel the same way as I do. We can build a better and brighter future for each other, together," Slick said.

The two Silver Serpents planted some forceful and passionate kisses on each other with their eager, forked tongues.

"Are you hungry yet? I'm getting kind of hungry again," Zelda replied.

"I could devour something," Slick said.

"Let's find something to devour around here," Zelda said.

"OK. I've heard that there are lots of nurse sharks in this area. Let's find some," Slick replied.

"Nurse sharks sound delicious! Let's find some to sink our teeth into," Zelda said.

The Silver Serpents patrolled that area and hunted for nurse sharks or any other kind of sea life that they could devour. They spotted a gam of nurse sharks ravaging a whale cadaver.

"There they are. Let's go get'em," Slick said.

"OK, I'm right beside you," Zelda replied.

The two Silver Serpents stealthily stalked the shiver of toothy nurse sharks. When they got close enough, they torpedoed their bodacious bodies at their targets with their brutal jaws wide open. They successfully clamped down on two nurse sharks each in their jaws of death. The Silver Serpents chomped down mightily on the sharks with devastating force and chewed them up. They completely devoured four nurse sharks in a flash.

"That hit the spot. Let's continue swimming towards our new piece of paradise at Oyster Island," Slick said.

"OK Slick. I'm with you all the way," Zelda replied.

The two Silver Serpents swam northwest toward Oyster Island. They were only about an hour away at that point. Slick and Zelda arrived at Oyster Island in exactly one hour. The time was about 7:00 pm.

The fiery, blood-red sun set on the grape colored horizon in the west.

"We are here. Isn't it dreamy and spectacular?" Zelda said.

"Yes, it most definitely possesses a charming atmosphere. Let's look for a clandestine cave that we can call our home," Slick replied.

"There must be some fabulous caves around here. We just have to keep our eyes out for the right one," Zelda said.

"You mean, keep my eye out. We need to swim deeper to find the caves," Slick replied.

"I'm sorry Slick. I didn't mean for it to come out like that. Let's swim deeper then," Zelda said. Slick chuckled.

"It's okay darling. No offense taken," Slick replied.

The Silver Serpents dove down deeper into the Atlantic's dark, icy-blue water. They spotted an enticing cave located around some imposing towers of forest-green and mustard-yellow sea vegetation.

"That's a marvelous cave. Let's swim inside of it and check it out," Slick said.

"OK. I'm right behind you," Zelda replied.

They swam inside the cave together. It was a good-sized cave with lots of seaweed and kelp along its edges.

"This is perfect. Let's move into this one," Slick said.

"I like it too," Zelda replied.

All of a sudden, a giant, yellow squid popped out from a hole inside the side wall of the mysterious cave.

"What are you doing in my cave?" The giant squid demanded to know. Slick wasted no time and attacked the giant squid. The squid sprayed its ink at Slick's face and attempted to vanish. The fearsome squid's oily, black ink felt and tasted like harsh, bitter chemicals on Slick's face and tongue.

Slick grabbed the squid with his upper limbs and stuck his blade-like claws into the squid's googly eyeballs. The squid attempted to wrap his tentacles around Slick's head, but Slick pulverized them into jam with his lethal rows of dagger-like teeth. Then Slick ripped the squid in half with his upper limb's claws and devoured it's bloody, inky, twitching body, guts and all.

"Now this cave officially belongs to us," Slick said proudly.

"It sure does. Thanks for getting rid of that horrid creature," Zelda replied.

"No problem. It tastes pretty good besides the ink," Slick said.

Zelda giggled and tasted the rubbery flesh of the squid for herself.

"Let's make ourselves comfortable. Let's make our bed out of spongy kelp and seaweed, so we may lay down next to each other for a while," Zelda replied.

"Good idea. I'm rather spent from our journey," Slick said.

"I am too," Zelda replied.

The Silver Serpents lovers gathered some cushy and colorful kelp and seaweed and made an enormous and comfy bed to lay in. Then Slick placed his two treasure chests and four jars of emerald seaweed in some large, jagged crevasses in the stony, cave wall. Then the Silver Serpent couple flopped into their heavenly bed of kelp and seaweed and dozed off for a while. They awoke at midnight in their new residential cave.

"Let's go outside and explore our new territory," Slick said.

"OK," Zelda replied.

They swam outside the cave and explored. Outside of their new cave there were lots of oyster beds, seaweed, kelp, and colorful coral reefs. It was an ideal environment for predators and potential prey. They swam up to the solemn surface and stuck their heads out of the glossy, obsidian water. They marveled at a little, remote island that was decorated with great, big, twisted trees and oddly shaped boulders.

"That must be Oyster Island. It's so magnificent and majestic," Zelda said.

"I know. It's like a Silver Serpent's heaven. We have everything we need here," Slick replied.

Chapter Twenty-Nine
The Oyster Island Boats

Another day's luminous sun presented itself over the expansive Atlantic, and it was Wednesday, August 30, 1904. Slick and Zelda awoke after a solid night's slumber and ventured outside their new cave. They swam to the surface and stuck their heads above the water. The fresh Atlantic sea air felt invigorating on their tough, scaly faces. Silver Serpents had a special cardiovascular system that enabled them to breathe underwater and out of water. The beaming, marigold sun was set high in the puffy, cumulus cloud covered sky.

The seagulls dove down into the water and attempted to catch jumbo white shrimp. Slick spotted a boat coming their way.

"Look Zelda. There is a boat coming toward us," Slick said.

"Let's descend further below the surface, so they can't see us," Zelda replied.

"Don't worry about it. I want to see who they are," Slick said.

"Why? So they can fire their harpoons and guns at you?" Zelda replied.

"No. So I can see who they are and what they do in this territory," Slick said.

"OK. I just don't want to see you get hurt again, my love," Zelda replied.

"Relax my darling. Don't worry so much. We'll be fine," Slick said.

"OK. I trust you," Zelda replied.

The boat approached closer and closer. Finally, it reached Oyster Island. It was an oyster boat named *The Sea Gem*. The Silver Serpents were about 150 yards away and they stuck their heads slightly above the surface.

"We better get out of here before they see us," Zelda said.

"We'll be just fine. They can't see us from all the way over there. Plus, the heavy current is making the water nice and choppy, so that helps to camouflage us even more," Slick replied.

"Are you sure about that?" Zelda said.

"Yes. You can go back to the cave if you don't feel safe here, my love. I don't want you to ever feel unsafe or uncomfortable," Slick replied.

"I think I will do that. I'll see you later, my love. Please be careful, Slick," Zelda said.

"OK Zelda. I won't be too long. I'll see you soon," Slick replied.

Zelda swam back to the cave. Slick decided to swim a little bit closer to the oyster boat. Nefarious, cumulonimbus clouds covered the bleak, gunmetal-gray skyline as it rained. The wind picked up and it created lively swells in the ocean. That was great for Slick's sake, because it made him harder to see. Slick reached within about fifty yards of the oyster boat. He saw them drop the oyster dredges into the water. The long-toothed bars attached to chain bags and lines, hit the ocean floor.

Slick was curious as to how the oyster dredges worked, so he swam closer to them to investigate. He observed how they were dragged across the oyster beds to collect the spoils of the sea, such as; oysters, scallops, crabs, clams, and sea cucumbers. Slick swam up to the surface to see if he could spot how many people were on the boat.

He stuck his spiky head above the tumultuous water and looked at the boat. He spotted about five or six people on the boat's deck. Slick observed them for about fifteen minutes as they dragged their dredges along the ocean floor and collected oysters and other varieties of edible sea life.

All of a sudden, another smaller fishing boat came out of nowhere. The fitful winds were whaling so loud, and the turbulent waters were so choppy that Slick did not see or hear the smaller fishing boat headed in his direction. One of the three fishermen on the small fishing boat spotted Slick's silvery head sticking above the water and his gargantuan body underwater. Slick spotted the fishermen too and dove deeper into the colder waters.

"Jumping Jellyfish! I just saw the Silver Serpent!" Alfonse exclaimed.

Alfonse was one of the fishermen on the small fishing boat named *The Trident*. The other two fishermen's names were Clarence and Seymour.

"Are you sure? There hasn't been a Silver Serpent spotted in these waters in decades," Seymour replied.

"I'm positive! I saw its gigantic body with a serpent's head and a serpent's tail. It was Silver with blue and green scales!" Alfonse said.

"Get a hold of yourself man. You've been in the sun for too long," Clarence replied.

"I'm dizzy and nauseated from these violent swells, but I know what I saw. As far as being in the sun for too long, what sun? It looks like a wicked storm is about to hit us," Alfonse said.

"The sun was out earlier when we set out here," Clarence replied.

"Nobody has seen a Silver Serpent in these waters for years. Why would a Silver Serpent suddenly appear in these waters?" Seymour said.

"I don't know. Maybe they migrate sometimes. I know that was a Silver Serpent. What else could it have been?" Alfonse replied.

"I don't believe you man," Clarence said.

"I don't either. You are probably just sea sick," Seymour replied.

"You guys have to believe me. Why would I lie to you fellas? You are my friends and my crewmates," Alfonse said.

"I don't know. To have a laugh maybe," Clarence replied.

"First of all, I'm not in the joking mood. Secondly, I would never joke about something like that," Alfonse said.

"Maybe you were just seeing things. Long hours at sea can do that to the mind sometimes," Seymour replied.

"How many times do I have to tell you that I wasn't seeing things? That was as real as anything I've ever seen!" Alfonse said.

"I don't know bud. That Silver Serpent legend has always been an enigma around these parts, because nobody we know has ever seen one. The only ones that have seen a Silver Serpent are dead by now," Clarence replied.

"What if Alfonse is telling the truth? If there really is a Silver Serpent lurking in these waters, we have to warn everybody before it does something devastating," Seymour said.

"That's right Seymour. I'm telling the truth by the way. We must warn everyone, and we must be prepared with harpoons as well. The Silver Serpent could demolish this boat and devour us in seconds," Alfonse replied.

"I don't know about all of that man. If you are telling the truth, then we have to warn everybody. We should also get the hell outta here before it comes back," Clarence said.

"I'm with Clarence. Let's hightail it outta here before that monster comes back. We are unarmed and helpless in a small boat. That beast would annihilate us in no time at all," Alfonse replied.

"Are you sure you fellas want to leave here based on something that Alfonse thinks he saw? We came all the way out here to fish, and now that we're here, you fellas want to leave?" Seymour said.

"For the last time I know what my eyes saw, damnit! It was the Silver Serpent! Let's get the hell outta dodge before we end up in its belly!" Alfonse exclaimed.

"Yes, let's book it. If the Silver Serpent does come back, we are history. It's better to be safe than sorry," Clarence said.

"I say that we stay out here and fish, but it's two against one. Let's go," Seymour replied.

"Wise decision Seymour. I'm telling you that creature was enormous," Alfonse said.

The Trident cranked up its motor and headed back to shore. The fishermen were disappointed that they didn't get to fish for very long, but they felt confident that they made the right decision. They knew in their hearts that if Silver Serpents existed, they were surely nothing they wanted to tangle with. At first, they thought that Alfonse was lying or seeing things that weren't there, but after they observed the look of pure fear his eyes, they figured that he was telling the truth.

The Trident headed back to shore, but the Sea Gem continued to collect oysters and other fruits of the sea with its dredges. Slick swam back to his cave to relax for a while. He entered his cave to find his beloved Zelda taking a nap on their gummy, kelp bed.

Slick lied down next to her and closed his eyes. He fell asleep and dreamed of the gruesome battles he has had with the humans through the years. Slick missed those days of battle, blood, and glory and he wished he could do it again, but he made a promise to his love, Zelda, that he wouldn't. He was going to try his hardest to keep his word. The Silver Serpents cuddled next to each other and took a divine nap for a couple of hours that afternoon.

They awoke in the evening and made love to each other. Then they headed outside of their cave to find some dinner. The Sea Gem headed back to shore with its plentiful bounty of oysters, clams, crabs, scallops, and sea cucumbers. The heavy rain, wind, and thunder passed. It was a crisp and refreshing night at Oyster Island with the chalky, crescent moon shining high above everything else in the raven sky. There were no boats around. Slick and Zelda had it all to themselves for now, and they knew that and cherished it.

Chapter Thirty
The Vultures

The next day came around and it was Thursday, August 31, 1904. Alfonse awoke at his house and decided to head down to the bait shop that he worked at. The bait shop was called The Bait Bucket. It was located in the harbor town of Cape Carnivore in Long Island, N.Y.

Alfonse jumped into his horse drawn buggy and rode down to The Bait Bucket. He parked his buggy and walked inside.

"Good morning. How is everyone doing?" Alfonse said.

"I'm doing well. How are you doing?" Sonya replied. Sonya was another employee at The Bait Bucket.

"Is Tony around?" Alfonse asked. Tony was the owner of The Bait Bucket.

"Yeah, he's in the back. Let me go get him," Sonya replied.

Sonya walked to the back room and notified Tony that Alfonse was looking for him. Tony walked into the store from the back room and greeted Alfonse.

"How's it going, Alfonse?" Tony asked.

"I'm good. I came here today, because I have some vital news that I need to share with you," Alfonse replied.

"What is the news that you have to tell me?" Tony asked.

"I saw a Silver Serpent yesterday when we were out fishing. It was monstrous and fearsome looking," Alfonse replied.

"You saw a Silver Serpent? Are you serious, or are you pulling my chain?" Tony said.

"I'm dead serious. It was at least 150 feet long," Alfonse replied.

"Where did you see that beast?" Tony said.

"I saw it at Oyster Island. It had an enormous, silver body with ferocious spikes and dazzling, blue and green scales. It dove down into the deeper waters as soon as it saw our boat," Alfonse replied.

"If what you are telling me is true, we have to do something," Tony said.

"I agree. I know a whale hunting crew called the Vultures. They are also serpent hunters, so they will definitely take advantage of an opportunity like this," Alfonse said.

"Where can we find the Vultures?" Tony replied.

"They like to hang out at a bar called the Electric Eel. We can find them there," Alfonse said. Alfonse and Tony left The Bait Bucket and climbed into Alfonse's horse drawn buggy. They rode to the Electric Eel, parked their buggy, and walked into the bar.

The Vultures were sitting at the bar and enjoying some drinks. There were four of them. They earned their name, because they never let any portion of their meals go to waste. They picked the bones clean, just like Vultures. Alfonse and Tony walked up to them.

"How's it going, fellas? My name is Alfonse, and this is my friend, Tony," Alfonse said.

"I'm doing okay. How are you doing?" Micah replied. Micah was the Captain of the Vultures.

"I'm doing alright. I have some news that you might want to hear," Alfonse said.

"What news would that be?" Creepy replied. Creepy was another member of the Vultures.

"I saw a Silver Serpent yesterday at Oyster Island," Alfonse said.

"Are you serious? A Silver Serpent hasn't been spotted around these waters in decades," Wilson replied. Wilson was another member of the Vultures.

"Of course I'm serious. Why would I lie about something like that? I heard that a wealthy sea captain from Staten Island, named Captain Golden, is offering a $10,000 reward to the slayers of the Silver Serpent," Alfonse said.

"Wow! A real Silver Serpent! We should attempt to slay the Silver Serpent for ten grand," Vincent replied. Vincent was another member of the Vultures.

"That's why we came to you guys. We were hoping that you would say that," Tony said.

"Sure. We'll slay the Silver Serpent and claim that bounty. Then we'll bask in the fame and glory as legendary heroes. We will go after it first thing tomorrow morning," Micah replied.

"That is great news! I know that if anybody can slay that beast, it is you mighty warriors," Alfonse said.

"No problem. We'll venture out to Oyster Island tomorrow. We just need to buy some silver harpoons. I heard that those are the only weapon that can slay it," Micah replied.

"I heard they sell those at The Flying Fish," Tony said.

The Flying Fish was a deep-sea fishing store.

"Yeah, I know that they sell silver harpoons at the Flying Fish. I saw some there just the other day," Creepy replied.

"I really hope that you guys can slay that beast and claim that reward. I would hate to hear about anybody from our own town slayed by the Silver Serpent," Alfonse said.

"I definitely believe that we can slay it. We are some of the best whale and serpent hunters in all the seven seas," Wilson replied.

"I believe it. I've heard that you fellas are the best in the business. Let's have a drink and toast the demise of the Silver Serpent," Alfonse said.

The Vultures ordered a round of beers for themselves and for Alfonse and Tony.

"How long have you fellas been whale and serpent hunting?" Tony replied.

"We've been in the sea hunting business for about ten years. We are all thirty something, and we started when we were in our twenties. In those ten years we've only seen one serpent. It wasn't a Silver Serpent, but it was most definitely a wicked serpent. It was blood-red with onyx-black scales, and it had fierce eyes that sparkled like polished emeralds. We called it the Red Serpent. We slayed it and mounted its head in our cabin. Very few people have actually seen the head though. That Red Serpent's mounted head is a sacred and prized possession to us, Vultures," Micah said.

"Wow! How did you guys find it and slay it?" Alfonse replied. We encountered it at Oyster Island hunting for prey. We slayed it by firing a bronze harpoon through its heart," Creepy said.

"That's astonishing. Did it die immediately?" Tony replied.

"Almost immediately. It thrashed about for a couple of seconds before it died. It wasn't going too far with a harpoon through its heart. It was a perfect shot. I was the one that fired it," Wilson said proudly.

"That's absolutely incredible! I'd like to congratulate your crew on that astounding feat and you have my sincerest admiration. Your crew has slayed a serpent before. That is good to know," Alfonse said.

"Yes, we sure have. It wasn't a Silver Serpent, but it was gargantuan and menacing. It had slayed some citizens from right here in Cape Carnivore that year. We felt obligated to protect our community, so we hunted it down and terminated it," Micah replied.

The bartender brought beers for everyone.

"Cheers to the death of the Silver Serpent!" Micah toasted.

"Cheers!" everyone replied. Alfonse and Tony drank a couple of beers with the Vultures and then left.

The Vultures stuck around the Electric Eel for a while drinking beer, and then they headed over to the Flying Fish to buy some silver harpoons. They bought five silver harpoons along with some food, water, and alcohol for their expedition. Then they rode home to get some rest.

Alfonse stopped by his crew's favorite watering hole, The Willow Tree. He arrived there and saw two of his crewmates, Clarence and Seymour, sitting down at a table having some drinks.

"What's going on, knuckleheads?" Alfonse asked.

"We're just taking a load off and having some drinks," Clarence replied.

"That's just grand. I could use a drink or two right about now," Alfonse said.

"How's it going, Alfonse? Did you tell anybody about the Silver Serpent yet?" Seymour asked.

"Yeah, I told a group of whale and serpent hunters called the Vultures. They have slayed a serpent before, and are rumored to be some of the best hunters around these parts. I also told them about the $10,000 bounty that Captain Golden put on the table. They are in," Alfonse replied.

"Is that so? They must be the real deal if they've slayed a sea serpent before," Clarence replied.

"That's what they said. It wasn't a Silver Serpent though. The Vultures said it was mostly red with black. They called it the Red Serpent. They slayed it by piercing its heart with a bronze harpoon," Alfonse said.

"That's interesting. Well at least they have one serpent kill under their belts. Did they look like straight shooters to you?" Seymour replied.

"Yeah those fellas seemed sharp as blades and looked tough as nails. I really believe that they can do it," Alfonse said.

"Great. When are they going after it?" Clarence said.

"The Vultures said that they would head out after the Silver Serpent first thing tomorrow morning. They just needed to buy some silver harpoons and some other supplies," Alfonse replied.

"That is fantastic news Alfonse. I'm glad that you spread the word to some real hunters that are capable of slaying that sea devil," Seymour said.

"I'm glad too. That monster needs to be destroyed before it claims the lives of any people from our community. I've heard the stories about the Silver Serpents. They are bloodthirsty killing machines," Alfonse replied.

"Why didn't it go after us yesterday? It could have attacked us if it wanted to," Clarence said.

"I don't know. Maybe it doesn't attack humans all the time. Maybe it didn't want to be seen, or maybe it wasn't hungry. It could have been any of those things," Alfonse replied.

"Only God knows. We're lucky that it didn't attack us," Seymour said.

"Even though it didn't attack us, we still don't want that monster in our territories, because it's dangerous and unpredictable. It can slay and devour any of us at any time," Alfonse replied.

"That's definitely true. I don't want that beast in the waters that we fish in. It will devour all of our fish and us, if it's really ravenous," Clarence said.

"At least we got somebody to go after it. I just hope and pray that they can get the job done," Alfonse replied.

"Let's raise our drinks and toast to the Vultures! May God be with them and see them through this honorable act of valor," Seymour said.

"Cheers!" Alfonse replied.

"Cheers to the Vultures!" Clarence and Seymour said.

The three crewmates drank beer and whiskey all night and went home marinated in liquor. The next day came around and it was the day that the Vultures were to set out to hunt the Silver Serpent. It was Friday, September 1, 1904. Micah woke up at 9:00 am despite being slightly hungover. He headed over to the boat launch.

When he arrived there, he saw his crewmates.

"What's going on, Captain?" Vincent asked.

"Today is the big day of our Silver Serpent expedition. Are you warriors ready to go out and slay that Silver Serpent?" Micah replied.

"Yes sir, Captain! We're as ready as we'll ever be!" Creepy exclaimed.

"I like your enthusiasm Creepy," Micah said.

"Let's accomplish this tremendous feat and make ourselves and the world proud," Wilson replied.

The Vultures loaded their personal bags, food, water, alcohol, and five silver harpoons onto their boat and set out toward Oyster Island. Their boat was aptly named, *The Vulture.* It was painted black and yellow with The Vulture spelled out in purple and a purple vulture underneath the letters, on each side. It drizzled as the Vultures rode out toward Oyster Island. The pewter skies were overcast and gloomy with the ripe scent of the mighty and mystical Atlantic Ocean in the crisp air. It took the Vultures a couple of hours before they arrived at Oyster Island. It was 12:00 in the afternoon.

The Vultures dropped their anchor and prepared the silver harpoons. Then they sat down and cracked some beer cans open.

"We should throw out some fishing lines just for the heck of it, to see if anything bites," Micah said.

"OK. I'll rig them up and drop them into the water," Creepy replied.

Creepy rigged up two lines and dropped them into the greenish-blue water. The Vultures fished and drank all afternoon at Oyster Island with no sign of the Silver Serpent. The ominous and leaden evening sky loomed and crept in like a grayish-black specter. Slick was out exploring and hunting that evening when he spotted the Vulture's boat with his beaming, ruby-red eye.

Creepy spotted Slick just below the surface, about seventy-five yards away from the boat.

"There it is! There's the Silver Serpent!" Creepy exclaimed.

"Pull up the anchor! Let's go after it!" Micah commanded. Wilson pulled the anchor up, and the Vulture's headed toward the

Silver Serpent. When they arrived at the spot where the Silver Serpent was sighted, Slick had vanished into the deeper, bluer waters.

"It's not here anymore! Where the hell did it go?" Creepy said.

"It probably saw us coming and swam away. Let's wait here for a while. Get the silver harpoons ready," Micah replied.

Creepy went to the cabin and retrieved the silver harpoons.

"Here they are, Captain. They are ready to be fired," Creepy said.

"Good. Hand me one and the other one to Vincent. Keep one for yourself and leave the other two within reach," Micah replied.

Creepy handed Micah and Vincent the silver harpoons and kept one. He set the other two on the deck close by.

"It could be anywhere by now," Wilson said.

"Wilson, go and grab your guns and be on the lookout for that sinister serpent," Micah replied.

Wilson went into the cabin and grabbed two rifles. Then he loaded them and returned to the deck. The Vultures were on their toes with their eyes wide open and glued to the water. They stood ready and vigilant with their weapons. Slick was debating pensively on whether to attack the boat or not. He thought about his love, Zelda, and the reasons why they had relocated to Oyster Island in the first place. Then he thought about the promise that he made to her and how much he truly loved, admired, and cared for her.

Then he came to the realization that he was what he was, a killer. It was in his nature and his blood. Slick realized that the humans would keep coming after him no matter where he went, because that's what humans did. They slayed creatures for their own personal gain and glory. They were monsters and killers also. Another reason why they hunted him was because they had deeply rooted fear and anger towards the Silver Serpent. Slick knew that the humans viewed him as a bloodthirsty killing machine, and they wanted vengeance for all of the humans that he had slayed and devoured. In that bloody, never-ending war against each other, violence only begot more violence. He deduced that he was going to attack them and their vessel. He gathered up his energy and launched himself above the water and toward the Vulture's boat.

"There he is! Fire the harpoons!" Micah exclaimed.

Creepy and Vincent fired their harpoons at Slick's upper body area between his upper limbs, where they assumed that his chest cavity and heart were located. One silver harpoon hit Slick between his upper limbs and just missed his heart. The other silver harpoon found its mark and pierced Slick's heart. It sent waves of excruciating pain through all of his veins and cells. Slick let out a savage and explosive roar that shook the Vulture's boat and their hearts.

Micah threw his silver harpoon also and hit Slick in the head, just above his empty left eye socket. Slick had three silver harpoons stuck in vital areas of his colossal and ferocious body. One silver harpoon was stuck in his head, while the others were stuck in his chest cavity and heart. His massive body crashed with a thunderous clap on top of *The Vulture*. *The Vulture* was destroyed and started to sink with part of Slick's upper body and head still on it. Slick attempted one last time to devour one of the Vultures, but his heart stopped, and he died. Slick, the mighty and herculean Silver Serpent, was dead.

His last vision was of his most beloved, Zelda. He envisioned her exotic pink and purple scales shimmering like precious gemstones on her sleek, silvery body. Then he gazed into her fiery, blood-red eyes that twinkled like polished rubies and glowed with love for him as his soul floated out of his body and into the eternal sea in the sky. Slick's soul met the one true God and reunited with his parents and his first love, Sandy.

"Holy shit! We're going down! Our boat is destroyed!" Wilson exclaimed.

"Quickly cut off the Silver Serpent's head, so we have proof that we slayed it!" Micah said.

Creepy and Vincent grabbed some long, razor-sharp machetes and started hacking away right below Slick's fierce, spiky head. His ardent, ruby-red eye was still open, but it saw no more of the physical realm. Finally, after several hacks, Slicks head separated from his body. It laid there on top of a net on the deck of the sinking vessel.

Slick's lifeless and headless body slid off the boat and started to sink to the bottom of the ocean. The damage to the boat had been done, and it was sinking steadily.

"We're not gonna last long on our sinking boat with this gigantic serpent's head weighing us down. Quickly call for help on the radio and cut the harpoon lines before that serpent's body drags us down with it!" Micah commanded. Creepy ran to the cabin and grabbed the radio. Vincent cut the harpoon ropes with the machete.

"Mayday Mayday, come in! This is the Vultures! Our boat was destroyed by the Silver Serpent and it's sinking fast! Please send help immediately to Oyster Island! We slayed the Silver Serpent and we have its head!" Creepy exclaimed. A nearby boat named *The Walrus* heard their cry for help on the radio.

"Ten-four. This is the Walrus. We're about ten minutes from Oyster Island. Sit tight. We're on our way! Over and out," Artemis replied. Artemis was the Captain of *The Walrus*.

"Ten-four! Oh thank God! Thank you Walrus! Please hurry! We don't have much time left! Over and out!" Creepy exclaimed

Artemis grabbed the helm and made a beeline toward Oyster Island. Creepy exited the cabin with the good news.

"Help is on the way! The Walrus is only about ten minutes away!" Creepy exclaimed.

"Thank God! That's great news! I can't believe we slayed the Silver Serpent! We're gonna be heroes!" Vincent said.

"I knew we could do it! We're the best serpent hunters to ever live!" Wilson yelled at the top of his lungs. *The Walrus* spotted the ravaged and sinking *Vulture*.

Chapter Thirty-One
Zelda's Revenge

Back at Slick's cave, Zelda started to worry about Slick, because he hadn't returned. She ventured outside the cave to investigate. She swam all around Oyster Island and searched for any sign of her lover. Then she searched the ocean floor until she came across Slick's headless body. Zelda swam up to Slick's lifeless and headless body and wailed hysterically. At that moment, she felt her heart drop and painful shock waves pulsated through her veins. She couldn't believe that the love of her life had been slayed. She roared a booming shriek of immense and utter agony. Suddenly boiling, fiery anger and pure desire for vengeance surged through her veins like scalding lava. Zelda needed to slay and devour those miserable humans that slayed her lover. She saw the Vulture's sinking boat above her and torpedoed herself up to the surface. She knew it was them that slayed her lover, Slick, because of their damaged and sinking vessel. *The Walrus* pulled up next to the sinking *Vulture* and offered help.

"Holy shit! It's another Silver Serpent!" Micah exclaimed. Zelda's spiky head rose above the surface and struck Micah like a vexed death adder. She grasped his torso in her jaws, crunched down on his ribs, and pulverized his internal organs. He died instantaneously, and she spat him out like a mangled rag doll. She eyeballed her next victim.

"Help us Walruses! Fire a silver harpoon through its heart!" Vincent exclaimed.

"Jesus, Mary, and Joseph! Give us the head before it slays you all!" Artemis replied.

"No! It's ours!" Wilson exclaimed.

"We need to give them the head! If we don't, then nobody will ever know that we slayed it!" Creepy said.

"What does it matter if we're all dead! These guys will probably say that they slayed it!" Vincent said.

"Just do it! "Creepy yelled. Just as Creepy finished saying that, Zelda snapped his head off in one clean bite and caused blood to spray out of his neck. Creepy's headless body collapsed onto *The Vulture's* sinking deck with a thump.

"We're all gonna die! Help us! Shoot that beast with something!" Wilson exclaimed.

"Give us the head, and we'll tell the world that you guys slayed the Silver Serpent. You said your crew was called the Vultures, right? We'll tell the world that the Vultures slayed the Silver Serpent, but we need the head as proof!" Artemis replied.

"OK. If we don't make it, then you guys better tell the world that the Vultures slayed the Silver Serpent!" Vincent exclaimed.

"You have my word on that!" Artemis replied. Wilson raised the net that was holding Slick's menacing head, while Gannon maneuvered the Walruses' net to catch it. Gannon was a member of the Walruses. Once both nets were in place, the Vultures dropped Slick's gargantuan head into the Walruses' net. Gannon pulled the Silver Serpent's head up onto their deck. It took up more than half the deck.

"Captain Golden is offering a $10,000 reward to the slayers of the Silver Serpent! Now help us before that beast slays us!" Wilson exclaimed.

"We're trying! Let us grab the ropes!" Artemis replied. Artemis seemed to be more concerned about the Silver Serpent's head than the Vulture's lives. He snapped out of it, grabbed some ropes, and threw them over to the sinking Vultures. Vincent grabbed the rope. Zelda saw that and honed in on her target. She slashed him in half horizontally at the waist with her claws the way that scythe blades chopped crops. His bloody torso clung to the rope for seconds before it splashed into the blood-stained water. Wilson was the last Vulture that still drew breath on the sinking *Vulture*. The marred *Vulture* was more than halfway submerged under the chaotic water. He stared directly into Zelda's wrathful, crimson eyes. She observed the pure and utter fear in his eyes and went in for the kill. She struck and snapped down on his head with a loud crunch. Then she chewed it up until it was just a bloody paste of brains and skull. All the valiant Vultures were dead meat, and their boat was almost completely under the deadly water.

"Let's get the hell outta here!" Lonnie exclaimed. Lonnie was another member of the Walruses.

"Crank up the engine!" Artemis commanded. Lonnie cranked up the engine, while Artemis grabbed the helm. Zelda stretched her long, slithery, upper body and head out of the water and stared at the Walruses with her blazing, ruby-red eyes.

"Grab the weapons!" Artemis ordered. Juju and Gannon rushed inside the cabin and grabbed a rifle and a harpoon. Juju was another crew member of the Walruses. Zelda opened her steely jaws and exposed her jagged, blood-stained teeth to the frightened Walruses. Then she let out an explosively wild and pained roar that rattled the Walruses to their bones. She struck at them with her jaws open wide.

"Fire the weapons now!" Artemis exclaimed. Just as Zelda was about to bite Artemis in half, Juju fired his rifle at her head, while Gannon fired his harpoon between her upper limbs. The bullet hit Zelda in the lower jaw, while the harpoon hit her chest cavity. It just missed her heart by a couple of feet. Those stinging hits slowed her attack down just enough for her to miss her target, Artemis, by a foot. Zelda was so close to Artemis at that point after her strike, that he could see the bloody, torn pieces of human carnage stuck to her lethal, razor-sharp teeth. He also got a pungent whiff of her rancid breath that stunk of fish and death. She ripped the harpoon out of her chest cavity and decided that she had suffered enough hardship and battle wounds for that day. Zelda grasped the Vulture's butchered remains in her claws and jaws and dove down into the enigmatic depths of the abyssal Atlantic. She was out of sight within seconds.

"It's gone! That foul creature disappeared!" Gannon exclaimed.

"For now, but we don't know if it's gonna pop up again. Bring the harpoon in. Keep the guns and harpoons loaded just in case. Let's hightail it outta here while we still have the chance!" Artemis said. Gannon pulled the bloody harpoon in as fast as he could. The Walruses had the Silver Serpent's prized head on deck and rode back to shore as fast as their boat could carry them.

"Did you see that? That was unbelievable! That Silver Serpent slaughtered those poor Vultures right before our eyes!" Juju exclaimed.

"How could I not have seen that? It was right in front of our eyes for crying out loud! That was beyond insane! The Silver Serpents really do exist! I had heard the myths and legends, but had never seen one for myself," Artemis replied.

"We saw one for ourselves live and in devastating action. Now we have the head of one as proof," Lonnie said.

"Let's haul its monstrous head back to land, so we can show it to the town," Juju replied.

"We could say that we slayed the Silver Serpent to claim that $10,000 bounty," Gannon said.

"We could say that, but that would be a vicious lie. We must give credit where credit is due. The Vultures made the ultimate sacrifice and paid with their lives for that Silver Serpent's head. It's our moral obligation to tell the truth and inform the world and Captain Golden that the Vultures were the true, valiant heroes that slayed the Silver Serpent. Maybe he will reward us for our efforts and honesty," Artemis replied.

"That's true. I agree one hundred percent with our wise Captain," Juju said.

"I can't believe that there's still another voracious Silver Serpent out there. What if there are even more than that? We must warn the people that there is still another Silver Serpent on the loose in these perilous waters," Lonnie replied.

"We will. First, we must tote the Silver Serpent's prized head safely back to shore, and then we'll plan our next move. This is precious cargo that we're conveying," Artemis said.

"Aye-aye Captain," Gannon replied. The Walruses rode back to shore at a steady pace under the serene, starry night's sky with the Silver Serpent's otherworldly head resting in a hug net on their boat's sturdy, wooden deck. They arrived back to shore at around midnight and unloaded their supplies and then they used their boat's net to place the Silver Serpent's prized head on two horse and buggies. The Walruses used thick chains and ropes to strap the ghastly head to their sturdy buggies. After that, they headed over to their warehouse. The Walruses placed the head in a spacious freezer to preserve it, and they locked up the warehouse. It took all four of them to drag it from the buggy to the freezer.

"Tomorrow we'll take the Silver Serpent's head over to the Cape Carnivore Tribune and tell them the true story of how we obtained it. We'll be much more respected for telling the truth, than for lying. The world deserves to know the truth. Plus, we owe the Vultures that much. They were the true heroes that paid the ultimate price and gave the ultimate sacrifice. They deserve the credit and they deserve to be immortalized and have their names etched into history," Artemis said.

"Aye-aye Captain," The Walruses replied. The Walruses said goodnight and rode home still in shock from the traumatic and mind-blowing events they witnessed that historic and unforgettable day. They felt proud that they were the ones that brought the legendary Silver Serpent's head safely to land.

Chapter Thirty-two
The Silver Serpent's Head

The next day it was Saturday, September 2, 1904. Artemis woke up in his bayside home and rode over to Juju's house. It was 11:00 am on a warm and breezy day in Cape Carnivore. Artemis picked up Juju, and they rode to Gannon's house. Gannon was outside watering his garden.

"How's it going, comrades?" Gannon said.

"Great. We came to pick you up, so we can take the Silver Serpent's head to the Cape Carnivore Tribune," Artemis replied. The Cape Carnivore Tribune was the town's newspaper.

"OK. Let me throw on some proper clothes and wash my face and hands. Then we'll get outta here," Gannon said. Gannon went inside, washed up, and threw on some nicer clothes and shoes. Then he walked outside and climbed into Artemis' horse drawn buggy.

"Are we gonna pick up Lonnie?" Gannon asked.

"Of course we are. Lonnie is part of our crew, isn't he?" Artemis replied.

"Yeah, I was just making sure," Gannon said. The Walruses rode over to Lonnie's house and knocked on the front door. Lonnie had just woken up and lethargically wiped the sleep from his eyes.

"Good morning. What's going on guys?" Lonnie said

"It's more like good afternoon, but hey, we all need our beauty sleep. It's time to take the Silver Serpent's head to the Cape Carnivore Tribune," Artemis replied.

"OK. Let me get dressed," Lonnie said.

"We're gonna need your buggy also to help haul the Silver Serpent's head," Artemis replied.

"Aye-aye Captain," Lonnie said. Lonnie threw on some clean clothes and walked outside and into his buggy. He followed Artemis' buggy over to their warehouse. Then they loaded the

Silver Serpent's head onto Artemis' and Lonnie's buggies and strapped it down with thick chains and ropes.

"We got it. Let's pay a visit to the Cape Carnivore Tribune. They're gonna eat this story up," Artemis said. They arrived there shortly and exited their vehicles.

"Lonnie, stay out here with the head while we go inside," Artemis said.

"Aye-aye Captain," Lonnie replied. Lonnie stood guard by the Silver Serpent's like a stoic sentinel, while his crewmates entered The Cape Carnivore Tribune. The Silver Serpent's head emitted a pungent, musty odor. Lonnie battled the noxious fumes and breathed in through his mouth.

"Good afternoon, gentlemen. How may I help you today?" Ivan said. Ivan was the Chief Editor of the Cape Carnivore Tribune.

"Good afternoon. A Silver Serpent has been slain. We have its head outside on our buggies," Artemis replied.

"Get out of town! Are you telling me that you have a Silver Serpent's head outside?" Ivan exclaimed.

"Yes. That's exactly what we're telling you. C'mon outside with us and see for yourself," Gannon replied.

"I have to see it to believe it," Ivan said.

"Follow us," Juju replied. Ivan and the Walruses walked outside. The Silver Serpent's head was there as clear as day on the two buggies. Lonnie was nauseated from the rancid stench, but he leaned proudly against his buggy.

"Holy Mary Mother of God! That is a Silver Serpent's head! It smells repugnant. Who slayed it?" Ivan said.

"A crew of serpent hunters called the Vultures," Artemis replied.

"How do you know that?" Ivan said.

"Because they are the ones that gave us this serpent's head right before another Silver Serpent slayed them," Juju replied.

"When and where did that take place?" Ivan asked.

"That happened yesterday at Oyster Island. My name is Artemis, and these guys are my crewmates. We're called the Walruses," Artemis replied.

"I'm Juju," Juju said.

"I'm Lonnie," Lonnie said.

"I'm Gannon," Gannon said.

"It's an honor to meet you gentlemen. My name is Ivan. I'm the Chief Editor of the Cape Carnivore Tribune. This is an incredible story that you are telling me. Do you mind if I print it on the front page of the Cape Carnivore Tribune?" Ivan replied.

"No, we don't mind at all. As a matter of fact, we were hoping you would say that," Artemis said.

"Great. Let's go back inside and sit down, so you guys can tell me all about it," Ivan replied.

"That sounds great," Artemis said. The Silver Serpent's head still looked menacing and fierce. Slick's dead, blood-red eye stared back at the humans, but it had lost that fiery, ruby-red glow. The razor-sharp teeth were still shiny, metallic silver with blood stains on them. They were still as sharp as freshly honed battle swords. The head showcased its malevolent spikes, and silver, leathery scales tipped with hues of sapphire blue and emerald green. Only, they didn't shimmer and sparkle with such dazzling brilliance and pizzazz any more. That one blood-red eye still stared back at the humans with wrath and bloodlust.

"Let's leave the head out here with your buddy, while you gentlemen give me the full scoop inside," Ivan said.

"OK Ivan. Lonnie, you stay out here and protect that prized head. Make sure nobody messes with it. There's a pistol under the driver's seat in my buggy if you need it. Holler at us if things get sticky and you need backup," Artemis said.

"Aye-aye Captain," Lonnie replied.

Lonnie stayed outside with the smelly Silver Serpent's head, while the other three Walruses entered the newspaper station with Ivan. Ivan pulled up some chairs for them and placed them around his desk. He offered them water and coffee. The Walruses sat down and told the epic tale of how they obtained the Silver Serpent's prized head from the Vultures.

"How did everything happen?" Ivan asked.

"We were going out to fish Oyster Island like we usually do, when we received a distressed call for help from the Vultures on our radio. They said that their boat was destroyed by the Silver Serpent and it was sinking fast at Oyster Island. The Vultures also informed us that they had slayed the Silver Serpent and they had its head. We immediately headed that way to help them. We arrived there and saw that their boat had been ravaged and was sinking fast. Half of it was already submerged in the ocean when we pulled up next to it. The Vultures had the Silver Serpent's head in their net, so we maneuvered our net to transfer the serpent's head from their net to ours," Artemis said.

"OK, go on," Ivan replied.

"After we transferred the giant head to our boat, we were going to throw them ropes, so that they could pull themselves onboard our boat. At that moment, another gargantuan Silver Serpent popped up from out of the blue and attacked and slayed them all. It bit their heads off and rendered their bodies right before our eyes. It almost bit and slayed me, but thank God my crew fired a rifle and harpoon at it and saved my life. The harpoon stuck in its upper body and the rifle round hit it somewhere in the lower part of its head. Those hits stunned it and caused it to barely miss me by a foot. I could smell it's putrid breath from that close, and I could see the pieces of the Vultures in its silvery teeth. My crewmates saved my life, and I'll never forget it. Then the Silver Serpent grabbed the remaining body parts of the Vultures with its claws and jaws and dove deep down into the Atlantic waters and out of sight. We never laid eyes on it again after that," Artemis replied.

"Wow! That is an absolutely rip-roaring tale! You said that the crew who gave you the serpent's head was called the Vultures, correct?" Ivan said.

"Yes, they were concerned that they wouldn't get credit for slaying the Silver Serpent. They made sure that they informed us that they were the ones that slayed it, and their crew's name was the Vultures. They also said that Captain Golden was offering a $10,000 bounty to the Silver Serpent's slayers," Juju replied.

"Holy smokes! Did you actually see them slay the Silver Serpent with your own eyes?" Ivan asked.

"No, we did not. But, how else could they have obtained a Silver Serpent's head like that?" Artemis replied.

"Maybe they dragged it in on one of their nets?" Ivan said.

"We figured that they were serpent hunters hunting the Silver Serpent and that they were attacked by one. We figured that their boat was destroyed by the Silver Serpent, but they were able to slay it and chop off its head before it sunk to the bottom of the ocean. That's the most logical explanation to all of this," Artemis replied.

"That's probably true, and that's the story we're going to print on the front page of the Cape Carnivore Tribune. The entire world needs to read and hear about this legendary story of heroism and bravery!" Ivan said.

"That had to have been what really occurred. It only makes sense," Gannon replied.

"Let's get back to the story. What happened after that?" Ivan said.

"That other Silver Serpent that slayed them was long gone. We assumed that it was a loved one of the slayed Silver Serpent, and it wanted vengeance," Artemis replied.

"That makes sense. Okay, go on," Ivan said.

"After that, we headed back to land. We transferred the Silver Serpent's head from our boat's net to two of our buggies and delivered it to the freezer in our warehouse. That's it and the rest is history," Juju said.

"Did you get a look at the other Silver Serpent that slayed the Vultures?" Ivan asked.

"Yes. We all got a very good look at it. It raised its long upper body and head right in front of our boat before it struck at Artemis like a Cobra. It was a magnificent and majestic looking creature. It was at least 150 feet long with a glistening, silver body and purple and pink tipped scales. It had fiery, ruby-red eyes with rows of sharp, metallic teeth that glinted like deadly daggers and swords. It had gleaming, jagged, silver spikes that ran along its head, spine, and tail. It was truly a spectacular specimen and an image that I'll never forget for as long as I live. That image is forever burned into the stitching of my mind," Gannon replied.

"Holy mackerel! That is a story and a half if I've ever heard one! I'm going to print it just like you guys told it. How does that sound?" Ivan said

"That sounds stellar!" Artemis replied.

"You said that you guys call yourselves the Walruses, correct?" Ivan said..

"Yes sir. That is correct. We earned our name because we are territorial, and we love to catch and eat fish, just like Walruses," Gannon replied.

"That name suits your crew well then. Did you happen to catch any of the Vulture's names?" Ivan asked.

"No. They just said that they were called the Vultures," Juju replied.

"OK, great. I have everything I need to write an excellent article for the front page. Let me go get started on that right away. First, let's go outside and take some photographs of your crew with the Silver Serpent's head, so I can post that on the front page as well. You said your names are Artemis, Gannon, Juju, and Lonnie, correct?" Ivan said.

"Sounds good Ivan. Yes, that is correct sir," Artemis replied. They walked outside and Ivan took photographs of the Walruses proudly gathered around the fearsome Silver Serpent's head.

"OK. That is all I need. I'll post these photographs alongside our article on the front page of tomorrow's paper," Ivan said.

That sounds great Ivan. Thank you for your help and your time," Artemis replied.

"It was my pleasure. Thank you gentlemen for your jaw-dropping story. The entire world is going to want to read and hear about this thrilling and heroic tale," Ivan said.

"It was our pleasure as well. I wrote down our names, addresses, and landlines inside if you ever need to contact any of us for more information. I believe we told you everything though. Feel free to contact us for anything anyway," Artemis replied. The Walruses shook hands with Ivan and said their farewells. They climbed back into their buggies and drove back to their warehouse to drop off the Silver Serpent's head in the freezer. Then they locked up the warehouse and rode to their favorite local bar called, The Tavern Wench. They parked their buggies and entered the bar. It was about 6:00 in the evening. The Tavern Wench was famous for their lobster tails, crab legs, whiskey, and ice cold beer. The Walruses found a table and sat down.

"Today is an epic and historic day my friends. We're gonna be famous," Juju said.

"You're damn right we're gonna be famous. The whole world is gonna learn of the Walruses. Everyone and their grandmas are gonna want to hear about this legendary tale of valor and triumph," Artemis replied.

"Let's celebrate!" Gannon said.

"First round is on me buddies," Lonnie said. Lonnie beckoned a waitress to their table. A voluptuous waitress came to their table.

"Hi, my name is Linda. What can I get you gentlemen?" Linda asked.

"Hi Linda. We'll take the coldest beers in this joint and some crab legs," Lonnie replied.

"What kind of beers would you like?" Linda asked.

"Some Green Marlin beers please," Lonnie replied. Green Marlin was a popular and locally brewed beer.

"OK, I'll be right back with your beers," Linda said. Linda walked back to the kitchen and placed their order. Then she retrieved four icy Green Marlin beers and strutted back to the table to distribute them among the thirsty Walruses.

"Thank you, Linda. You are an absolutely stunning woman if you don't mind me saying so," Artemis said.

"Thank you sweetheart. That is very kind of you to say. You're very handsome if you don't mind me saying so," Linda replied with a bubbly giggle and an inviting wink.

"Of course I don't mind. I'll take all the compliments that I can get. My name is Artemis. It's a pleasure to meet you," Artemis said.

"It's nice to meet you as well, Artemis. Your crab legs should be right out. Let me know if I can get you gentlemen anything else," Linda replied.

"Thank you, Linda. You're a real doll," Artemis said. Artemis and Linda flirtatiously smiled at each other. There was definitely a coquettish spark between them.

"Cheers to transporting the Silver Serpent's head safely to land and cheers to the Vultures! And last but not least, cheers to becoming famous!" Gannon said.

"Cheers to the Walruses!" The Walruses exclaimed.

"Cheers to us and the Vultures! Without them, none of this would have been possible, and that Silver Serpent would still be out there wreaking havoc on the human race. Another one is still out there," Lonnie said.

"Cheers to the Vultures!" The Walruses replied.

"I feel bad that the Vultures not only lost their lives, but they didn't get to claim that bounty for slaying the Silver Serpent." Juju said.

"I do too. That reminds me. We should find Captain Golden and inform him that the Vultures slayed the Silver Serpent, and we brought back its head," Artemis replied.

"That's true. Where can we find him?" Gannon said.

"He lives in Cape Crusade. We should head over there tomorrow after the newspapers are in circulation. That way we can show him the front page as proof of our story," Juju replied.

"That's smart thinking, Juju. After we buy some copies of the Cape Carnivore Tribune for ourselves. We'll head over to Cape Crusade to locate Captain Golden. A man as rich as that can't be too hard to find," Artemis said.

"Sounds like a plan, skipper. Cheers to the Cape Carnivore Tribune and to Captain Golden!" Lonnie replied. The Walruses drank their beer and devoured their king crab legs with lemon and garlic butter. They caught a good buzz and felt proud that they accomplished their mission. They were on cloud nine at that moment in their favorite bar, and they were relishing every second of it.

"Don't forget to buy tomorrow's paper!" Artemis commanded.

"Aye-aye Captain!" The Walruses replied. The joyful Walruses climbed into their buggies and rode out. Artemis dropped Gannon off at his house, and Lonnie dropped Juju off at his. The Walruses slept soundly that night and dreamed about their names being on the front page of the Cape Carnivore Tribune, next to the legendary Silver Serpent's mighty and menacing head.

Chapter Thirty-three
The Front Page

The radiant, golden sun arose the next day amid a picturesque Cape Carnivore skyline. The day was Sunday, September 3, 1904. Juju woke up at noon and rode over to the newspaper stand to purchase an issue of the Cape Carnivore Tribune. Juju paid the newspaper vendor a nickel and received a copy of the daily newspaper. The front page read: The Silver Serpent's Head! There was an electric article and some captivating photos of the Silver Serpent's head and the Walruses on the front page. Juju read the article. The article read exactly like the Walruses explained it to Ivan. It gave credit to the heroic and valiant Vultures for slaying the Silver Serpent and credit to the Walruses for delivering its head safely to land. It mentioned the names of the Walruses, of course. The bold and captivating article also informed the readers that another Silver Serpent slayed the Vultures as they attempted to board the Walruses' boat. Juju felt especially proud and honored to have had his and his crewmates' names and pictures on the front page of the Cape Carnivore Tribune, standing next to the ferocious head of the legendary Silver Serpent. Juju finished reading the article and marveled at their pictures. Then he rode over to Artemis' house. He parked his buggy and knocked on the front door made of solid oak.

"Well if it isn't my loyal and trusty crewmate, Juju. What's the skinny buddy?" Artemis said.

"Greetings, Captain. I just read our article on the front page of the Cape Carnivore Tribune. It's right on point. Look, I bought a copy, so you can feast your eyes upon it," Juju replied.

"Outstanding Juju! Come on in, and make yourself comfortable, so I can read it," Artemis said. Juju walked into Artemis' house.

"Did you just wake up?" Juju asked.

"Yes, about thirty minutes ago. I was just having a cup of coffee. Would you like some?" Artemis replied.

"Sure, I'll take a cup of Joe," Juju said. Artemis poured a cup of coffee for Juju and handed it to him. Juju handed Artemis the newspaper. Artemis' eyes lit up like lanterns when he saw the pictures of him and his crew standing next to the Silver Serpent's menacing head.

"Would you look at that? There we are on the front page of the Cape Carnivore Tribune. We look sharp as shark fins if I do say so myself," Artemis said proudly as he sipped his creamy cup of Joe.

"We sure do, That's us alright, bright and clear as day. The photographs came out really swell," Juju replied. Artemis read the article as excited as a fisherman landing a whopper of a catch. He read it from start to finish and smiled from ear to ear.

"Hot dog! That's exactly how we explained the story to Ivan. I couldn't have written it better myself," Artemis said joyously.

"Yup. It explained it exactly like it happened, word for word. That way, nobody gets smoke blown up their asses. That article is one hundred percent accurate and truthful," Juju replied.

"Brother, that is truly beautiful. I've never been so proud of our crew in my entire life. I gotta go get some copies for myself. What newspaper stand did you purchase it at?" Artemis said.

"That stand located on Melon St.," Juju replied.

"Are they still a nickel over there?" Artemis asked.

"Yup, they're still a solid nickel, Captain," Juju replied.

"We've inscribed our names into the history books. This is a historic and monumental event for the town, state, nation, and world. I wonder if Lonnie and Gannon have seen it yet. Let's ride to their houses and find out," Artemis said.

"Sounds good skipper," Juju replied. They finished their cups of coffee and exited Artemis' house. Then they hopped into Juju's buggy and rode over to Gannon's house. They climbed out and knocked on his front door.

"What's going on comrades? Today's the big day!" Gannon said.

"Have you seen today's paper yet?" Juju asked.

"Not yet. I was just on my way to the newspaper stand to buy one. I see that you guys already have a copy. Let me see that! Come on in guys," Gannon replied. Juju handed Gannon the newspaper as they walked inside his house. Gannon looked at the front page and smiled.

"Would you take a gander at that! The Walruses are famous!" Juju said.

"Walloping wahoos! Today is a historic day for our town and our crew," Gannon said.

"It sure is buddy. We are all immensely proud," Artemis replied.

"The photographs that Ivan took came out really keen. The Silver Serpent's head looks mighty fierce. We don't look too bad ourselves," Gannon said.

"You got that right. Read the article," Juju replied. Gannon read the article.

"Holy smokes! That article was thrilling and captivating. I liked how he ended it with: Beware! There is still another Silver Serpent out there on the loose!" Gannon said.

"Let's go see if Lonnie has seen this," Artemis said.

"OK, let's go," Gannon said.

"I'm two steps ahead of you," Juju replied. The three Walruses walked out the door and into Juju's buggy. They rode over to Lonnie's house feeling proud and on cloud nine, as they discussed the captivating article. The crew parked their buggy and knocked on Lonnie's door. Lonnie answered the door.

"What's going on, brothers?" Lonnie said.

"The Walruses! That's what's going on!" Artemis exclaimed. Artemis handed Lonnie the Cape Carnivore Tribune.

"Take a gander at that!" Juju said.

"I've been dreaming about seeing that article. C'mon in," Lonnie replied. The Walruses walked inside Lonnie's house.

"How does it feel to be famous?" Gannon asked.

"It's exhilarating! Our crew is on the front page of the Cape Carnivore Tribune! Not too many people can say that," Lonnie replied.

"Read the article buddy," Artemis said.

"Would you sand crabs like anything to drink?" Lonnie replied.

"Do you have any cold beer?" Juju asked.

"Of course. I always keep some cold beer in the fridge. What kind of question is that" Lonnie replied.

"A simple yes would've sufficed, but okay. I'll take one," Juju said.

"I'll take one too," Artemis said.

"I'll wet my whistle," Gannon said.

"This is cause for celebration! Let me grab those beers," Lonnie replied.   Lonnie fetched the beers and distributed them to his crew.

"Your house is looking sharp Lonnie," Artemis said.

"Thanks bud. Sit down guys, and make yourselves comfortable," Lonnie replied. The Walruses sat down in the living room with their ice-cold Stingray beers.

"Go ahead Lonnie. Read it," Gannon said. Lonnie read the article.

"That was the best article I've ever read in my life. I know Cape Carnivore, New York, the nation, and the entire world are going to salivate over this splendiferous read," Lonnie said.

"We're famous and chiseled into the stone tablets of history," Juju replied.

"Let's go to the newspaper stand, so we can buy ourselves some more copies of the Cape Carnivore Tribune. Then let's head over to the warehouse, so we can pick up the Silver Serpent's head. I want to drop it off at, Real Nature Taxidermy. I want to have that head mounted, so we can proudly display it at our warehouse. We'll need to bring your buggy too, Lonnie, to help carry the head. Then we'll ride over to Cape Crusade to locate Captain Golden," Artemis said.

"Aye-aye Captain," The Walruses replied. They climbed into Juju's and Lonnie's buggies and rode over to the newspaper stand on Melon St. There was a mob of excited people buying the newspapers and talking about the front page story.

"Look at all these people buying the newspaper. The word on this riveting story must be spreading like wildfire," Gannon said.

"Let's purchase some copies for ourselves before they sell out," Lonnie replied. The Walruses parked their buggy and made their way through the buzzing crowd to the stand.

"Hello there, my good man. I want to buy seven copies of today's paper, please," Artemis said.

"Sure, that'll be thirty-five cents," the vendor replied. Artemis paid the vendor thirty-five cents. The vendor grabbed seven copies of the Cape Carnivore Tribune and handed them to Artemis.

"Thank you," Artemis said.

"Thank you for your business. Get them while you can, because they are selling like hot cakes," the vendor replied. The Walruses took their newspapers and worked their way back to their buggies through the boisterous mob. They each owned two copies of the Cape Carnivore Tribune. The Walruses rode over to their warehouse and loaded the cold yet pungent Silver Serpent's head onto their buggies with ropes and chains. After that, they rode over to Real Nature Taxidermy. Real Nature Taxidermy was the most renowned taxidermy shop in Cape Carnivore. They arrived at Real Nature Taxidermy and parked their buggies.

"Gannon, stay outside with the head while we go inside and negotiate," Artemis commanded.

"Aye-aye Captain," Gannon replied. Gannon stayed outside with the buggies and the slightly decayed Silver Serpent's head, while the rest of the Walruses walked inside Real Nature Taxidermy.

"Good afternoon, Walruses. What may I do for you gentlemen today?" Jerry said. Jerry was the proprietor of Real Nature Taxidermy. He was the best in the business and did outstanding work on all types of creatures.

"Good afternoon, Jerry. We want to mount a Silver Serpent's head. It's outside on our buggies," Artemis said.

"Leaping Lizards! Is it really outside? I read about that head and your crew in today's paper!" Jerry exclaimed.

"Of course it is. Would I pull your chain about something like that? C'mon outside and see it with your own eyes," Artemis replied. Jerry shot up from his chair and followed the Walruses outside. His eyes lit up like fireworks when he saw the gigantic, monstrous Silver Serpent's head resting on top of the two buggies.

"Good Lord! It's true! It's magnificent!" Jerry exclaimed.

"Can you mount this type of head?" Lonnie asked.

"You bet your bottom dollar. I can mount any type of head on God's beautiful planet!" Jerry replied enthusiastically.

"That's wonderful news. How much is that gonna cost us?" Artemis asked.

"Since this is an extremely special and exotic type of mount because of the type of creature it is and because of its unique scales and skin, I'll mount this head for $500. You can pay half up front and the rest when you pick up the finished product," Jerry replied.

"Is that as low as you'll go?" Artemis asked.

"That is low as I can go, considering the cost of materials that I'll need and the amount of specialized work hours it will require," Jerry replied.

"OK. That sounds reasonable," Artemis said. The Walruses put their money together and came up with $250. They handed it to Jerry.

"Here you go, Jerry. When will it be ready for pick up?" Artemis said.

"With something as rare and jumbo as this, give me about six months. Just give me your phone number, and I'll call you when it's ready for pick up," Jerry replied.

"OK, sounds good. It was nice doing business with you," Artemis said.

"It was a pleasure doing business with you gentlemen as well. Congratulations on obtaining and bringing in this prized gem of a head. Would you guys deliver that huge head to the garage at the back of the shop? I'll open up the garage door and meet you back there," Jerry replied.

"Of course," Gannon said.

"Great. I appreciate it," Jerry replied. Jerry walked back inside his shop and to the garage, while the Walruses steered their carriages and the Silver Serpent's prized head toward the garage. Jerry arrived at the garage first and opened the garage door for the Walruses and the Silver Serpent's head. The garage was also used as a workstation. Jerry had the head of an impressive trophy buck and a fully-grown, pristine blue marlin that he had been working on in there.

"You can set it down right here. I'll get started on it ASAP," Jerry said. The Walruses pulled the heavy, massive head down from the buggies with thick ropes and chains. Then they shook hands with Jerry and exited the taxidermy shop. They decided they only needed to take one horse and buggy to Cape Crusade, so they dropped Juju's buggy off at his house.

Chapter Thirty-four
Captain Golden's Bounty

"OK. We've taken care of that. Let's ride to Cape Crusade to locate Captain Golden," Artemis said.

"Aye-aye Captain," The Walruses replied. The Walruses rode southwest towards Staten Island. They arrived about two hours later. It was 6:00 in the brisk and balmy evening.

"Where should we go first?" Lonnie asked.

"Let's head over to the Sandbar. I heard that's where the fishermen and whale hunters hang out. I'm sure they'll know where to find Captain Golden," Artemis replied. The Walruses rode towards the Sandbar and arrived fifteen minutes later. They climbed out of Lonnie's buggy and entered Cape Crusade's most beloved watering hole, The Sandbar. They sat down and ordered a round of Yellow Crab beers. They were trying to get a feel for someone that might know where to find Captain Golden. The Knight Sharks sat at another table and drank beer and devoured fried sea trout.

"Those guys over there look like they are fishermen. Let's go ask them about Captain Golden," Artemis said. The Walruses walked over to the Knight Shark's table and introduced themselves.

"Good evening, gentlemen. My name is Artemis and these are my crewmates, Gannon, Juju, and Lonnie. We're a fishing crew from Cape Carnivore called the Walruses," Artemis said.

"I thought you guys looked familiar. It's nice to meet some fellow fishermen. I'm Clayton, and this is Augustus, Ringo, Rodney, and Zeus. We're a local fishing crew from here in Cape Crusade called the Knight Sharks. We read about your crew today in the paper. It's such a relief to learn of that Silver Serpent's demise. We give honor and credit to the valiant Vultures that slayed the Silver Serpent, and we pay homage to your crew for bringing its head safely to land. We lost two beloved crew members to that virulent monstrosity. I can't believe that there is still another one out there. It's an honor to meet you all. What can we do for you gentlemen? Let me guess. You want to know where to find Captain Golden, so you can show him the newspaper in case he hasn't read it yet, and possibly claim that reward money," Clayton replied.

"That is correct. We want to make sure that he knows that it was the Vultures that slayed the Silver Serpent, but it was us that brought its hellacious head to land," Artemis said.

"That's what I figured. Our crew would've done the same thing. You can find him at his boat shop. It's called Captain Golden's Boats. It's just about five miles up the road from here. You better hurry though, because he closes shop at 7:00 pm. Just go north on Seahorse St. and east on Grouper Ave. It'll be on your left hand side. You'll see the big golden letters on his sign. You can't miss it," Clayton replied.

"Thank you so much for that information. We better get going before he closes shop for the night," Artemis said.

"No problem Walruses. I really hope Captain Golden pays your crew that reward money for hauling that treasured head to land," Zeus replied.

"We really hope so too. Thanks again gentlemen. It was a pleasure making your acquaintances. Your next round of beers is on us. Take care and good luck in your future fishing endeavors," Gannon said.

"We appreciate that. The Walruses are always welcome here in Cape Crusade and at the Sandbar. God bless and good luck in your future fishing expeditions as well," Clayton replied. The two fishing crews shook hands, and Artemis bought the Knight Sharks a round of Yellow Crab beers. Then they exited the Sandbar and hopped back into Lonnie's buggy. The Walruses rode northward on Seahorse St. and eastward on Grouper Ave. Then they noticed the sizable and flashy golden letters on their left hand side that spelled out Captain Golden's Boats. They entered the parking lot and parked their buggy. It was 6:45 in the brisk evening. Then they walked into Captain Golden's office with a copy of the Cape Carnivore Tribune. Captain Golden sat at his polished desk and revised important sales documents. He sipped on some bourbon and soda with keen satisfaction. He was a stocky, dapper man in his sixties. He had salt and pepper hair and a well trimmed beard. He appeared very relaxed but gleamed with astuteness and confidence.

"Hello. Welcome to Captain Golden's Boats. How may I help you gentlemen this evening?" Captain Golden announced.

"Hello. Are you Captain Golden?" Artemis asked.

"Yes indeed. In the flesh. Who might you gentlemen be?" Captain Golden replied.

"It's an honor to meet you good sir. I'm Artemis, and this is my crew. We're called the Walruses and we've journeyed here today from Cape Carnivore in Long Island," Artemis said.

"AHH yes, Cape Carnivore. I've heard that's a great fishing and whaling town. What brings you to Cape Crusade today? Are you looking for a boat? I've got the best boats in all the land," Captain Golden replied.

"No sir. I'm sure you do. I don't know if you've read today's newspaper, but we came to inform you that the Silver Serpent has been slayed," Artemis said. Artemis handed Captain Golden the Cape Carnivore Tribune. Captain Golden looked it over.

"Take a look at that! That's your crew with the Silver Serpent's head in the photos! No, I haven't read today's paper. That's great news! Was it your crew that slayed it?" Captain Golden replied.

"No sir. It was another sea crew called the Vultures. They transferred the Silver Serpent's head to our boat. We tried to save them, but just before they could grab our ropes, another Silver Serpent popped up from out of the blue and slayed and devoured them right before our eyes. After that, we hightailed it outta there with the Silver Serpent's head and brought it back with us to Cape Carnivore. We wanted to let you know personally, because we heard that you offered a bounty to the slayers of the Silver Serpent," Artemis said.

"I'm sorry to hear that the Vultures didn't make it, but that is one incredible story. I'm glad that you gentlemen found me to deliver this message personally. I appreciate your honesty and efforts. Because you were honest about it and because you brought the Silver Serpent's head to land, I'll reward your crew with the $10,000 bounty prize. What do you all think about that?" Captain Golden replied.

"That's the greatest news we've ever heard and today is the best day of our lives! Thank you so much Captain Golden. Words cannot express the joy we're feeling and our eternal gratitude for you. You've just made us the happiest fishing crew on the planet! God Bless you!" Artemis said ecstatically.

"Thank you so much Captain Golden! You're an awe-inspiring and honorable man!" Gannon exclaimed.

"Thank you so much from the bottom of our hearts good sir! God Bless you always!" Juju exclaimed.

"God Bless you Captain Golden! Thank you! Thank you!" Lonnie exclaimed.

"You're welcome gentlemen! I'm just glad that a Silver Serpent has been slayed. I can't believe there is another one still out there. I might have to offer another cash reward for that one as well. I'm very grateful to your crew for carrying the Silver Serpent's head to land. What are you gonna do with it?' Captain Golden replied.

"I can't believe it either sir. I'm sure that cash reward will inspire more serpent hunters to hunt the other Silver Serpent that's still on the loose. We're having the head mounted by a taxidermist in Cape Carnivore. He said it should be ready in about six months," Artemis said.

"I'm sure it will too. Having that glorious head mounted is a grand idea. When the job is complete, let me know if you want to sell it. I'll pay a small fortune for that head," Captain Golden replied.

"We'll keep that in mind Captain Golden," Artemis said.

"Fantastic. C'mon, let's go get your crew's money. Follow me," Captain Golden replied.

"Yes sir," The Walruses replied. Captain Golden led the Walruses out of his main office and into a smaller back room. Inside was a desk, a chair, and a steel safe. Captain Golden entered the combination to the safe's lock and opened the door. There were stacks of crisp bills inside of all denominations. Mostly large bills. Captain Golden pulled out ten stacks and set them on the desk. Each stack was $1,000. The Walruses eyes lit up like stoked embers.

"There you go gentlemen. That's $10,000 in mint bills right there. Enjoy it and don't spend it all in one place!" Captain Golden said as he chuckled.

"Thank you so much Captain Golden! You've made our day and our lives, today. Our families thank you too. May God Bless you always good sir!" Artemis said.

"You're welcome Walruses. Thank you for your honesty and for your efforts. I might offer another bounty for that other Silver Serpent still out there. Just leave me your names and phone numbers, and I'll let you know if I do," Captain Golden replied.

"Will do, good sir. Lonnie, go and fetch the satchel from the buggy," Artemis said.

"Aye-aye Captain," Lonnie replied. Lonnie walked out of the building and to his buggy. He collected the satchel and returned to the backroom. Lonnie handed the satchel to Artemis. Artemis placed the $10,000 in the satchel and closed its latch. Then he threw the satchel's strap over his shoulder.

"Thanks again Captain Golden. If you only knew how much you've changed our lives for the better. You are truly a Godly and honorable man," Juju said.

"Thank you dearly, Captain Golden. If there is ever anything that we can do for you, please don't hesitate to ask," Gannon said.

"It was my pleasure gentlemen. Spend and invest that money wisely and it will go a long way. C'mon, let's go to my office, so you can write down your names and numbers, in case I need to contact you in the future. I'll give you mine as well," Captain Golden replied.

"Yes sir," the Walruses said. They followed Captain Golden into his main office where he handed them a pen and paper. Each crew member wrote down their name and phone number on that paper. Captain Golden wrote down his name and number on a piece of paper also and handed it to Artemis. The Walruses thanked Captain Golden again and shook his hand. They promised to keep in touch. Then they walked out of his office with a satchel full of money and huge smiles on their glowing faces. They climbed back into Lonnie's buggy and headed back to Cape Carnivore. The Walruses felt extremely joyous, proud, and $10,000 richer.

"We'll divide the money up equally when we arrive at our warehouse. Then we'll have some shots of rum and some beers to celebrate this heavenly day. Everyone will receive $2,500 each. Not a bad day's pay!" Artemis said proudly.

"Aye-aye Captain!" The Walruses exclaimed.

Chapter Thirty-five
Slick's Bloodline

The next day it was Monday, September 4, 1904. Zelda awoke in her cave, lonely and heartbroken. She was still in shock and devastated by Slick's death and missed him immensely. All of a sudden, Zelda felt something move in her stomach. She was pregnant she thought to herself. She felt her stomach with her upper claws and felt a living thing moving around. That told her that she was pregnant. Zelda felt a brief sense of joy despite her overwhelming and consuming sadness. She was happy and proud to be pregnant with Slick's offspring. Their bloodline was guaranteed to continue. She thought about how proud Slick would have been if he was still here with her. They had talked about having little Silver Serpent's of their own. Once the female Silver Serpent became pregnant, it usually took about two to three months before she gave birth. Zelda had always dreamed of becoming a mother and having a little Silver Serpent of her own to love, nurture, and care for. She laid back down on her spongy, kelp bed that Slick had made for her and closed her ruby-red eyes. She envisioned Slick swimming and hunting in the eternal sea in the sky. Then she envisioned herself giving birth to a fierce, male Silver Serpent that looked just like Slick, and that made her smile. Zelda was content to know that even though Slick was gone from the physical realm of earth, a piece of him would remain here. Zelda opened her eyes, and she realized that she was a lot hungrier than usual. Her pregnancy cravings had started already, she thought to herself. She had another life inside of her that she had to feed as well. She ventured outside her cave to hunt for her and her baby's next meal. The Atlantic Ocean was very quiet and tranquil. The only sea creatures that moved around were some king mackerel that glided over some oyster beds. Zelda pursued the lustrous kings. There were six of them, and they made her jaws salivate. She launched herself toward them like a rocket and rapaciously grasped two of them in her jaws and two of them in her upper claws. Zelda chomped down with purpose on the two kings that dangled in her jaws and crushed them into fish stew with her steely teeth. After Zelda swallowed those two down her gullet, she placed the other two mackerel in her jaws. She crunched down savagely on their slippery bodies and pulverized them into a fish jelly. Her taste buds rejoiced in delight and savory satisfaction. She decided to swim over to Slick's headless corpse and say a prayer for him. She arrived at Slick's massive, headless cadaver and saw that a frenzy of lemon sharks and bull sharks feasted on it. They had devoured over a quarter of Slick's corpse. Slick had always said that when he died, he wanted his body to be devoured by the sea creatures so that his flesh and blood could nourish their bodies. He believed in the circle of life concept and the food chain. And that all creatures had to devour other creatures to survive. It's nature's way of balancing the universe out, Slick would always say. Zelda could hear his voice in her head, saying that, at that moment. Zelda positioned herself right next to Slick's headless, Silver Serpent body and prayed for him.

"Oh all-knowing, almighty, and merciful Lord in the wondrous and eternal sea in the sky; please protect Slick's soul on its journey into the afterlife. May you bless his majestic soul and protect it with your blood until it finds its final resting place in your divine and glorious kingdom. I loved Slick with all of my heart and soul, and I hope and pray to be reunited with him again someday in the heavenly sea in the sky. Life won't ever be the same again, without him, but I will try to stay strong for myself and our young one on the way. Please bless and protect my baby Silver Serpent on the way, so that he or she may grow up to be fierce, intelligent, and powerful like their Daddy, Slick. Amen," Zelda said. Zelda kissed Slick's corpse with her slithery, forked tongue and swam away as she wept sparkly, silver tears out her blood-red eyes. A gam of great white sharks had smelled the flesh and blood from Slick's cadaver and they joined in on the feast. Usually sharks fight each other off for meals, but there was enough of Slick to go around for all the them. The ferocious and voracious sharks tore solid chunks of flesh from Slick's bones, which exposed more of his colossal skeleton. Zelda swam to the surface and scoped out the scene from above. The canary-yellow sun blazed like a fireball in the pristine, cornflower-blue sky. There were some fishing boats out trying to bring in some worthy catches for that day. The squawking seagulls hovered around the boats and tried to get a quick and easy meal tossed their way. Zelda submerged her head in the water and spotted a gargantuan whale shark that cruised toward here like an iron submarine. It was Bo. Zelda recognized him and swam towards him.

"Hi Bo. How are you doing?" Zelda said.

"Hello, Zelda. I'm doing well. I just devoured a swarm of copepods. How are you doing? Where's my best buddy, Slick?" Bo replied.

"I'm not doing well. I'm afraid I have some terrible news about Slick. He was slayed by some serpent hunters. He's gone," Zelda said as she broke down again into glittery, silver tears.

"What? No, it can't be! Not Slick!" Bo exclaimed.

"I wish it weren't true, but it is. Slick was slayed the day before yesterday. His bones are not too far from us, on the ocean floor. The sharks feasted on his flesh," Zelda replied.

Bo broke down into tears.

"That is the saddest and most devastating news I've ever heard in my entire life. Slick was my best friend in all of the seven seas. He was my brother," Bo replied.

"I know you two loved each other like brothers. I loved him too more than anything in the world. I still can't believe it either," Zelda said.

"I thought you two relocated out here to get away from all of that dreadful, serpent hunter violence," Bo replied.

"We did. I told Slick not to mess with them anymore, and he said that he wouldn't, but in the end, it was just in his nature. I don't think he could help himself when it came to those serpent hunters. The war with them was in his blood," Zelda said.

"Yes, that was unfortunately true of hard-headed, Slick. I'm so sorry for your loss, Zelda. I know that you two loved each other with all of your hearts and souls," Bo replied.

"Thank you Bo. Yes we did. I'm so sorry for your loss as well. I know that you and Slick were the best of friends and loved each other like brothers," Zelda replied.

"Yes, we did. Slick was my brother, adviser, hunting buddy, and security all wrapped into one. He was the true king of the ocean. He will be sorely missed and irreplaceable. He will never be forgotten and he will always live in our hearts and minds," Bo said.

"Yes, he will. I said a prayer for his royal soul and its journey into the afterlife in the eternal sea kingdom in the sky. A piece of him will remain here on earth with us. I'm pregnant with his offspring. I can already feel our little Silver Serpent moving around in my belly," Zelda replied.

"Really Zelda? That is amazing! A true blessing from the almighty Sea God. I can't wait to meet the precious, little rascal! When are you due to give birth?" Bo said.

"I can't wait either! The reproductive cycle for us, Silver Serpents, is usually between two to three months. They grow rapidly in our bellies," Zelda replied.

"Is it going to be a male or female?" Bo asked.

"Silly Bo. I won't know that until the little serpent pops out," Zelda replied. Zelda giggled and Bo chuckled.

"What I meant to say is, I wonder if it's gonna be a male or female. Congratulations Zelda!" Bo said.

"Only the great Sea God knows. We'll have to wait and see. Thank you for coming around here, Bo. I really needed a friend to talk to. My soul has been crushed since Slick's death. Today is the first day that I've had a glimmer of hope again," Zelda replied.

"You're welcome Zelda. I had to check up on my loved ones," Bo said.

"Awe, you're such a sweet and gentle giant. I consider you a loved one too, Bo. I'm just so devastated about Slick's death. It's difficult to find the strength to go on without him. I know I must though, not only for myself, but for our little Silver Serpent growing inside my belly. I just miss him so much. I keep seeing his fierce and handsome face and hearing his deep and powerful voice in my head," Zelda replied.

"I know you do, Zelda. I miss him more than words can say, too. Rest assured that I will take care of you and your little Silver Serpent with my life, just like Slick would have wanted me too," Bo said.

"Thank you Bo. I hope and pray that we can survive in this perilous ocean with so many serpent and whale hunters around," Zelda replied.

"I guarantee we will. Keep your head up. We are stronger than we know. I will do everything in my power to protect our lives and our future," Bo said.

"You are true sweetheart, Bo. I know why Slick loved you so much. Let's go grab a bite to eat," Zelda replied.

"That sounds like a splendid plan. I can always eat. Let's go," Bo said. Bo and Zelda swam off together and hunted some fresh Atlantic Ocean prey. The natural cycle of sea life always restored itself, only, it missed its true king of the ocean, Slick the Silver Serpent. At least Slick and Zelda's bloodline was most certainly guaranteed to live on through their offspring. Slick's soul took joy, pride, and comfort in that from the eternal sea kingdom in the sky. He happily reunited and hunted with Sandy, Oliver. and his parents up there in that heavenly sea. Slick praised and thanked the One, true, almighty God, and prayed that He protect his loved ones from the whale and serpent hunters. He prayed for God to guide and shield Zelda, their offspring, and Bo, with his loyal love, righteousness, justice, and eternal light. God appeared to Slick in the form of a beautifully glowing, royal-blue orb surmounted by an exquisite, dazzling golden cross. God spoke to Slick.

"Greetings Slick. I am the One true God," God said.

"Hello God. It's an honor to finally meet you," Slick replied.

"I present myself to you today, because I have heard your prayers, and so that you may know the truth. All of your life you worshiped the Sea God. I am the God of the sea, the land, the earth, and the heavens. On the third day I created the land, the sea, the plants and the trees. On the fifth day I created all of the sea creatures and the flying creatures. On the fifth day I created the progenitors that originated your bloodline. You have slayed many humans, but I can't hold that against you, because I created you do that. I wanted to humble the humans for all of the slaying that they were doing and for their haughtiness. I looked into your heart and mind many times, and I could see that your thoughts and intentions were pure, and you had true love inside. You worshiped and praised the God of the Sea, which is Myself, with everlasting love and faith, and that is why I have saved your soul. I will do my best to protect your loved ones, but it has become more difficult, because evil has entered into the hearts of some humans. The ones who turn their heads and hearts away from Me and refuse to acknowledge My existence. They refuse to worship and fear Me. That is because of the devil's work, but he shall never defeat Me. It's a constant battle between good and evil, but evil shall never surmount holiness, and darkness shall never overtake the light. I am the eternal light, love, justice, and righteousness throughout all of the earth, seas, and heavens. I'm a savior to all those who truly love, worship, and fear Me. I will bless your soul, and I will bless your loved ones on earth. Welcome to the My eternal and glorious Kingdom of heaven," God said.

"Wow! I always had unconditional and unbreakable faith that You truly existed, and my faith has been rewarded. No matter how dark or difficult the times were, I could always feel Your presence, light, and love in my heart. You would send me signs of beauty, clarity, love, and joy that assured me of Your existence. You blessed me with strength, wisdom, courage, and vision. I never feared anything on earth, but I always feared and loved You. Thank You for Your loving embrace and for welcoming me into Your pristine, heavenly Kingdom of holiness, love, peace, and splendor. And thank You for answering my prayers. We can both watch over my loved ones from here," Slick replied.

About the Author

Author Andy Bazan has released his debut novel, *The Silver Serpent*. Bazan hails from McAllen, TX. He loves to write and play sports. He excelled at baseball, soccer, and tennis in his youth. He traveled throughout Texas playing high level baseball and soccer tournaments. Andy also traveled all over the state and nation competing in USTA tennis tournaments. He was ranked top 10 in the state of Texas for three years in a row when he was 16-18 years old. He was ranked top 200 in the nation for those three years as well. Andy competed in the junior national hard courts in Kalamazoo, Michigan for two consecutive years. He broke his left leg playing baseball, in his senior year of high school in Mexico City. That ended his tennis career. After a year of recovery, he played one year of college baseball at Ranger Junior College but was never the same player after that serious injury. Andy still works out regularly and enjoys athletic activities. He graduated from Texas A&M International University in Laredo, TX in May of 2013 with a Bachelors of Science in Fitness and Sports. He has a beautiful and gifted 9-year old daughter, that is his pride and joy, Cassie Victoria Bazan.